FIRED UP

AMY BRIGGS

Dani,
Enjoy the Heat!!
xo

♥ AmyB

Fired Up

By Amy Briggs

Cover Design copyright © 2016 Concierge Literary Promotions

Editing by Cassia Brightmore of LJ & CB Creative Images and Services

DEDICATION

For my parents.

TABLE OF CONTENTS

JO

I couldn't find anything suitable to wear to my own dad's funeral. Everyone was going to be there, wearing their Class A Dress Uniforms, which was completely acceptable, since he was a Fire District Chief, but I won't be wearing mine. I haven't worked at that department in almost a year, and it just doesn't seem appropriate at all. My aunt also informed me that my father's only daughter shouldn't be dressed like a boy the day he's laid to rest; her words of reprimand have been ringing in my head all morning.

At least my best friend, Matt will be there, along with his brother Brian and the rest of the department of course. Brian was actually appointed into my father's position when he died last week. We have a bit of a history. We had a moment really; a hot, steamy moment that I'd never be able to get out of my head apparently. I felt a moistness pool between my legs thinking about his beautiful green eyes, his

1

well-defined muscles and the tattoos that couldn't be more perfectly placed on his chest and arms. *Jesus Christ, it's your dad's funeral, get your shit together, Josephine Meadows.* That was a one-time thing, just kiss, a really great kiss. No matter how great it was, or how much deep down I actually wanted him, having those thoughts at this time and place was inappropriate. I shook my head to clear it; reminding myself that Brian was a cocky asshole anyway.

Matt was picking my aunt and I up, she was my only biological family left now and my dad's older sister. My mom died when I was three, leaving me and my dad to fend for ourselves for the most part. After she died, he never dated, or married again; he was more or less married to the fire service. He worked the job until his last breath; when he passed away from a heart attack while out on a call. It was no secret that the stress of firefighting made heart attacks the number one killer of firefighters, but their shitty diets certainly didn't help either, no matter how hard I tried to get him to be healthier.

"Josephine! Matt's here, let's go!" Aunt Molly yelled from downstairs. I finished putting on my favorite red lipstick that I never wore except to go out or for events, grabbed some black heels that were probably a bit too high for walking around all day, and took a deep breath as I went downstairs. It was going to be a long day, but everyone that I'd be greeting loved us, they were all our family.

BRIAN

It's the day of Jack's funeral, a day I've been dreading as I felt like I lost my own father. He was my fire chief for as long as I can remember as I moved up the ranks. Technically, he was the only father figure I had. My dad left my mom with me and my little brother when I was five and he was three. Our mom, and Jo's mom had been friends, and Matt and Jo have been best friends since they were born. The two were born in the same hospital in the same week; making them almost inseparable for as long as I can remember.

When our dad left, Jack Meadows stepped in to help out; teaching us how to be boys, and then how to be good men. He and our mom stayed friends and I always thought there might have been something going on there, but who knows. Jack was an honorable man, and when his wife died, around the same time our dad left, he made it a point to check on my mom, and that was good enough for us. From what I know, he never really involved himself

4

with a woman again. They ended up being really close. When we were old enough, we couldn't wait to join the fire department, and we've both made a career out of it. That fire department was our calling and definitely our family.

It was time to lay to rest the only father I've ever known, and to make sure his family had everything they needed from the fire department; that was my responsibility now and we looked out for our own. I adjusted my uniform, making sure it was all in place and thought about Jack's family. His only family besides the department was his sister, Molly who lives out of town, and Jo.

Josephine Meadows. I started to get a little twitch in my dick; she was always so fucking sexy and had absolutely no clue how hot she was. She was a firefighter too, it was in her blood. We used to all ride together, and my God, her ass in a uniform. It would stop you in your tracks if she walked by. She was off limits though, her dad had been my boss, and my brother was her best friend--that's like two bro code fails in one. I haven't seen her all that much since we drank too much, and got a little handsy with each other at one of the fire academy graduation parties last year. We said some stuff to each other that probably should never have been said.

JO

We'd decided to do only one service, viewing, whatever you wanted to call it. My dad knew it would be a production, he was a Fire Chief, and as humble as he was, he was a fucking good one, and well respected across our state as well as several others. We'd casually discussed what he wanted over the years. It's something you got comfortable talking about in emergency services; you knew how short life could be. We were going to the funeral home, then straight to my dad's house for a reception that the fire department stepped in and took care of for me.

In traditional fashion, I was up at the front of the room by the memorial, thankfully with my aunt, and I had asked Matt to be with me too. Normally, he would have come with the rest of the fire department, but as a show of support, he arrived with me instead. Dressed in his Class A uniform, he stood by my side, ready to be my crutch if I needed it. It was a lot of people, he knew everyone, and could help me say and do the right thing. I honestly think I was still in shock, I had yet to shed one single tear. Matt was a little worried about it, but I knew it would happen after all the "business" of the funeral was over. Matt's mom, Catherine, was also sitting in the front row, she'd been really close to my dad, and I could see she was grieving as well, dabbing at her eyes with a beautiful little white lace handkerchief that appeared to have tiny blue flowers embroidered on it.

My dad was cremated, as per his wishes. He was a firefighter, and as sick or crazy as it sounds, he thought it was amusing to be cremated. Whatever, it was what he wanted, and at the end of the day, what did it matter? It was the only thing my aunt and I disagreed on about this whole situation, she felt that he should be traditionally laid to rest. We compromised, and I let her buy a plot and a headstone, and I'd promised that we'd have a private non-burial sometime after the service, but not that day.

My feet were killing me from my heels already, and the service had barely started. The fire department had wanted to do an honor guard and I asked them not to, but they were all there, showing their support. There was a sea of navy blue uniforms, and I truly appreciated their presence even though it was a little overwhelming. My heart thumped against my chest thinking of how supportive these people all were. I've shown up to a lot of these in the support role myself, always knowing this day would come, but was still in awe at the amount of people in attendance.

Matt leaned over to whisper to me. "How are you holding up?"

"I'm alright. I probably should've worn more sensible shoes though," I giggled, and my aunt threw me a glare. I leaned over to her. "You know my dad had a sense of humor, lighten up a little bit." She took my hand and squeezed. She knew I was right and that even if we didn't know all of the firefighters, EMTs and police officers coming through to pay their respects, they had all been touched by my father in some way. It was important for us to not make their hurt any worse either. We were a family, a big crazy family that most folks didn't understand, but family nonetheless. He had even indicated, should he pass, that we should play upbeat music at his "funeral." We did just that, turning the service into an almost cheerful gathering.

Matt checked his phone and smiled. "Looks like our department is here, just got a text from Brian." They could all be so annoying and crude, but would do absolutely anything for you. I basically had one hundred brothers, which was the coolest thing since biologically, I was an only child.

"Ok, so here we go. No crying."

"You can do whatever you want you know. I'm here for you." He put his arm around me and gave me a squeeze. He looked down at me with a soft smile, eliciting a small smile from me in return. Matt always knew how to keep me calm and I was so grateful he was there for me.

"I really appreciate it, Matt, thank you. I just want to be strong, he was so loved by everyone, I really want today to be a celebration and I know that's what he would want too." I sighed.

Matt smiled and leaned into me. "I think that's exactly what he would want."

The funeral director came over and let us know people were arriving and that he'd direct them where to go. I thought it was pretty obvious where to go, and we already knew, but I kept my mouth shut for a change. I was planning to really make the effort to not offend anyone or give too many of my opinions which would be a change of pace for me. The first to walk in the door was Brian, and the rest of the guys filed in one after another. I noticed those goddamn sexy eyes right away, and felt myself getting warm and flushed in his presence. Brian looked me straight in the eyes and nodded, before holding the door for his men to come in and pay their respects. They were so professional looking. I mean they were professionals, it's just that I grew up with so many of them, sometimes I'd forgotten how handsome and well put together they could all look when they needed to, especially right now.

Each of the emergency services well wishers that came through the line, said something wonderful about my dad, gave me and my aunt a hug, shook Matt's hand, and then took residence in the back of the funeral home. That's how it worked, the "family department" basically stood watch at these events to see if anyone needed help. Brian didn't come through the line with the rest of the guys, which seemed odd. I spent the greater part of the afternoon shaking hands and hugging my friends, my dad's friends and several people I didn't actually know. That felt like it went on for an eternity and I was growing uncomfortable from all of the talking and hugging. My uncomfortable shoes weren't helping me either.

As the guys from my old department, which was my dad's department came through I thought about all the things I loved about each of them, and what I know my dad loved about them too. Scotty was always the driver, and ran the pumps. He was kind of young for a full time driver with that much responsibility at twenty-three, but he took it in stride. He was also our engineer, he could get water to flow out of anything, and was often called upon to teach rural departments how to get water when they had hydrant problems or couldn't get water at all. He was so smart, and had such an instinct for reading a scene and knowing where equipment needed to be efficiently and effectively.

Our engine officer, Kevin Taylor, was quiet and cool all the time. Never lost his head, always had a good answer to a question, and could read a fire like nobody else. He was almost forty, and had never settled down himself. He was actually older than Brian who was thirty-five and now our chief. Taylor had ladies throwing themselves at him, but he never took the bait, at least not in front of any of us. He could be a bit of a loner, but I had the best late night conversations with him in the kitchen at the firehouse, I could have sworn he was the most interesting man in the world like in those silly beer commercials.

Jax was, well he was Jax. Seth Jackson was actually his real name, but he reminded us all of a tall, Australian guy on a soap opera we saw one time, named Jax. It just stuck once we started calling him that as a joke years ago. He was tall, blonde, blue eyed and handsome like a model. An ex-marine, he was so fit and good looking, he was always beating the girls off with a stick. Matt lived with Jax. He bought a house when he got out of the marines, and figured he'd offset costs by having a roommate. I think all those years in the marines, he didn't really like being alone that much, even though he was kind of quiet. We always got along well, and he was a great firefighter. Always training, and reading about the latest thing in fire suppression. He was a walking encyclopedia of new technologies.

Matt was usually on the same shift as me when I was riding regularly. He's also an engine guy. Back in the academy, I had to coax him off of a fire escape that we were training on when he got paralyzed up at the top. It's no joke, and if I wasn't helping him myself, we were partners on that training exercise, I probably would have frozen too. That's the thing I love about firefighting, you always, and I do mean *always* have a partner; it was actually a very common rule. No going off on your own and freelancing at a fire, everyone has a partner. Since we're so close personally, we work together really well and were usually side by side until I left the department to work several part time and per diem jobs at different departments and for the county, which seemed like a great way to branch out at the time. . He dates the worst girls ever, I hate them all, and that's not because I have a secret crush on him, I saved that for Brian. Matt just has horrible taste and dates the dumbest girls I've ever met in my life, but they sure do love firefighters. Most girls love a sexy firefighter, we've all seen the movies. As a female firefighter, it was both nauseating and hilarious to watch the dating rituals of the guys around me.

I tried to smile as much as I could and worked to not think about what I was going to do with myself at thirty-two years old with no parents left. When you're little, your thirties seem so old, but here I am, and I'm not ready to have no parents. I'm not ready to let go. Sure, I had the fire department, and I had my aunt, and Matt of course, but I was basically out of family and it was starting to hit me hard, causing a pain in my chest that felt like a hole being drilled right through my heart. As I felt that hole get bigger, my eyes started to well up. *Well shit, here it comes, now I'm going to cry.*

Last to come through the line was Brian. He gave my aunt a kiss on the cheek, and stopped in front of me. He was obviously sexy, but he looked so well put together and handsome in his uniform. He reminded me of my dad a little, looking very serious and very much in charge. I'd tried to avoid eye contact, I *was not* liking how he was consuming my thoughts throughout the day today and at this point, I was definitely going to cry at any moment and I didn't want to do that in front of him or anyone else for that matter.

BRIAN

Fuck she's beautiful. Seeing those steely blue eyes filled with tears, I just wanted to grab her and take her someplace away from all this madness. These things can get really crowded, and with someone as awesome as her dad, I knew this would happen. I watched her from the back of the room for two hours, just smiling at people, sharing stories, thanking them for coming, I don't know how she can look so calm. She's a fucking warrior. The thing is, when this many firefighters, cops and EMTs get together, it becomes overwhelming, even for some of us that know to expect it, and that includes her. She's a firefighter, one of ours, and always will be, even if she isn't riding with us right now. There's stories to tell, guys you haven't seen in forever, and then the responsibility of looking after the family. It can be a lot to deal with, when they're grieving themselves. Everyone would want to share their "Jack story" with her. Jo knew all of that, but something inside me wanted to protect her anyway. I sure as fuck wasn't going to let anyone know that. I didn't go through the receiving line with my department when we arrived, I hung back and kept an eye on things, not quite ready to face her.

Once it was time for me to go up there, I had to say something. "Jo, are you okay? I know we haven't spoken in a while, but I'm so sorry about your dad. I'm sure you know how I felt about him."

"I'm fine, Brian. Congratulations on your promotion. I'll be by sometime next week to get both his and my stuff from the station." she said calmly.

"That's not even a little bit important right now. Please let me know if there's anything that I, or the guys can do to help you out. You know we're all family." And I meant that.

"I'm okay, thank you." She gave me a quick, friendly hug. I felt an electric charge, and I could smell the orange blossom or whatever it was in her hair. I had to walk away, immediately. It was not okay to have those thoughts about her, and definitely not at that moment.

I was Jack's Deputy Chief, and was recently appointed to take his position temporarily, possibly full time later. As far as I was concerned, that meant looking out for everything he cared about, which included Jo, whether she liked it or not. The last time we had a real conversation just between the two of us, she told me what a fucking asshole I was. She also mentioned how I needed to grow up, and how she felt that I wasn't the person she thought I was. I've been thinking about that conversation a lot this week, but at the time, I was only concerned about my career and getting laid. Messing around with her wasn't going to make either of those things work. So, maybe she was right. Today, I'd sent the Ladies Auxilliary to Jack's house to handle the reception, so Jo could stay here as long as she wanted before going back to the house and continuing to entertain people. It was the one small thing I could do, and since she *did* speak to my brother a billion times a day, he helped me arrange her okay with it.

I went back to my post at the back of the room and watched the last of the people trickle through. The crowd had dwindled as people were leaving to go to the reception, and I saw Jo's demeanor change suddenly. She went from a wistful sadness to what appeared to be pissed off in an instant. Some guy that I sort of recognized, but wasn't sure from where, was standing next to her and as I watched, he grabbed her arm. What the fuck was that about? I watched my brother grab the guy's arm, and motion for him to leave. I saw red. I rushed to the front of the room, grabbed the clown by his jacket lapels and got in his face.

"Is there a problem here?" I snarled at him.

"You need to get the fuck off me, bro. I'm talking to my girlfriend right now, you can back the fuck up." I looked over at Jo to confirm what this jackass was saying.

"I'm not your goddamn girlfriend, you fucking asshole, and you have absolutely no business being here. This isn't the time or the place, and regardless, we have nothing to discuss. Please leave." she literally hissed at him. She turned toward me and my brother. "Brian, Matt, it's fine. Danny, please leave, you don't belong here." She pointed to the door.

"Fine, I'll leave because you're causing a scene at your own father's funeral, but we aren't done talking, Josephine. Not by a long shot." The douche stormed out of the funeral home.

"Well that was fucking perfect. Sorry, Dad." Jo said to the sky. "Thank you both for being here, I really do appreciate it." She huffed. "I think it's time to get back to dad's house so I can hug some more strangers and hear fish stories about my dad. At least I can have a drink there, cause damn, I sure need one."

"Well, I'll take you there now and we'll do some drinking for your old man," Matt said. She smiled and walked toward the door with her aunt who didn't respond to the scene at all, and Matt hung back to talk to me.

"What the fuck was that all about, man? That guy is a douche. Are they seriously together?"

"That was Danny, Jo's *ex* boyfriend, the lying, manipulative Fire Inspector from Station 19. He went to the academy with me and Jo and was a prick then too. Well he never got any better, and somehow, they dated for the last year, and big shocker, he cheated on her the entire time. Anyway, she has some stuff at their old apartment together she wants to get back. He wants to get back together and he thought today, at the funeral, would be the perfect time to approach her about this." His eyes got big, letting me know he thought it was a dumbshit idea just like I did. I'm actually kind of surprised Jo didn't punch him right in the throat.

"That guy is a dick. What the fuck did she date him for? We need to go get whatever shit she left there for her." I'd be damned if I let her go anywhere with that guy. I couldn't believe he'd grabbed her, I'd like to rip him apart for that alone.

"I honestly don't know why she dated him. I was actually going to ask for your help, I wasn't sure you would though."

"Why wouldn't I?" I was offended.

"Listen, Jo and I never discussed whatever it was that happened between you two last year before she started dating, Danny the Douchebag, but it's no secret that something went down. I know you haven't spoken more than two words at a time since then, and it's fucking awkward, man. I don't really want to know but I know you well enough to know you can't keep your dick in your pants with the ladies, so how about you not do that to my best friend who not only lost her dad, your boss, but is basically family to us."

Now I was mad. "I'm not going to talk about that with you now, but I will tell you that I would do anything to help her out. That's it. Just call me later and let me know what you need. I'm going to meet the guys at her dad's, I'll see you there."

I was fucking pissed. I know what I did, and at the time, it seemed smart, but now I felt like a fucking asshole. It gave me a pain in my gut thinking that I might have hurt her and drove her into the arms of that prick; although I didn't think I did at the time. I glanced over in her direction, and she nodded back at me, but it was icy and expressionless. Her black dress hugged her body in all the right places, and those fucking heels. Goddamn, I wanted to bend her over a chair and fuck her until she saw stars. And there it was, she still made my dick hard as a rock and I needed to go before that became noticed.

JO

What the fuck was Danny thinking
showing up at my dad's funeral? Thankfully,
Matt was with me, and before it got really
nasty, Brian came up to help too. That was nice,
but also kind of strange. I never even saw him
coming, he just appeared and grabbed Danny.
Every time I glanced in his direction today, he
was staring at me. Piercing me with those
goddamn green eyes that I couldn't stop
thinking about. What the fuck for? I wanted to
hate him, but I also kind of wanted him to
punch Danny in the face for me, and I actually
think he might have done it if I'd asked. I'll have
to deal with Danny another day.

I waited outside with my aunt for Matt
to finish talking to Brian so we could leave for
the reception back at my dad's. Well it was my
home now, but still definitely felt like his. Matt
chauffeured us to a reception full of well-
wishers, most of which I had just talked to at
the funeral home. I saw many of these people
on a regular basis, but my aunt didn't have the

privilege of hearing the stories about him retold over and over, so I wanted her to enjoy that. When a lot of firefighters, cops, EMTs get together, it's a lot of storytelling. If you don't do it for a living, it can be really fun to hear what people have to share, and I knew Aunt Molly would love that.

After awhile, I went to go get some air out back, and found Brian leaning against the railing on my back deck, just staring off into space.

"Hey there, what are you doing back here?" I asked him. I felt a little smile form on my face, I wasn't entirely sure why, but I was happy to see him and had a little flutter in my chest. He took his sunglasses off as I got closer and smiled back.

"I'm so sorry, Jo, for everything," he took a deep breath in. "I miss him a lot." I could see his beautiful green eyes start to look glassy from tears and I took the two steps closer and reached out to embrace him. He pulled me into his broad chest with his muscled arms, and hugged me. I mean seriously hugged me, holding on tightly, as if he needed to. I could feel his warm breath on my neck, giving me chills. It sounded like he was trying to hold back tears from the way his breath hitched. I pulled away from the hug to look at him, those sparkling eyes were now bloodshot and sad. I reached up to touch his face and smiled again. I could see that he was truly hurting over the loss of my dad, they were very close and had been working side by side for several years now. My heart ached for him, I wasn't used to seeing him this torn up over a loss, or anything else for that matter, and yet I completely understood.

I hadn't been very nice to Brian the last year, I took a huge blow to my ego and skid marks were left across my heart when he blatantly rejected me and I wanted to hide my hurt and anger. That didn't change how I truly felt about him deep inside my core, buried deep so no one would know. I fell in love with Brian when I was sixteen-years-old, I'd always loved him and quite possibly always would. Seeing him like this, tearing up over losing my dad, tugged at my heart strings, bringing those old feelings right back to the surface in an instant. I wanted to comfort him the way I needed to be comforted. I wanted to make him feel better, not so alone in his grief. I know that my father was the only father Brian had ever really known, and their bond was special and unique, as was his loss.

"You know you were very important to him, right? Not just at work. He loved you and Matt as much as he loved me really." He gave me a much bigger smile then, looking like he might even laugh.

"How do you always know how to make people smile?" Leaning in close to me again, he rested his chin on top of my head for a moment, hugging me again. He smelled so good, I inhaled his manly scent and forgot about the day for just a moment, lost with him. He let me go, and moved to lean back on the railing of the deck and put his sunglasses back on. Mine were still on top of my head, so I slid them down and took up the spot next to him, letting out an audible sigh.

"Anytime. That's one of the many things that our little family is for." I gave him a little elbow to his rock hard abs and mused to myself a bit. It was kind of nice just hanging out with Brian, not uncomfortable at all. The last time we were alone ended in an argument about a kiss we shared, which seemed unlikely to happen at this moment thankfully. I thought about it quietly, hoping that maybe we were past the point of avoiding each other, and potentially leaving room for us to be friends again. I'd always want more, but I'd certainly have taken friendship over nothing at all.

I wasn't sure how much time had passed, but I realized I had been gone for a bit, and needed to get back to the reception. "I've got to go back in and say goodbye to some people, but anytime you want to talk, you know where to find me," I gave him a tiny peck on the cheek, leaving me with a little electrical charge.

"Thanks, Jo, and obviously the same here. We'll talk later okay?" he said as I walked back inside.

Finally, the reception was over. My aunt had decided to head back to her place, which was about two hours away. I was staying at my dad's, like I have been since I moved out of Danny's apartment. I never saw Brian leave, but I was now alone, like I felt I needed to be. Truthfully, I'd had enough men and firefighters, and questions about my life to last me a lifetime. I felt like I might be able to be friends with Brian again and that was nice too even if deep down I'd always want more. I wanted to drink, and I wanted to forget about being sad. Or maybe I wanted to think. Either way, I definitely wanted some quiet. I sent Matt home with the rest of the guys, they were all going out to the local watering hole.

It had been a couple hours since everyone left, and I wandered around my dad's house, touching pictures, talking to myself as if talking to him. *What am I supposed to do now without you here?* I heard a knock on the screen door and jumped. It was Florida, and a typical 80 degrees in October, but no humidity so I had the door open for some fresh air.

"I'm sorry I scared you, may I come in?" Those green eyes penetrated right through me. Brian was dressed in a black t-shirt, jeans that hung low on his hips and showed just a bit of that V leading to...oh you know. His beautifully sculpted arms were covered in tattoos that I couldn't admire earlier today, and I think I forgot to reply while assessing him as he repeated his question. "Jo, can I come in and talk to you?"

"Oh, yeah sure, come on in, Brian. Did you need something?" *Besides fucking me on this recliner? I obviously need to stop drinking, there's something wrong with me.*

"No, I don't need anything at all. I wanted to come and see you, check on you really. After the drama with your ex, and well, just everything, I wanted to make sure you're alright." He looked like he meant it, but I was in no mood at that point in my day. I was feeling kind of angry about life and losing my dad and I didn't want to be bothered. I'd been nice and understanding all day and while I did love admiring him physically, and daydreaming about those arms around me, he definitely

31

wanted to come and play Chief of the Department with me right now and I wasn't up for it.

"Look, Brian, it's me, not some random civilian that doesn't get how this all works. You don't have to come over here out of obligation from the department and take care of anything. I'm perfectly capable of handling my shit. I appreciate you having words with Danny earlier today, but I can certainly take care of that situation myself," I was being mean, and I felt bad, but didn't stop myself. I felt like lashing out at someone, and he was an easy target.

"Listen here, Jo. I've known you your entire life, you can be pissed off at me, the fire service, the world, or whatever you want, sweetheart, but it *is* my responsibility to look after you whether you like it or not and not just because I'm the Chief. And while we're at it, we're eventually going to talk about what happened last year, because we can't keep ignoring each other forever. Today was the first time we've spoken more than two words to each other since last year. You need to let me be here for you now!" he raised his voice, making me angry and turned on at the same time.

I got in his face and put my hand on his broad chest in a gesture to push him away, but he didn't move an inch. "I don't need anyone's help, definitely not yours. Thanks for stopping by." He stood in front of me without moving just like a statue, and it was as if there was a magnet between us. I didn't move my hand either, it was glued to him giving me a warm static charge I couldn't let go of. I stared into his eyes, full of fire and wasn't sure whether this was a standoff or we were going to just argue about it, then he did it. He kissed me. For the second time in my life, he kissed me, drawing me into him like a tornado, consuming all of me.

BRIAN

I didn't know why I did it, but I grabbed her face and planted my lips on hers in a kiss like no other, and she let me. She didn't push me away, she let me devour her; it was so fucking hot, my cock was hard in an instant. Holy shit, she tasted like strawberries and wine, I wanted to ravage her. I ran one hand through her beautiful short hair, and the other I used to pull her close into me; she had to feel how fucking hard I was. She gave in, and even let out a sexy little moan as I shoved her up against the wall by the door where I walked in, and started to kiss her neck, inhaling her intoxicating scent.

After a moment, I stopped and looked into her dark gray eyes. "Look at me, Jo." I ordered her as she tried to look away. She obeyed and I swear to God, something inside me melted. Literally, I felt like my insides were turning to fucking jello. *What is going on here?*

"Brian, you should go. I don't know what that was about, but we're obviously both grieving in our own ways, and I don't want us to do something we'll certainly regret." I didn't want to let go of her. She was wrong—this was something else entirely, it wasn't my grief or my desire to console her. It was something different.

"I came to talk, I'm not going to apologize for what just happened though, it was fucking hot, and I know you can feel what you do to me." Yes, I meant my rock hard cock. It was fucking aching, pressing up against my jeans, begging to be freed.

"I can feel it alright, and I'm not interested anymore, we've been down this road. You need to go. I have things to do here at the house, we can just forget about what happened here tonight, and any other night for that matter. I'll be by the station next week to pick up my old stuff I know my dad kept as well as his things." She pushed me away.

"You really want me to go?" I couldn't believe she was kicking me out. We were both flushed, and she was fighting it hard.

"Yes, I do. Please go, now is really not the time for this discussion or anything else," she looked down at the floor and wouldn't make eye contact with me.

"I'll do as you ask today, but we're not done talking, and after that," I waved my hands in between us. "We have more than talking to do." I wanted to press my body up against her again, and own her right there in the living room.

As soon as she'd stopped kissing me, I was missing it, feeling a pull to her. I've never felt that way. Ever. I loved it, and I was going to get to the bottom of it, but not today, I honestly don't want to upset her today, she doesn't deserve that. I probably shouldn't have pushed her today, I'm kind of a dick. We'd just spent the whole day at her dad's funeral and I even leaned on her for support. I definitely shouldn't have done that; I looked down at my cock, who clearly had a mind of his own.

"I'm sorry, Jo," I walked out the door, got in my truck and headed to the bar. I was off the following day, and I needed to drink off and shake the feeling that had come over me. I texted my brother and some guys from my shift and told them I'd meet up with them at Haligan's, the usual firefighter hangout.

JO

Oh, shit. What just happened? I touched my lips and my breath hitched; I cannot believe he just did that. I didn't even fight back, I melted like butter right into him and it was so good. I was tingling all over, and even though it was so *so* wrong, I wanted it to happen again. Immediately. Ugh, how did I find myself in these situations? Well, it can't happen again, I won't let it. He's just upset about my dad, and we got carried away. It would crush me if he rejected me again like last time and there's no way he'd changed since then.

Brian was a notorious skirt chaser, and I already made the mistake of catching feelings for him a long time ago when we were growing up. Last year, when I told him how I felt and after the best kiss of my life, we parted ways with him saying, "we can never be together," I was crushed. I was drunk as hell and shouldn't have said anything to begin with, it was just a childhood crush anyway, but he was so cold about it that night. I can't even believe he brought it up again. I'm certain that my dad knew how I felt about him, and that he secretly hoped I'd end up with Brian someday, but that clearly wasn't going to happen. From what I knew, he couldn't keep his dick in his pants, and he was definitely not a one woman guy, which I always knew, and I was more of a serial monogamist.

I went back to rummaging through my dad's things, and fussing with things nervously around the house. I tried doing the last few dishes that were left out, and put away anything leftover from the reception, all in an attempt to not think any more about Brian. I should have been thinking about my dad, not about getting shoved up against the wall in a way that left me getting moist between my legs and shuddering with excitement.

I decided I didn't really want to be alone quite as much as I thought I did. Isn't that always the way. Most of my friends and a few people that were my dad's friends were all gathered at Haligan's, which wasn't really a surprise, that's where everyone in emergency services hung out. Since some of my dad's friends were going to be there, I felt like I needed to spend some more time hearing about how awesome he was, and also getting hammered. Drinking more would definitely take my mind off of that glorious kiss, and touching Brian's perfect body. I rolled my eyes at myself, remembering that I didn't think it could ever work out seriously, so it was a waste of time to keep fantasizing. But I still got butterflies thinking of his hands on me. I hoped he wouldn't be there tonight, but I think deep down I knew he would be.

BRIAN

I went straight to the bar from Jo's house, completely afflicted by her touch. Her lips on mine were all consuming to me and after waving my friends down, I headed straight to the bar to order a beer and a shot. I needed to get this damn woman off my mind. She's right, she isn't really just my responsibility, certainly not in the way I was making it, but I was feeling like I wanted her to be. That had to be my closeness to her father. She was practically my little sister if you think about it. Somehow my cock doesn't know that though. Just thinking of her gave me a stiff dick and I had to adjust myself under the bar.

Matt and a bunch of the guys from the department were all there, the place was packed. "Hey, bro, what's going on?" he asked me.

"Not much, stopped by to see Jo before coming here. She wasn't in the mood for company though." *Except when she kissed me back,* I thought.

"Yeah, she sent me on my way too, but I guess she changed her mind, she's on her way here now too."

I tried to hide my anxiety, or was it excitement? "Oh that's cool. I'm gonna go play some pool with the guys." I ordered another beer, and headed over to the pool tables, which had a perfect view of the front door. I'd be able to see when she came in. There were way too many people here for me to look like something was up, and I didn't think I'd be able to talk to her about what happened between us yet after she pushed me out. Hell, I'm not even sure I would know what to say. All I really knew was that I wanted to get my mouth on hers again, as soon as possible. About fifteen minutes later, she walked in and headed straight to Matt and a couple of the guys at the bar. I couldn't hear what they were talking about, but they both looked in my direction, and I caught her eye. I held up my bottle of beer in greeting and smirked at her. She froze like a deer in headlights and darted her gaze away. I wasn't letting her off that easy. I wouldn't confront her in front of everyone, but there was

42

something going on between us, and I was determined to find out what it was.

I played a couple games of pool absent-mindedly; I couldn't stop looking over at her talking and laughing with a crowd of guys around her. It was pissing me off. I knew they were her friends, and friends of her dad's, but something's different, and I didn't like all that cock hovering around her. I couldn't take watching all those guys around her, and before I could even think through what I was doing, I was storming over in her direction.

"Jo, I need to speak with you," I growled in her ear.

"I'm busy, Brian." She wouldn't look me in the eye.

"Look at me. We need to talk, right now." She met my eyes, and my heart started racing.

"Ok." she said quietly. "Hey, I'll be right back, need to go talk to Brian about something real quick." She walked past me, toward the back door and disappeared outside. I followed closely behind. I was pissed.

"What is your problem, Brian? I was talking to the guys and having a good time," I could see she was getting drunk, her words were slurred and she was smirking at me, almost taunting me.

"Yeah, I can see that. You had a crowd of sharks swarming around you. You need to stay away from that." I couldn't believe how mad I was; I was jealous. I was the only shark that should be circling. She leaned up against the building, and I caged her in with my hands on either side of her face.

"Seriously, what are you doing? Why are you giving me a hard time? I told you I'm not your responsibility once already today." She looked me dead in the eyes and I felt it in my chest. I leaned in close enough to feel her breathing.

"You *are*," and I crushed her lips with mine. God, she still tasted so good. I grabbed her behind the neck with one hand, and pulled her close at the small of her back with my other hand, pulling her into me. She opened her mouth, and I explored her with my tongue. I swear to God, I was seeing stars and angels and

I don't know what the fuck else. She had one hand on my chest, and the other reached around to my back. It was like a raging inferno where she touched me. I felt like I was getting a fever from the heat between us.

She came up for air and looked down, I grabbed her chin and lifted her eyes to mine. "Don't look away, Jo," I said softly, still pulling her close to me with my other hand.

"What are we doing? I mean really, what is this?" she asked me sounding exasperated.

"You know I care about you. I don't know what this is, but I don't want you being available to those other guys." That probably wasn't exactly what I should have said, but my dick was rock hard and it was true.

"Oh, I see, so this is some kind of ownership thing all of a sudden? It doesn't work that way after one kiss this afternoon," she started to push me away.

"There's something going on between us and you know it. Don't deny you want me as much as I know you can feel I want you." I pressed the hardness between my legs up against her. I wanted to take her right up against the building. She softened up a little bit, and I took advantage and edged my face into her neck, she smelled so good. Like flowers blooming on a fresh morning; fresh and sweet. She leaned her head to the side a little giving me access and I licked and kissed her neck, I wanted to continue the same treatment on her entire body. Her legs started to give a little and I steadied her with the hand I had on her back, bringing her in tight to me again.

"Let's get out of here," I whispered in her ear.

"I don't know if that's a good idea," she whispered.

"It is by far; the best idea I've had all year. Let's get out of here," I whispered to her again, and kissed her softly.

"Okay," she said quietly and smiled up at me. I took her hand and walked us to my truck, which was conveniently parked out back.

JO

Oh, my God, he was so sexy. I was a little drunk, but honestly, since I was a teenager I'd wanted him, and you know what, even if it was a fling with my best friend's brother, my dad's protégé, and a damn manwhore; I was going to have myself some fun. Fuck it. He's so possessive and demanding and it makes me feel sexy. The way he grabs me to kiss me, and then turns soft has my panties completely soaked. He took my hand and practically dragged me to his truck.

"I need to tell Matt I'm leaving," I said. He was texting and didn't look up.

"I just texted him and said I was taking you home," he opened the passenger door of his giant truck. "Hop in."

"What about my car? I can drive it." Which probably wasn't true, my head was swimming a little.

He laughed. "Sweetheart, you're not driving anywhere. You're coming with me, and

47

I'm going to show you exactly how much I want you." He smacked me on the ass as I climbed in. Well, okay then. I wanted to be mad, but I was so turned on by him that all I could think about was his giant arms wrapped around me, and his huge, and I do mean huge, package pressed up against me twice today.

"Where are we going?" I asked quietly, forgetting he'd already told me. I was starting to sober up, and wondering if this was a good idea, even if I really did want him to do bad things to me.

He grabbed my hand while he drove with the other and looked over at me. "*We*, are going to my house, where *we*, are going to talk and explore each other and see what's going on between us. Just us. I'm going to kiss every inch of you, Jo. That's where *we*, are going." He brought my hand up to his lips and kissed it gingerly.

Holy shit, I think I just came hearing him say that. That's the hottest thing I've ever heard in my life. Danny and I'd had sex obviously, we were together for a year, but never was I turned on just from the words he spoke. We had a pretty vanilla relationship. Not that I was into kink per se, but a little feistiness in the bedroom was a turn on, but that was not his thing, at all. With just Brian's words I was going to melt right into the seat. I forgot to respond I think because then he asked, "is that ok with you, Jo?

I looked up at his face and smiled before whispering my reply. "Yes."

We pulled into his driveway, he had a beautiful home. Really nice for a single guy. It was a typical Florida bungalow style house with a perfectly landscaped yard in the front, and the back. I'd been there before for events and parties; he had the perfect backyard for entertaining. We hopped out of the truck and he came over to my side. "When you're with me, you need to let me open the door for you." He kind of growled under his breath at me.

"Okay," When our eyes met, it was like he could see through me. He leaned down and kissed me softly on the lips, then taking my hand and leading me inside. This was happening.

BRIAN

I'm actually a little nervous, and I'm never fucking nervous. I also never bring women here. I have had my fair share of action, but I preferred going to their place, or anywhere that isn't mine, so I could get out of dodge when the party was over. This was different, she needed to be with me, in my space. We walked inside, me still holding her hand, almost dragging her behind me. I was acting like a caveman, but I wanted to claim her as mine.

She was standing in front of me, staring at me looking confused and nervous too. "Can I get you something to drink?" I asked. I was forgetting my manners, and practically my own name right now. I walked to the fridge and got us both a beer.

"Thank you." She took the beer from me and never broke eye contact. We stood in the poorly lit kitchen in silence for what seemed like a really long time. I needed to do something. She broke the silence first.

"We don't have to do this, Brian, I think we got carried away in the heat of the moment and—" I stopped her right there, slammed my beer down and lunged at her, ramming my tongue into her mouth, and wrapping her up in my arms. She was still trying to hold her beer, while kissing me back, letting me explore her mouth with mine. I grabbed the beer bottle from her, without breaking our kiss, and put it on the counter, and she grabbed me roughly. She was so fucking hot. I lifted her up, she wrapped her tiny legs around my waist as I shifted us over to the island in the kitchen and set her on top of it. She had her hands under my shirt at my back, and I was groping every inch of her. I yanked her tank top over her head.

"Fuck you are so gorgeous, Jo," I grabbed some of that sexy short hair and pulled her head to the side giving myself access to her neck. She moaned softly at my touch. "We need to take this to my room," I scooped her up and carried her, legs wrapped around my waist.

I put her down gently on the edge of the king size bed, and took my shirt off. Her breath hitched, and I smiled. "You like what you see?" I workout a lot, and my job demands I be in shape; it certainly looked like she was pleased.

She stood up, and started to lightly touch my abs, and kiss my chest. I was going insane. "You need to lose the pants," I said as I unbuttoned her jeans. She started to lower her hands to the hardness pressing up against my jeans and I thought I'd explode right there. I had her pants off, and she was standing there in nothing but a lacy black bra, and matching panties. Fuck me, she was hot. She had a cardinal tattoo and some flowers that went around her shoulder and back, they were so colorful, on her pale, beautiful skin; I couldn't take my eyes off of them.

She finally spoke. "Fair is fair, time to lose your pants," she unbuttoned my jeans and reached in freeing my aching cock from the constraints of my boxers. She was still kissing me softly and her touch set my skin on fire all over again. She was starting to kiss me lower, and I stopped her. If she put her mouth anywhere near my cock I was going to come apart, I wasn't going to let that happen so fast.

I pushed her back down on the bed and climbed up next to her. I kissed her softly and reached around to undo her bra, taking it off with one hand. Her nipples were stiff little peaks, and I began to suck and knead one, and then the other. I reached down between her legs and groaned. "You're soaked, Jo," I ran my finger along her slit under her panties and felt her juices. She was so wet for me. I brought my fingers to my lips and licked them. "You taste so sweet."

"Brian, are you sure you want this?"

"Woman, I'm about to taste you, all of you. I've never wanted anything more in my entire life." I had no idea how true that was.

JO

I was coming undone. He sucked on my nipples and started to kiss me lower, I just leaned back on his bed and let him. He was like an animal, sniffing and licking me and I loved it. He took charge, and was going to have his way with me, and I wanted to relish in it. My entire body was flushed and when he got to my panties, he growled, and ripped them off. I let out a little startled sound and leaned up on my elbows.

"This is mine, Jo, once this happens, it's mine," he looked me in the eyes, and I was mesmerized and speechless. "Say it. Josephine," he demanded, and used my full name. I fucking loved it when he called me Josephine.

"Yours," I barely get the word out. I could feel his hot breath between my legs, a little bit of five o'clock shadow grazing my thighs and I wanted him to touch me so badly I could hardly think. I would be his any which way he wanted at that moment.

"That's right." He began to lick me softly between my thighs, massaging my clit with his tongue, and I swear to all that is holy, I saw heaven in that moment. He slid one, and then two fingers inside me, massaging me from the inside while licking my clit soft and slow. I've never had anyone make me feel this way, I was literally coming apart from the inside out. I was going to explode at any moment. I didn't want this feeling to end, I was shaking all over and ready to lose it.

Once he began fucking me with his fingers, I lost control and he was coaxing it out of me. "Yes, Jo, come for me. Come on me now!!" He demanded while pumping in and out of my hot, wet pussy. I obeyed, and lost complete control, screaming his name while he continued to lap at my clit like he couldn't get enough. It felt like he was feeding on me, and he was starving.

"Oh, Jesus, Brian! It's too much, oh, my God," I screamed. When the raging orgasm subsided and I leaned back panting, he crawled up over me and kissed me hard. I could taste a little bit of myself on him as he devoured my lips with his. That tongue of his was soft and rolled around in my mouth like it was finding it's home, it was so sexy and I was still recovering from the orgasm I had just had, getting turned on again just from him exploring my mouth with his.

"I'm not done with you yet. I need to be inside you, Josephine," he was hovering above me now, my hands on his broad shoulders. "I don't think I can be gentle, baby, you have me too hot, I need to fuck you. I need to fuck you hard." He growled and leaned in to lightly suck my neck, sending shivers through me. He reached over to the nightstand and grabbed a condom then looked at me intently, awaiting a response to what he said.

"Please, Brian, yes, I want you so bad," I uttered, wanting him more than anything I could fathom. He rolled the condom on, and grabbed my ass underneath me pulling me to him. He lined his cock up to my slit, I honestly couldn't imagine it fitting inside me it was so big and hard. With one thrust, he was filling me and I was seeing stars.

He groaned on top of me. "Jesus Christ, you're so tight and so wet, fuck!" He pulled almost all the way out, and began pumping into me hard. I felt another orgasm welling up inside me almost immediately, forcing me to call out. "Fuck yes, Brian, oh, my God!" He was ramming his length inside me, so hard, but he was connected to me. He never took his eyes off me. I was ready to come, and I knew he was too as he moved faster, and harder and we both began to lose control. I felt him come with me, even through the condom and he yelled out my full name. "Josephine, my God!" When we finished, I was shaking all over and he grabbed my face and planted soft sweet kisses on my lips and all over my face. He was still pumping lightly into me, as I felt the aftershocks of the greatest orgasm I've ever had in my life.

"You're so beautiful," he was staring into my soul, and I was letting it happen. I was so fucked.

BRIAN

I was so fucked. That was the most intense sex I've ever had in my life. "You're so beautiful," I whispered to her while staring into her eyes. I pulled out of her with a groan, and went to the bathroom to get rid of the condom and to grab a towel to clean us both up.

"Thank you," she said quietly as I cleaned her up. The room smelled like sex, and she was glistening from a little bit of sweat. I was starting to get hard again already. I laid down and pulled her to me, she rested her head on my chest and sighed. It was the most comfortable I've been in my entire life except that she was so quiet, which was definitely not like her in general. One of the things I loved about her is that she says whatever she's thinking. Except in this case; she was quiet, staring off a little.

"What are you thinking about, Jo?" I was almost afraid to ask, but I needed to know what was going on in that pretty little head of hers.

She giggled before answering. "Well, it's been a hell of a day." Thinking back to the events of the day, her dad's funeral, our argument at his house, the bar, and now me holding her, yeah, it had definitely been a hell of a day. I relaxed and laughed too, "Yes, babe, it sure has. Are you okay?" I kissed the top of her head. She hesitated, and took a deep breath.

"Uh, yeah, I'm okay," she propped herself up on her elbows and looked at me. "I just want you to know, that uh…This doesn't have to mean anything, okay? It's been a kind of fucked up day, and we both know this isn't what you do really, so—" What just happened? Now I was pissed off.

"Whoa, wait a minute there, Josephine. We just had mind-blowing sex, and now you're here, with me, at my house and I'm trying to talk to you. Please give me the benefit of the doubt for like five fucking minutes, woman. What I *want*, since you failed to ask me, is *exactly* what's happening *right* now. Without all the angry yapping though. Jesus Christ." I huffed, and she started to giggle. "What's so funny?"

"You are. I'm so sorry, I didn't mean to upset you. I just don't want either one of us to feel like we have to turn this into something it's not. We're both grieving right now, we've been drinking, and these things happen, and I just didn't want you to think I had some kind of expectations," she laid her head back down on the pillows and sighed.

"What kind of expectations?" I genuinely didn't know exactly what she meant, and I wanted her to clarify before I argued with her. I leaned up on one arm staring at her intently.

"I don't know, Brian, can we just change the subject?" she sighed again and I wasn't going to let her off that easy. I didn't really want to push my luck, but pushing my luck was kind of my thing, and after today, I wasn't going to be taking no for an answer.

"Let me be clear. I do have expectations. I told you that you were mine, and I meant it. I don't want you messing around with other guys from the station, any other station or anywhere else. While we're doing whatever this is, and we'll definitely be doing it again, you're mine." There, I said it. I meant it. I've never given a shit before now, but fuck that, I would kill another dude if he went near her. And this was absolutely not a one-time thing. I was feeling pissed off just thinking about it. And I'm pretty sure I sounded like a fucking caveman or something and I didn't care at all.

She sat up, looked me in the eye and smiled. I pulled her to me and kissed her, I was marking her as mine, again. She climbed up on top of me and I was instantly hard again. The things this woman did to me, where the hell did this come from? She whispered in my ear, "I want you. Again. Now. And, I'm on the pill." Knowing we're both clean from our normal FD physicals every six months, she slid herself on top of my length. I sat up with her tits right in my face and started sucking on her stiff little nipples while she slowly bounced up and down on my cock. We had clearly come to an understanding. I massaged her breasts and continued licking and sucking on them until she picked up the pace, and I felt my balls start to swell again. She felt so fucking amazing. She grabbed the headboard behind me, and started fucking me hard. "Brian, I'm so close!" I could feel her body tensing up, and I let myself go too, coming inside her and thrusting as hard as I could; holding her hips to mine. I didn't think I'd ever stop coming, and I could have died a happy man in that exact moment. Oh, I was definitely fucked.

JO

Wow, well that was an interesting turn of events. What the fuck was going on with me? Not only had I just fucked Brian, the hottest man on the planet—*twice*—he called me his. At first, I thought about saying I don't belong to anyone, but him demanding and saying those words, *you're mine*, entranced me. It was hot. He did things to me, and I knew it would not end well. I slept next to him for a while, I was downright exhausted from the best sex of my life and an emotional day in general.

When I woke up, he wasn't there, but I heard noises in the kitchen. I grabbed one of his fire department t-shirts, I had the exact same one, but his smelled like him, and was so big to fit that ridiculously ripped body of his, that it hung down to mid-thigh on me. I looked for my panties, then remembered he ripped them off of me last night. Damn, they were cute too, *oh well it was worth it*, I giggled to myself. I opened a few of his drawers until I found a pair of his boxers, and put them on. I went to the bathroom, and tried to make myself presentable, which was damn near impossible. I settled on washing off the prior day's makeup at least.

I tiptoed to the kitchen and what I saw made my jaw drop. A perfect specimen of a man, shirtless, wearing basketball shorts was humming, and cooking. I just stared at him, he was so fucking hot. He turned around and caught me; giving me the biggest smile with the whitest straightest teeth I've ever seen.

He came over to me. "Leannán," he said, kissing me softly.

"What does that mean?" I asked, kissing him back.

"It means lover in Gaelic. You are my 'leannán. Mianach. Mine." He said it again, and I felt myself get flushed all over. How did I not know he used Gaelic phrases. Who cares, he should do it all the time. I kind of wanted him to fuck me on that kitchen island we started on last night.

I settled for a very soft, "Yes." This was intense.

"I made breakfast, and there's coffee over there," he pointed to the counter and just like that, the intensity was gone, like it never even happened. The whole thing was so crazy. When I turned around to walk to the coffee maker he smacked me on the butt. "Nice outfit. You're lucky I'm hungry and I know you need to eat or I'd take you right here again." He gave me a devilish grin. I really am a sucker for a great smile, okay, I'm a sucker for *his* smile.

"Thank you very much. I forgot to eat yesterday, I'm actually starving. And you know, coffee makes me very happy too." I made myself a cup, and he brought breakfast over to the table for us to eat. He set the two plates down and got himself a cup of coffee too.

"I have off today, which you already knew. I was thinking we could get out of town for the day and go to the beach. Get away from everything for a while, what do you think?" he asked.

"You want to spend the day with me?" I was kind of surprised we were even having breakfast together, let alone discussing spending the day together.

"Of course I do. Plus, I thought maybe a day of not being busy would be a nice change of pace for you. And it's a great day for the beach, I mean it's too cold to swim, but the sun is shining, it should be nice."

God his smile was amazing. He should seriously do toothpaste commercials or something. His eyes were sparkling as he tilted his head like he was waiting for an answer.

"Um, sure. That would actually be really nice. I need to get my car from the bar, and I would like to shower and get a few things from the house first. Is that okay?"

"Of course. I showered earlier so after we eat, we'll go get your car and drop it off at your house. Now eat..." he looked so serious. I'm not withering away, that's just not genetically possible. I have come from a long line of people with a pretty round ass and some curves.

"Yeah yeah, I'm on it," I laughed. This was kind of surreal. I wasn't really sure what' was going on, but I didn't hate it. We couldn't let anyone know about this at all though. I mean good lord, in this town? But a day away, on the beach, sounded absolutely glorious and he's right. I totally deserved a day to just kind of be free. I figured that I would take what I could get for a day and deal with real life another day.

BRIAN

After we got her car back home and she took a shower, we headed out. It was all I could do to keep myself from getting in the shower with her. I could hardly be in the same room as her without getting turned on at that point. I really wasn't sure what the hell was going on, but I liked it. I liked *her*. A lot. I wondered if I always felt this way. I mean I've always been attracted to her. She's beautiful. I was such a dick to her last year, but things were different. Her dad warned me very clearly that my intentions had better be on the up and up and I was not willing to get involved in anything that would jeopardize my relationship with him. I was pretty sure she didn't know her dad talked to me, and it was probably better that way.

It's about an hour drive to the coast and it was a really warm day for October. But that's Florida for you, it was basically second summer here. We could hang out on the beach and get some sun. It's good for the soul, and I thought it would make her happy. Making her happy made me feel happy. Yep, I was fucked.

She was staring out the window, and we were jamming to some early 90's alternative rock so we didn't talk much on the ride; it was making me a little nervous. I wanted to know what was going through her head, she looked deep in thought. I put my hand on her tan thigh just below where her skirt ended and she jumped and looked over at me startled. "Are you okay?" I asked her. I could feel myself scrunching my face at her.

She relaxed and smiled. "Yeah, I'm good. Just thinking about things is all. It's a beautiful day," she took a really deep breath in and sighed out with a smile. I took her hand and brought it to my lips, kissing it softly.

"What are you thinking about? Your dad?" I didn't want her to be sad, I was hoping to give her a distraction from all of that.

"No actually. I was thinking about last night," she laughed and was definitely blushing. I started laughing too, and took her hand in mine again, weaving our fingers together.

"Pretty great night. There's more where that came from. I could barely stay out of your shower this morning." There went my dick again, with a mind of it's own, getting excited. "We're going to have a fun day today, Jo," and I meant it. She smiled back at me and rested her head on the seat. She looked so relaxed, I couldn't wait to get to the beach and just put my arms around her.

We got to the beach in record time, and I specifically chose one we could drive the truck out onto. It was a perfect sunny day, the sun was warm and there was lots of people there enjoying the surf. That's Florida living man, it's like no other. There were surfers out there, people fishing, kids playing. I pulled out a huge blanket I had in my truck, and a picnic basket, yeah I have a picnic basket that my mother gave me years ago, and set up a spot for us just beyond where I parked us. Jo had already hopped out and walked to the water. I watched her kick off her flip flops halfway there, and lift her skirt up a little bit, even though the water didn't stand a chance of getting her clothes wet. She never really showed her body off in a provocative way at all, and that made her that much sexier. She was never on display.

I watched her get her toes wet, and jump a little. I had told her that water was too cold. It was adorable watching her keep sticking her little feet in. I finished setting up a spot for us, kicked my shoes off and quietly snuck up on her. She was staring off into the water; her hair was blowing a little in the gentle breeze. I watched her for a minute, thinking about how perfect she looked, so relaxed and beautiful.

I put my arms around her from behind, and inhaled her scent. She smelled like flowers and that, mixed with the smell of the ocean, was my idea of heaven. I buried my face in her neck and just breathed it all in. "You look happy. It's nice."

She held me a little tighter. "I am. I love the water. Even with all the activity here, it's so peaceful. Thank you for bringing me here today. It's definitely what I needed."

"I want to make you happy, Jo." I turned her around and brought her closer to me;

kissing the top of her head. She was intoxicating. She felt like home. She relaxed into me and we both sighed. She's it for me, I didn't know when it happened, but in a moment somewhere in the last twenty-four hours, she had my soul. I couldn't possibly imagine not holding her and having her in every day of my life. She was meant for me.

"I am happy," she pulled away and smiled up at me with her perfect little mouth. She leaned up on her tippy toes and gave me the sweetest kiss I've ever felt in my life. Her lips were like little pillows, so soft. It wasn't even an erotic thing, even though I was basically at half mast in her presence at all times, it was like sweet sugar on my lips. She took my hand and walked us back to the blanket. "Come on, let's have a drink, and enjoy the view!" She cheerfully pulled me along and plopped down on the blanket, her flowing skirt falling around her.

I grabbed the mimosas we made back at her house out of the cooler, and poured two cups, handing her one. They were really delicious, not nearly as delicious as her lips, but it would do for the moment. I sat down next to her and we both faced the ocean. "Do you remember when we used to come out here fishing with your dad?" I was hoping that wouldn't upset her, I really was having some fond memories sitting here with her.

"I do. They're some of my favorite memories. Not at the firehouse, just sitting out here waiting for fish to show up," she laughed. "My dad loved it here. I think he wanted to retire on the water and just fish, or pretend to fish, all day," she smiled. "We had a lot of fun as kids before you grew up first and became a big jerk." She poked me and laughed.

"Aww, come on now. I'm trying to make up for it now. That's gotta count for something." She was right, I was kind of an asshole as a teenager to her and my brother, and then again as an adult. I took myself way too seriously.

"Well, maybe you should keep trying, buddy," she said and gave me that look. The kiss me right this fucking minute look. And I did. I grabbed the back of her neck and brought her to me. She started exploring my mouth with her tongue and I felt myself wanting to climb on top of her right there in front of everyone.

Until a little kid yelled, *eww* at us. We both started cracking up and immediately stopped our public show. She rolled over on her stomach and couldn't stop laughing. "What is up with us, Brian?" She was still laughing.

"I don't know, but I like it." I smiled down at her.

"I do too." She rolled over on her back and I settled in next to her on my side, just looking at how sweet and beautiful she looked.

She didn't look at me as she spoke. "Did you talk to my dad a lot lately?" I wasn't sure what she meant exactly.

I rolled over on my back next to her, and nudged my arm around her and she laid her head on my shoulder. I Inhaled the salt air before answering. "I'm not sure what you mean. I talked to your dad every day when we were working together, and then when you taught him to text, we communicated daily more or less." I kind of chuckled about that.

God, Jack learning to text on the smartphone Jo bought him was hilarious. He used to get so pissed off at it like it was the phone's fault he couldn't get it to understand the words he wanted to send. He was the king of autocorrect fails and it never disappointed on making me laugh.

She giggled. "No, I meant about anything besides work. He had seemed kind of distracted the last couple weeks, and I was wondering if he ever talked to you about it. Like was he extra stressed out or anything?"

I thought about it, and Jack was always kind of a chill guy unless he was pissed off at his phone, or one of us for doing something careless. He seemed like maybe he didn't feel well the last couple weeks, but I didn't realize it at the time. I decided to keep that to myself for now though.

"I don't think so, babe, he was mostly his usual self from what I could tell. I'm not sure that he would have told me if something was troubling him, or if he wasn't feeling well." Which was true. We have a 'man up' philosophy in the fire department. Basically, if you don't feel well, suck it up pussy. So, if he didn't feel well, he wouldn't have told me unless he thought it was serious. I didn't think she meant his health though.

"Hmmm, I was just wondering," she said, seemingly in thought about it.

"Do you think something was going on with his health?" I asked. He wasn't as fit as the rest of us, but he was also a lot older. He certainly could have worked out a bit more, and maybe staved off the heart attack longer, but our job was stressful, and it could happen to fit guys too.

"Well, he wasn't the poster boy for health and fitness, but no. I don't think that's it. Maybe it was nothing, I'm just doing a lot of thinking about the last year, and how much time we spent together. That's all. It's nothing really. Just thinking," she said.

I squeezed her closer and kissed her forehead. "Babe, you know you were everything to him right?"

She squeezed me back tight. "I do know that. I just miss him, and I wish that I'd talked to him about a lot of things before he was gone."

"I know, baby, I know." I didn't know exactly what to say, but I knew she needed me to hold her. She sighed deeply, and snuggled into me. She was the perfect little fit in my arms. I was holding her hand on my chest, and had my other arm wrapped around her. It was the most comfortable I've ever been with a woman.

We spent the rest of the day sharing stories about her dad, drinking mimosas, and just enjoying each other's company. I can honestly say that I kind of always thought I'd be solo, playing the field. Sure it would be nice to have someone to come home to after a long shift, someone to worry about me being in danger, but that's the job. I found plenty of people to keep the sheets warm, but if this is what a relationship is like, I've been missing out. It was awesome; I'd never felt so relaxed and content in my life.

JO

It had been the best day I've had in as long as I could remember. Brian was so kind, sweet and gentle all day. Not at all like the last couple years. Talking about my dad, talking about the fun we had as kids, it's just been so fun and relaxing, and it's not the mimosas talking. I didn't want the day to end, but I knew it would have to. Then it's back to real life. I was going to push that off for as long as I could. We watched the sunset, and Brian asked if I wanted to head back to town.

"If we must," I said wistfully. It was kind of like a vacation fairy tale.

"We can stay here all night if that makes you happy, Jo. You happy is all I want today." He sounded like he really meant it, but the escape had to come to an end at some point.

"We should head back I guess. It's been nice being away from reality all day. Thank you so much," I rested my forehead on his chest and sighed. He put his arms around me.

"What's wrong? You seem upset." He asked and I tensed. Having this conversation was really the last thing that I wanted to do, but I realized we probably should.

"I'm not upset; I'm just not thrilled about going back to reality is all. I mean it's been a wonderful day, but we have to get back to our lives," I didn't want to say separate lives, but it was what I meant knowing deep down that the other shoe was bound to drop, I was sure of it.

"Back to our lives isn't so bad. You've got a lot of support back at home, Matt, the station...me," he looked at me questioningly. He knew where I was going.

"You're not suggesting this become a public 'thing' are you? We can't be together in public, Brian if that's what you're implying," Okay, there I said it. I stiffened up, and he pulled away from me, looking angry. It needed to be said by me, before he did.

"What do you mean we can't be together? I thought we established this last night. And this morning." He was furious.

"I don't want to go public. We don't even know what this is. Especially after last year, and my dad, everything that's happened. I don't need people thinking that I fell into the arms of the guy that got my dad's job at my old firehouse. And to be perfectly honest, this has been an amazing day and I don't want it to end, but I don't think either one of us is ready for what showing up 'together' really means, do you?"

I was feeling exasperated but it had to be said. I was anxious and paranoid just thinking about it. The last thing I needed is the public humiliation of this falling apart after a weekend fling the day after we said our goodbyes to my dad. Seriously, I didn't need the gossip at the station or the county for that matter and I didn't need the heartbreak that he was going to lay down on me, I mean let's face it, I was hooked. I'd been hooked my whole life on him. But he's a heartbreaker plain and simple. I felt tears welling up in my eyes, and now I'm going to cry too? If only a bolt of lightening would've stricken me down right at that minute. He was staring at me, and he looked hurt and angry, like really pissed off. I felt like a caged animal and I wanted to flee. But I meant what I said.

He took a deep breath, shutting his eyes for a moment. I was waiting for him to raise his voice at me, and I was holding my breath anxiously. "Look, Jo, I honestly don't know what this is between us, but I can tell you that it's been one of the best days of my life sitting out here with you all day, touching you, kissing you, and watching you smile. I know what I said to you last year was shitty, and we can talk about it at some point. I promise I will explain, but not now. Right now, it's me and you, baby, and nothing else really matters. I need to be with you, inside of you, around you, and I know you feel it too. If you want to keep this a secret, I can agree to that for now, but I refuse to never kiss those delicious lips again." He leaned in for a kiss, and I met him halfway. It was soft and deep and felt as if it were meant to prove something. It did, I was getting hot and wet, and I almost forgot everything I had just said. I lost myself when he touched me. I always lost myself with him.

"So, you're suggesting that we sneak around?" I whispered when we stopped kissing. I was resting one hand on his chest and holding myself up in the sand with the other.

"No, *you're* saying we have to sneak around. I'm willing to go along with that for now because I crave you, Jo. I'm not nearly done with this, and I know you're not either, if I have to sneak around behind people's backs to get to you—I will. It's not like we have to climb out the bedroom window and sneak away from our parents, people know we're friends. I've known you your whole life." He grabbed me and rolled on top of me in the sand, holding himself up and caging me in between his huge arms. "But make no mistake, you're mine, Jo. There's no one else in the picture while this is going on. Understood?" He looked me right in the eyes.

"Does that go both ways?" I had to ask, and he let his lips spread wide in a handsome grin; trying to disguise his urge to laugh.

"Yes, it goes both ways. I mean it, both of us. Only you. Only me. I know that you don't believe me, but you'll see." With that, he leaned in for another kiss. It wasn't the animalistic crazy devouring kiss we had so often, it was deep and loving, and I forgot my name when it happened. He literally took my breath away. This couldn't possibly be real, could it?

BRIAN

Honestly, I wanted to flip the fuck out when she said we couldn't 'go public' whateverthefuck that even means. I'm actually totally impressed with myself that I didn't, and I somehow came up with a game plan on the fly. I usually do what I want and generally, especially when it comes to women, I get what I want. That being said, I didn't want to scare her off and I sure as hell didn't want to stop fucking her. I didn't really love the idea of having a secret from my brothers at the firehouse, or my actual brother for that matter, but if it kept this thing going longer then I was all for it. I couldn't get the woman off my mind and if it meant sneaking around to see her naked and otherwise, then so be it. For the time being.

I'd never actually had a girlfriend that I brought out with me anywhere anyway, so this was fine until I figured out what is really going on between us. I was going to ride this out because I'd get to see her, and she wouldn't be seeing anyone else. Apparently, I'm more fucked than I thought. When did I start becoming such a pussy? God, I needed to get to the gym and workout or something. *Do something manly.*

We pulled into her driveway, and she reached to open the door. "Hey!" I snapped at her.

"What?" I startled her and hopped out of my side.

"What did I tell you about letting me get the door for you?" I smiled across the bench seat at her.

She immediately blushed and smiled, so my mission was accomplished, as she took her hand off the door. I came around and opened her door for her, taking her hand and helping her out of the truck.

"You've become quite the gentlemen, Cavanaugh," she took my hand and we walked to the front door of her dad's old place.

"You like it?" I caressed her face with the back of my hand.

"I do, very much," she whispered.

"Are you going to invite me in, Jo?" I kissed her softly.

"Would you like to come in, Brian?" she smiled up at me, her gray eyes sparkling.

"Why yes, I would like to come in and get you out of that dress. Immediately please," I started reaching up under her dress, finding her wet, just how I liked her.

She opened the door, and pulled me in behind her. I shut and locked it, turning to pin her with my stare. Her back was to me; I stopped her and pulled her into my chest. Kissing her neck, I slid one of the straps of her dress off her shoulder and she leaned into me more, making my cock hard as hell. I was wearing basketball shorts, so there was no hiding what she did to me.

"Let's go to my room," she whispered and took my hand, pulling me behind her. We got to her room and she turned to face me, grabbed the hem of her dress and pulled it up over her head in one motion. Standing in front of me, braless, wearing nothing but a pair of white lacy panties, she smiled and then looked down.

"Álainn...beautiful...you're so beautiful. Look at me, Josephine," I took her chin in my hand and lifted her face to meet my eyes. "Don't look away, baby," I told her as I yanked my shirt up over my head. Looking into my eyes, she didn't say anything and it made me question if she was okay. I took her face in my hands again, bringing her close. "Talk to me, Jo," I stroked her face gently.

"Now is not for talking," she smiled and leaned in to kiss me. My heart was racing, as I pulled her in tight to take her mouth to mine, all the blood in my body rushed right to my cock again, igniting my need to be inside her. Playing with the waistband of my shorts, she reached in and freed my cock and sunk to her knees, dragging my shorts down with her. Taking me in her mouth, she licked the tip of my cock which was just starting to drip, and then took my entire length.

"Oh fuck, Josephine, that feels so fucking good," I was holding the back of her head as gently as I could while she used one hand to stroke my shaft, and the other was massaging my balls. She used just the right amount of pressure with her tongue as she bobbed her head up and down on my aching cock. My balls were getting heavy and I was going to cum any minute. "I'm going to cum baby, you gotta stop," I tried to gently push her away.

My girl grabbed onto my ass and began sucking even more vigilantly, I couldn't take it anymore, I let every bit of cum I had hit the back of her throat and she swallowed every drop. I yelled out with my release, grabbing the back of her head as gently as I possibly could at that moment, which wasn't very gentle.

Holy shit, was that fucking hot. When I was done, she let my cock out of her beautiful mouth with a pop and she looked up at me, still on her knees with a satisfied smile on her face. Goddamn she's so hot and so beautiful, and she's mine was all I could think looking down at her like that. "Oh, my God, that was amazing. Now get up and turn around," I demanded. I was going to fuck her so hard she'd feel me all day tomorrow, but not before I taste her sweet pussy again.

She got up slowly, touching me softly all the way up, kissing my torso, my abs and my chest on her way up, rubbing those full perky breasts up my body. She turned around, her back to me, rubbing so closely and softly against me, I was instantly hard again. "Bend over," I demanded gruffly and she obeyed immediately, leaning her hands onto the bed with her ass in the air toward me, still wearing those white lace panties.

I softly rubbed the small of her back, and gently rolled her panties down to her ankles and helped her step out of them, widening her stance, and running my hand back up her leg between her thighs. She took a breath in, and I caressed that perfect round ass with my other hand and gave it a squeeze. I fucking loved her ass, I was going to get it eventually, but not yet. I got down on my knees, and bent her further over on the mattress, her legs spread wide in my face, and began licking her sweet juices.

She started moaning softly, and I stuck a finger deep inside her, lapping at her wet pussy. "Oh, Brian," she called out, sticking her ass even further into the air, and pumping her sweet little clit on my finger. Just as she started to cry out, ready to cum, I pulled my finger out, stood up, and thrust all of my cock inside her. She cried out. "Oh, my God, Brian, fuck fuck fuck!!!" She met me, pushing back into every thrust, calling out my name. I fucking loved it when she screamed my name.

I could tell she was almost ready, she was panting and clawing at the sheets on the bed. "Come with me, Jo, come with me, baby!" and I fucked her even harder, with everything I had, while she screamed my name out into the mattress, arching her back and pulling the sheets toward her. I pumped her pussy full and when we were both done, I practically collapsed on top of her, my heart beating out of my chest. We were both shaking and panting, relishing in the aftershocks. I scooped her up onto the bed, planted a kiss on her lips, and went to the bathroom to get something to clean us both up.

When I came back, she was laying on the bed, totally naked, smiling at the ceiling. I stopped for a minute and she looked over in my direction. "Hey you," she grinned.

"Hey, beautiful, whatcha thinking over here," I climbed on the bed next to her, and cleaned us both up with a warm washcloth. "That was pretty amazing, Jo."

"Yes, yes it was. I think I'll be feeling that tomorrow," she laughed.

Feeling some pride, I replied. "That was the plan. Gotta have me on your mind tomorrow," I dropped the towel on the ground, and scooted in next to her, pulling her close. She sighed into me, and I squeezed her a little tighter and planted several kisses on the top of her head. Inhaling her scent, that freshness that reminded me of spring mornings when the orange blossoms were blooming, I felt more at ease than I ever remembered feeling and the more time I spent with her like that, the more comfortable I became.

"Oh, I'm sure I'll be thinking of you tomorrow, Brian." She gave me a squeeze, then started to get up.

"Where are you going?" I reached out to keep her in place next to me. She dodged me, and went over to her closet and grabbed some little shorts and a fire department t-shirt to put on.

"I'm not going anywhere, but the shower, however you gotta get home," she laughed. I frowned back at her, I didn't want to go. I wanted to wake up next to her. I was about to throw a temper tantrum.

"I think I'd rather just stay here in bed with you.

"Yea, as nice as that would be, and it would be nice," she came over to the bed and kissed me. "We both have early shifts tomorrow, babe, and my house is pretty much on everyone's way to work, so your truck needs to not be sitting in my driveway in the morning," she got back up off the bed.

"How about this? How about if I join you in the shower, and then I'll go home to my lonely bed without you tonight if I absolutely must?" I tried to negotiate.

"That sounds like a fair deal, Cavanaugh, I like how you do business." Her smile was so bright it gave me butterflies. She came back over to the bed, leaned over me and planted a sweet kiss on my lips, taking my hand, and dragging me with her to the bathroom.

After stripping down again, she leaned over and turned the water on, and I stood watching her in awe for a moment. It was like watching art that you couldn't understand, but you loved anyway. As my eyes roamed her beautiful body, taking in her colorful tattoos, I was hard again. She turned around to look at me and a smile formed at the corners of her mouth "Come on, let's get in, babe." she whispered. Okay, yeah I loved it when she calls me babe. I loved it when she calls me anything actually, but that, I really loved, it sent a warm sensation straight to my chest.

I followed her into the huge walk-in shower, unable to keep my hands off her. She was standing under the water, and pulled me in to kiss her. "This is really nice, Brian," she whispered with her lips just barely touching mine.

I wrapped my arms around her and agreed. "Yes it is, baby, we'll have to make this a habit." I seriously couldn't stop smiling around her. She's sexy, smart, she's everything, and my carnal need was beginning to take over. I grabbed the body wash and some poofy sponge thing and started to wash her. She had a perfect body. She wasn't tiny, she was fit and strong, curvy, with that nice round ass that I couldn't get enough of.

She started to make quiet moaning sounds as I rubbed her body down gently, the hot water rolling over both of us, wrapping us in warmth. She in turn, was rubbing soap around my shoulders and neck, massaging me with just enough pressure to send tingles through my whole body. I was so relaxed, and so turned on that I dropped to my knees in the shower, and pushed her against the shower wall. I grabbed her leg and threw it over my shoulder, I was going to taste her delicious pussy again right now.

I looked up at her, and she was watching me, smiling and breathing heavily while the water continued to roll over both of us. "Baby, I need to taste you again," I started to circle her clit with my thumb, watching her react to me by touching herself, massaging her own breasts, and pinching her hard pink nipples. Fuck, that's hot. My dick was aching to be inside her, but I was hungry for that pussy.

I went in with one finger, and started to lick that hard little nub causing her to suck in air and cry out softly. "That feels so good!" She was trying to steady herself on one leg, leaning into the shower wall and reaching out on the tile, but I was holding onto her so tight, she wouldn't fall. I kept licking and sucking at her folds, pumping two fingers inside her slowly, coaxing out her release.

As she got closer, she gently grabbed onto my head with her other hand and started to moan and cried out, "Brian, I'm going to cum! Oh, my God, baby!" Her whole body shook and I could taste her juices as I continued licking gently, making it last as long as I could. When she was done, I stood up and kissed her hard, wanting her to taste herself on me.

"Do you taste how delicious you are?" I growled at her, pressing my hard cock against her. "I need to be inside you, baby," I said, not waiting for her answer. She looked satiated and I wasn't done with her by a long shot.

"Yes please," she whispered to me, and gently bit my bottom lip, then ran her tongue across it.

I grabbed her by the ass, lifted her and pressed her into the shower wall as she wrapped her legs around me. I slowly guided her down on my cock which was aching for her now. She grabbed onto me, yelling out as I thrust into her. Fuck her pussy was so tight, I could feel it adjusting to my size inside of her, squeezing my dick just enough to send chills all over me while I was slowly pumping into her and holding her against the wall. Sex has never been this amazing, it's like bees buzzing all around me.

"You like that, baby? You like my cock inside you?" I whispered in her ear. She was holding on to me tight while I fucked her against the wall.

"I can't get enough, baby," she panted.

I could feel my release coming, and I was trying to hold off until she was there. I started to try moving faster, and she moaned; giving me the go ahead. I started pumping into her hard, causing her to cry out with each thrust, driving me even crazier than I already was.

"Oh yes! Brian! Fuck me, baby, that's so good!" She started to shake, and I could feel her pussy tighten around my dick, bringing me to my climax, I pulled her down on my cock as hard as I could and let myself go inside of her, crying out myself.

"Jo, oh, God!" I yelled out as every bit of cum I had was released inside her. I fucking loved coming inside her, there's no greater feeling. As we both finished, I gently let her down to her feet again, and just pressed my body against her, under the steaming hot water, relishing in the moment.

"Damn, that was amazing. You have no idea how fucking sexy you are, do you?" I looked down at her beautiful, gray eyes looking back up at me.

She smiled. "That *was* fantastic, baby," she said. "I've never had shower sex, we'll have to keep this on the regular list of things to do in secret," she laughed.

After we got out and dried off, we dressed in her room. She put on leggings that had me staring at her ass and forgetting everything else. I laid down on her bed and sighed.

"Tired, babe?" she climbed on top of me straddling her legs around me and looking down at me smiling that beautiful smile of hers. I grabbed her hips and rubbed the sides of her legs.

"Not really, just super content actually," I smiled from the inside out. "I'm really happy, Jo, I really like being with you." Her presence was so warm and inviting, even when it wasn't sexual, which it was for me almost all the time, but it was something different. I just wanted to be near her.

"I'm happy too, Brian," she replied, but she looked like she had something else to say.

"But? It sounds like there's a but," I pushed myself up, causing her to put her arms around me to stay upright.

She held on tight to me, bringing me in for a hug, and playing with the hair at the back of my neck, sending tingles through my head. "There's no 'but', this is actually really wonderful," she kissed my temple sweetly, and rested her head on my shoulder. I brought her in tight, rubbing her back softly while she sighed into me. I'm in, one hundred percent. This chick is all that's right in the world. How did I even consider saying no to this in the past? I have seen the error of my ways, everyone should feel this content with someone.

"I promise you, it will always be wonderful," I pulled her away just enough to get lost in her eyes. "I'm serious. You need to understand I don't consider this a fling, something is happening here." God, I almost wanted to tell her I love her right now, but I've never said that to anyone, ever.

"I don't consider this a fling, Brian, honestly I don't," she smiled sweetly, leaning in for a kiss. I wrapped my arms completely around her, kissing her as softly as I could. She stirred up an animal need in me, but the passion in just that sweet kiss overwhelmed me. I held onto her in a hug that felt almost desperate, like I was afraid to break it and let her go. She sat up and released me first, to my dismay. I could have held her all night.

"As much as I'd love you to stay, babe, you've gotta go," she crawled off me and walked across the room, grabbing a sweatshirt and pulling it on over her head. She looked kind of like she just woke up, she was fucking adorable.

"Alright, alright. You win this time, but I prefer waking up next to you, in my bed. So that needs to get on the schedule asap," I was going to insist on this in the very near future.

She slinked her sexy ass over to me, and put her arms around my midsection and looked up. "I think that can be arranged," I leaned down and kissed her. God, I'd never get tired of kissing her, I needed my lips on her constantly. "Now next time you swing by, park out back. That big truck of yours is a pretty huge eyesore in my driveway for all to see," she gave me a sideways glance, meaning business.

"Ugh, Jo, I hate hiding. Do we have to hide? Seriously?" I was still holding onto her and rolled my eyes.

"Yes, we do if you want to keep doing this. It's not anyone's business anyway. And before you ask, no, I'm not telling Matt either, so don't think it's easy for me. This is just the best for now, trust me," she laid her head on my chest.

Kissing the top of her head, I agreed. "Okay, for now. But let me be clear, this isn't just about sex. Do you understand me?" Honestly, I'd do anything to keep her, to keep this feeling. She was like a drug and now that I'd had her, I couldn't get enough.

"Yes, I understand," she reached around me and scratched my back softly, sending chills up my spine. "Now get your ass out of here," she laughed.

"Booo. Fine. I'll text you later, baby," I cupped her face in my hands and kissed her.

I left her house a few minutes later, after we made out like teenagers in the doorway. Even though it was getting a bit late, I went to the gym at the firehouse. I called my brother and he said he'd meet me there. While I had a twenty-four hour shift the next day at seven a.m., a shitload of paperwork due to the new Chief appointment, I seriously needed to hit the gym a little tonight. Jo gets me so fired up, and I just couldn't fathom how Jack dealt with all the bureaucracy and red tape bullshit that comes with being Chief.

Matt was already there when I pulled up. "Where have you been all day, bro?" he asked me.

"I went fishing at the beach," I lied, like she wanted me to.

"You don't have any poles in your truck, man," *Christ, I suck at this lying business already apparently.*

"Well, I went to the beach intending to fish. Since I didn't have my poles, I basically just hung out. It's been kind of a long couple days dealing with everything here at the station since Jack..." I trailed off.

"Yeah, it has. I sure do miss the old man. Closest thing to a dad we ever really had. It's not the same without him giving us shit." Matt chuckled. He was right. "It was probably nice out there just relaxing. We should actually go fishing like we used to out on the beach soon."

"Yea, let's definitely do that soon. Come on, let's pick up some heavy shit and put it down," I laughed. Okay, so I covered myself that time. I was gonna have to get better at that though. I grabbed my cell out of my pocket and sent her a text.

My lips need to be all over you. When can I see you?

She replied immediately *You just left!*

I'm already hard thinking about you. When? I couldn't help myself.

Oh please lol. I can come by the station tomorrow after my shift at 19 to say hi, but we can't do anything there. Day after maybe when you're not working.

You're working at 19 tomorrow? We need to discuss that. And maybe nothing. You're mine. Tomorrow. Now I was pushing my luck but fuck it. I was already getting half hard just thinking about it. And as for her working at 19 with that dickbag? No. That needed to stop immediately.

I have to work, there's nothing to discuss. And we'll see about tomorrow. Goodnight, Cavanaugh.

Goodnight my beautiful, Josephine. She has no idea who she's messing with. I get what I want. We were absolutely going to discuss her not working at all these different places though. And definitely not with that Danny asshole, something about him really bothers me. He's shady as fuck and I don't trust him. I put my phone away and killed my upper body at the gym.

JO

I loved that he called me by my full name sometimes. No one did really, even my dad rarely did. Actually he and Brian are the only two people to call me Josephine, ever. It was my mom's middle name. Everyone else called me Jo. After he left, I laid down on the couch and thought about how excited he makes me. I wondered if he really meant what he said, that it wasn't about sex, that it was something more. Lord knows it was something more to me, but I just wasn't sure with him.

I was disappointed that I told him to leave, and I was almost disappointed in myself that I was letting this happen, but it felt so good. Couldn't really be bad, could it? Something that felt so right? Okay maybe, but maybe it was time for me to start living a little instead of being so wound up all the time. I had a reputation for being pretty high strung and fussy. Not in a girly kind of way, just particular about things. Around the firehouse, even as a young girl, I was like the "mom" of the group always making sure nobody got hurt if I could avoid it, always knowing all the "rules". That probably had a bit to do with my dad too, but it was my nature to look after people. It was in my genes to take care of people.

I really needed to make some decisions about work too; I had too many part-time jobs. I had been working per diem at another fire department —Danny's fire department actually, and as a fire inspector I picked up some work, in addition to co-teaching a class at the community college in fire science of course, and a part time gig as a per diem paramedic sometimes, but I had not picked up any shifts at Station 23 in quite a while. I wasn't sure why I had been avoiding working there, it was actually my favorite place to work. I didn't have to prove myself anymore, and I liked just about everyone there. My teaching semester was over, and Matt had suggested I talk to Brian about picking up some shifts at the station and stopping work at Station 19, since it was the same department Danny belonged to. I needed to be there for work tomorrow though, I had been on the schedule a while. I'd need to think that over. Brian certainly didn't like it. I didn't like personal issues becoming work business, but Danny showing up at dad's funeral was too much. I didn't need him making work unsafe. Something about his behavior really gave me the chills.

After my shower, I made myself a sandwich for dinner, and sat down at my dad's desk. I wanted to go through some of his papers, and start getting things in order. Since I was living at Danny's until a couple months ago, I didn't have another place except here, and I was planning to stay here until some other plan came to mind. I needed to start sorting through my dad's stuff and getting rid of some of the junk he'd been collecting. And the papers, that man had notebooks and papers everywhere. He kept regular and meticulous notes on calls he was on, in case he ever needed to refer to them in court, or for his reports. I turned the scanner on; I liked the background noise, and hearing what emergencies were going on across the county actually made me feel safe, and sometimes

107

people said some really hilarious, and dumb, stuff over the air.

There was a small car accident on the other side of town, an MVA, with no injuries, and some fluids on the ground. A boring gig for a firefighter, you're basically spreading cat litter all over the road to soak up the oil and grease, and sweeping it up. There was a respiratory emergency at the nursing home, which didn't require the FD, just an ambulance. That was a pretty common call unfortunately. That, and slip and falls. In Florida, you're required to be both a paramedic and a firefighter to work, and I admitted, with the exception of helping the elderly, and people that have been in car accidents, fire was really my favorite. The camaraderie of the brotherhood as we call it, is a lot like police or guys in the military. They become your family, and really you're only as good as the sum of your parts on the team. Everyone has a specialty of some kind, something that they love about the job, and a role they have on a truck. There were no calls for our department, which made me feel good. As fun as it is to be a firefighter, when the tones drop, you don't always know what you're walking into, and I did always fear for the safety of my friends.

My favorite was engine work; I just wasn't a ladder girl. I hated ladders at the academy, and I'd climbed on top of buildings to do work when needed, but I really hated it. I hated carrying heavy shit up a ladder even more. That vertigo-like sick feeling that you're going to fall. I'd read someplace that there are only two fears we're born with, the fear of falling, and a fear of loud noises. You didn't grow up in a firehouse maintaining a fear of loud noises, in fact, I loved the sounds of the trucks, the saws, the sirens. The fear of falling, that never went away.

I was smaller than most of the guys, so rescue in tight spaces was usually my job. I was on the tactical rescue team, which was ideal since I could squeeze into cars that are all smashed up to help stabilize patients, crawl in a storm drain to save baby geese easier, things like that. I could haul hose wherever it needs to go, and carry all the same stuff the guys could, we just all have our specialty and our preference. On a fire, I was usually on the hose, or doing some searches, that kind of thing. The engine was for fire suppression and water supply and the ladder was for ventilation, search and rescue. This was all relative, and depended on what you saw when you showed up at a scene and what other stations or equipment were available.

My dad insisted that if I was really going to make a career out of it, that I get certified in basically everything there was and made myself as good as possible at every activity in the service I could. He knew that even with him at the helm, I'd face some challenges as a female firefighter, and he knew I didn't want special treatment. Even though he felt the real learning was on the streets, there was something to be said for attending all of the classes, for exposure to other departments, and for credibility later on. It's actually helped me a lot, I'd kind of become a jack of all trades and literally, I had a laundry list of certifications that while interesting, aren't especially common.

Brian was a ladder guy, so we didn't ride the same truck usually, although he didn't ride a truck that much anyway now since becoming deputy chief, and now chief of course. He had his own duty truck to take to scenes. Ladder guys, or truck guys, love climbing on roofs, going up ladders, hell as a kid he loved climbing trees and stuff like that so I guessed it made sense. Matt and Brian are actually on the same schedule and typically work together most of the time. I used to be on the same shift pretty often as well, just a different truck than Brian. We used to have a lot of fun at the station. I was the only woman, but our department is progressive, so it was never an issue really, plus I guess looking back, my dad being the chief meant that people would respect me, or at the very least be nice to me. In fact, I think that people expected a lot more out of me than others sometimes because my dad was so good at what he did.

Matt and Brian have been in my life literally since Matt and I were babies, and Brian was three. We grew up together. I didn't want this fling with Brian to ruin what little family I really have left, but I also couldn't stop thinking of getting him back in bed. As long as it remained a secret, that was okay. I wished it didn't have to be a fling, but I knew that we could never go public, and to be totally honest with myself, there's no way that he could be serious about me for long. It's just not who he is.

BRIAN

Thinking about her working at Station 19 was making it a long day. It made my blood boil, I knew that douchebag Danny was going to do something, I just didn't know what. He rubbed me the wrong way for more than one reason, there's something just off about him, I didn't want him anywhere near Jo. He's up to no good, and I made a mental note to do some digging on the guy. She needed to just come back to this department already. I was sitting at my desk with a mountain of paperwork in front of me and a huge cup of coffee, but I couldn't concentrate, I tapped my fingers, just being pissed off about her working there, and also half turned on because I was thinking about her.

I pulled out my phone to text her, *Morning, beautiful. When are you coming by?*

I sat and waited for her to reply. I know she doesn't have a call, because I've been listening to the scanner, and I would know if there was a fire or an EMS call in her district. After what seemed like forever, but probably was a few minutes, she replied.

Hey, there. After my shift I can swing by.

Everything okay? I ask.

Yeah, why wouldn't it be? I'm just working. Like you.

You're working where we both know you shouldn't be. I was going to be honest. She definitely shouldn't be there.

Look, I'm just working. Please don't give me a hard time.

I'm protecting what's mine.

I don't need protection, I'm just working. I'll be by after my shift around 4. Now settle yourself ;)

Okay, I got the wink, so she wasn't pissed. *Just be careful. I miss you. ;)* I don't care if I sound like a pussy, I do miss her.

Be careful too. And then she sent a second text, *I miss you too.* I grinned like an idiot and stared at my phone. She missed me and I loved it.

The tones dropped, and I hopped up and shoved my phone in my pocket. I was listening for the dispatcher to announce where the call was and what we had in store for us today.

"Engine 23, Ladder 23, Visible Smoke in the area of North Orange and Virginia Ave," I heard over the intercom. I was wearing my duty radio, so I replied on my way to my new Chief's truck. "Central, 2300 responding." The rest of the guys were racing to their trucks, and they also responded accordingly.

Normally we'd have an actual address, but since it was the middle of the day, someone must had spotted smoke, and called it in. That meant we'd either have to find which house it is, or it would be really obvious which house it is. Because it's a home on the end of town, the neighboring town's trucks were called as well. We all went lights and sirens to the scene, something I'll always love. The rush of excitement that comes with getting to the scene is something you just can't describe unless you've done it. I arrived first, and immediately saw which house it was and called it into dispatch. I threw my jacket and helmet on, and walked around the house doing my 360, sizing up the scene.

The other trucks arrived shortly after I did, and I instructed them where to set up. It looked like there was a fire somewhere in the back corner of the house, probably the kitchen. The smoke alarms were audible now, and I could see a lot of smoke in the kitchen window. It appeared that no residents were home, but we still needed to do a search. My guys ran like a well-oiled machine. I went back to my vehicle to set up command, and instructed the ladder to set up and conduct a search to make sure there was no victims in the house. Then instructed the engine to attach to the nearest hydrant and prepare to go in the back side of the house. The interior crew reported that there was no visible fire, however there was smoke coming from the wall near the oven.

I sighed. That meant that if they didn't find the hot spot with the TIC (thermal imaging camera), they'd have to start ripping the wall apart looking for the fire. That could go a lot of different ways for us, and get complicated. In a concrete block house, you couldn't exactly just rip the walls apart obviously, and it could be a little trickier to find the source of the fire. Also, our job was not just to find the fire and put "the wet stuff on the red stuff", but we had a moral responsibility to try not to do a bunch of damage to personal property as well. The house had an addition to it, so it wasn't traditional cement block like most homes in Florida. It definitely had a truss roof construction on the addition of the second floor, and I was pretty concerned there was fire in the addition walls making its way to the roof. In central Florida, most of the homes start as one story cement block, and they're on relatively small plots of land. The only way to have a bigger house is to move outside the city, or build up. This house had done that, and it wasn't looking good for the likely pricey addition. I called for additional personnel to the scene, it was definitely a fire and we'd need reinforcements. It was going to be a long job.

JO

I heard Station 23 get tapped out for what sounds like might become a real fire. That made me a bit tense. The thing is, firefighting isn't really what you see on television. There aren't that many fires in real life. Yes, in a city, there's more than our fair share, however it's not racing from one fire to the next, so when you do have a legitimate fire, it's a big deal. Brian knew what he was doing and those guys are really the best around, so I was sure it would be fine. It's unlikely for me to get called there, it's all the way on the other side of town. I decided to listen to the call on the radio to stay up-to-date.

I'd been avoiding Danny all morning, who wasn't supposed to be on the schedule, and yet somehow miraculously was on shift. He's up to no good, and while I probably should talk to him to make arrangements to get a few things I left at his place, I'd almost rather buy new shit. He approached me this morning when I got in, and I told him I needed to go check my duty rig. I was not riding a fire truck today, I was medic du jour today, and my partner was another girl who's also a per diem. I didn't know her that well. Her name was June, and she was a tiny thing, about three inches shorter than me, and I'm only five foot four, and she means business. I'd partnered with her before, and she was a nice chick and not competitive, which was a wonderful change of pace in a medic partner. I prefer when everyone just shows up ready to do their job and that was definitely June.

We hadn't had a call all day, and so we were sitting in the engine bay listening to Brian's call. They called for additional staff, so there was definitely a fire. I loved hearing him on the radio, he sounded gruff and sexy. I felt myself grinning hearing his voice give orders and provide updates.

"Central, place all companies in service, and request back-up EMS. Active fire in progress." I heard him demand over the air. This perked me up, that's pretty serious around here. Suddenly, our tones dropped too.

"Rescue 19, EMS Fire Response to North Orange & Virginia for active fire." My partner and I hopped up and headed to our duty rig. I replied immediately over the air. "Central, Rescue 19 en route."

The fire was actually about fifteen minutes in traffic away, it's a congested area, and even with lights and sirens it's difficult to get through it. It was "my treat", which basically meant, my partner drove, and I got the first patient. In those situations, you took turns unless a call was something that was the one thing that you "just can't" and you made a deal. In this case, it was just my treat, so I rode shotgun, and laid on the sirens, a lot. I was a little anxious knowing that Brian was there. It would be the first time I'd see him since everything that was going on, and we were both working. It was never an issue when I had a mad crush on him from afar, but I felt invested differently. I was there to do a job, so that's what I'd do. I was actually relieved that he wasn't interior fighting the fire himself, although all of my other friends were.

My partner knew that Station 23 had command, and that it was my old station. "Hey, do you know if it's your old shift on today?" June asked.

"Actually, yeah they are on today. It's Matt, his brother, and our friends inside right now." I laid on the queue hard, people drive like assholes here and they needed to get the hell out of our way for Christ's sake.

"Must be a fucking mess for us to get called all the way out here. I didn't think the county was that busy today, although I was napping this morning, so what do I know?" June laughed.

"It's actually busy as hell today, I think all the other rigs were out and that's why we got called all the way over here. You'd think it was a full moon or something. I'm actually more than happy to get out of the station today. At least we can sit outside and watch the firefighters." June knew about Danny, and commented this morning over coffee why he was on the schedule when he wasn't supposed to be. She never cared for him. The more time that passed it seems nobody really liked him.

We were rolling up to the scene, and I saw my dad's old truck, now Brian's truck.

June pulled up next to Brian and yelled out the window. "Hey, Chief, where do you want us?" He had a serious look on his face, and when he looked up, he looked right at me and smiled.

"Pull back out in front of my truck. Thanks for coming," He went back to what he was doing; he had several guys around him providing reports and waiting for orders. It was such a turn on watching him. He had on his Class B uniform, but he had his turnout coat and helmet on and was pointing at the rear of the house where you could see brown smoke puffing out of the roof seam steadily. He looked so commanding, and honestly, it was making me wet. I was definitely staring at him.

He looked up and waved us over once we'd parked, and had our equipment in hand. We were really on standby, there were no active injuries at this time. "Meadows, Cruise, thanks for coming. Looks like a busy day in EMS, and fire too it seems. You can hang out here for now, we already have a rehab unit set up in the neighbors yard over by the B side of the house. I'm hoping not to need you...for EMS." His gazed locked with mine. Damn that was smooth. I felt myself get hot, and not from the fire.

"Sounds good, Chief," June replied, and we wandered a few yards away to watch the scene and stay out of the way. We stood off to the side of Command, where Brian was and watched the crews go in and out of the house, listening to the ops channel on the radios we were wearing. The ops channel is the channel you switch to once your scene is active, so you're not clogging up the dispatch channel. Everyone on the scene switches to that channel so you can talk to each other about what's going on with your job, what you need, all of that kind of thing.

The interior crew was able to find active fire in the attic, which was part of what looked like an addition to me. The fire probably started in the electric in the kitchen, it was an old house, but had two stories, which is not at all traditional for Florida homes. I knew Brian knew all of that, so I just minded my own business, I was there as EMS support, and with a different station. He's the boss and it was his show. He was kind of always the boss, since he was ahead of most of us at the academy and all, but I have to say it was strange to be at a mutual aid call like this and not see my dad running Command. It made me a little sad.

June seemed pretty bored, and to be honest, if it weren't for lusting after Brian, leaned up against my ambulance, I'd be pretty bored too. She wanted to see if we could leave after we'd been there about an hour. "I'm gonna go ask Command if we can get out of here; it's been over an hour and our shift is almost over. They can get a crew that's closer by now, you cool with that?" she asked me.

"Yeah, that's fine," I actually wanted to stay and more or less stare but she was right. We could leave then, sit in traffic, and probably get to our station just in time for our shift to end. That would mean I could totally avoid Danny today. She walked over to Brian, and although I couldn't hear the conversation, he glanced at me, and he looked annoyed. I didn't know what he wanted me to do, they didn't really need us here since by now the scene was secured, the fire appeared to be out, and they had another crew that was doing rehab that could be assigned. He was going to be there for awhile, but that wasn't my job today.

"He seemed grumpy about it, but he released us from the scene. The fire is out anyway; they don't need us loitering." She hopped into the driver seat, and as I was climbing into the passenger seat, I caught Brian's eye. I gave a little wave and got in my rig. He didn't wave back, and that made me sad, even though we were at a scene. Well, I'll just have to deal with it later, I'd text him or something when I got home. He wouldn't be done here, and back at the station when I got done, so there was no point in planning to stop by. Based on his scrunched up face, I'd be hearing from him sooner rather than later anyway, and that was alright with me. Watching him in action today, made me feel proud, like he was *my* hero.

BRIAN

Even though I didn't need Jo and her tiny partner on scene anymore, I was still annoyed when they left. I looked at my watch when Cruise came over, and immediately realized that I wouldn't be done here by the time Jo was originally planning to stop by and see me. Both myself and my cock were very disappointed. I grabbed my cell off the tailgate of my truck, and sent her a quick text and then put my phone in my pocket.

I'm still getting my hands on you tonight. I didn't wait for a reply, I really wanted to wrap it up here, and I needed to go take a look inside the residence so I could write my reports up. Jack was very serious about maintaining records, and that is something he taught me very early on. He said that it could save your ass if a resident came back and thought we did something wrong, or needed to use our report in court to back up their claims against a shitty contractor, or a million other reasons. He made it very clear that complete concise reports, even for fires, not just EMS, were critical.

I felt my phone vibrate in my pocket, and knowing it was her gave me a stiff dick. I couldn't wait to get the hell out of there and see her. But I still had some work to do.

We finished up about two hours later, and it was hot. I was sweating from the Florida heat, my guys were exhausted, and it was finally time to head back to the station. I checked my phone to see what Jo's reply was, and I grinned at the screen.

Hope you're thinking of a creative way to make that happen, Chief.

Oh I most certainly was. I couldn't stop smiling, and Matt came over to me as we walked back to the trucks to leave. "What are you all smiley about? You look like an idiot," he laughed at me.

I quickly shoved my phone back in my pocket. "Ah nothing, just a girl." Well, it wasn't a lie, it was a girl. It was my girl.

"Oh, you've got a new one do you? What's she look like? Got a picture of this one?"

he asked and leaned in to nudge me to take my phone back out, which obviously I wasn't going to do.

"No, but you know she's hot." I laughed and walked off to my truck. Fortunately for me, this was pretty typical banter between us when it came to the opposite sex. Matt and I really don't discuss these things outside of your typical chiding. None of us has been in a real relationship for as long as I could remember, so our conversations were always pretty superficial. I didn't even think anyone in our little circle even tried seriously dating anyone. That made me think of Jo and I, and how this would all play out. I was already completely unwilling to let her go. That was pretty much the long and short of it, she needed to be with me always, and I needed to figure out how to make that happen. In any event, she would be stopping by to see me later, and the nice thing about working twenty-four hour shifts at a giant firehouse is that there are plenty of places to disappear to when you needed some "alone time." I'd be making sure we had some of that one way or another.

In the meantime, I also had another little surprise for Jo. I wasn't sure she'd love it, but I thought she'd be open to it.

JO

I was just getting out of the shower when I got a text from Brian letting me know they were back at the station finally. It really did take forever to clean up a scene sometimes. I was already home, and fussing with myself over how I was going to play this tonight. Was I going there as a casual friend stopping by? What was my real excuse for coming there? I didn't really want to come off suspicious. This whole sneaking around thing in public was a little harder than I anticipated.

I texted back that I'd be there in a half hour or so. I kept fussing with my hair, which was short and black, and had kind of a messy pixie thing happening which I actually loved in my general line of work, it was never in my way. I stared at myself in the mirror, swiped on some red lip gloss, and called it a day. I was going to the firehouse, not out to dinner. I had on ripped up jeans that even I thought made my ass look pretty good, a white t-shirt that was probably a little more snug than it had to be and a black bra, since I was feeling a little feisty. Fuck it. Time to go.

The anticipation of seeing him was making me nervous and excited at the same time. It seemed every time I thought of him, I got tingles and butterflies, and I could already feel myself getting wet in anticipation. I didn't know if I'd be able to touch him at the firehouse. I mean it's definitely not something they encouraged, fraternization. Whatever, Brian is the Chief now, and I'm just stopping by to "talk". I actually giggled to myself like a teenager. I was literally giddy with anticipation.

I pulled up to the station and parked in the visitor parking in the back of the building. The bay doors were open, so I walked around and entered that way; where I ran into Matt.

"Hey, what are you doing here?" he asked genuinely surprised. Usually I tell him what I'm up to. Since the thing with Brian started I actually haven't talked to him that much. I'll have to catch up with him later, it's only been a couple days.

"Oh, I'm just here to talk to Brian about my dad's stuff. I saw him at the fire today, and he said he'd be doing paperwork and stuff tonight if I wanted to stop by since it would be convenient," I lied innocently.

"Ah, that's cool. Well, I'm going to the day room to watch a movie and hopefully fall asleep in a recliner. Text me later and we'll catch up," he laughed.

I laughed too, that was pretty typical by the last third of a twenty-four-hour shift. Sleeping in a recliner and hoping for no calls. "Alright, sounds good. He in his office?" I was already walking in that direction.

"Yep, sure is," he pointed in the direction of Brian's office, which obviously I knew where it was. I walked toward the back corner of the building where the offices and conference room were. It was getting kind of late, so most of the lights were off, but there was a glow coming from below the closed office door. *Why did I feel like I was sixteen-years-old all of a sudden and too nervous to knock on the door?* I sighed to myself.

Just as I raised my hand to knock, the door swung open and Brian literally ran right into me like a brick wall. I didn't even see it coming, and as I was falling to the ground, he grabbed me and pulled me into him.

"Oh, my God, Jo, I didn't know you were standing there, are you okay?!" he grabbed my face with both his hands and was inspecting me. I started laughing immediately.

"Yeah, I just got hit by a super hot truck, but other than that, yes, I'm fine," I really thought it was hilarious. He looked at me like I was crazy for a moment, then pulled me into his office and shut the door behind me. Before I knew what was happening, he had his mouth on mine, and he was exploring me with his tongue so passionately, I melted right into him again. He had me pushed up against his office door. I started to wrap a leg around him, pulling him in closer. I simply couldn't get enough of his taste and I was drinking him in.

"I've been waiting to do that all day," he said in a raspy, low voice.

"Me too, Brian," I managed to breathe out. He had his hand at the small of my back, drawing me closer to him, something I could never get enough of, and his other was caressing my face while he planted soft kisses on my lips. I swear, our lips were molded for each other, every time he kissed me, I just wanted more. I didn't want to undo his uniform, so I had my hands on his back pulling him into me, and I could feel his hardness pressing up against me. He reached next to me and locked the door.

"What are you doing?" I was surprised.

"I'm going to have you right here in this office. I can't wait another second, or couldn't you tell?" Oh I could tell. I was going to pretend to be coy and shy about it, but we both know why I'm here, so I took a step back, and grabbed at his utility belt, undoing it, and freeing his huge cock from the restraints of his thick uniform pants. He yanked my t-shirt over my head, and admired my lacy black bra.

"So fucking sexy, Josephine," he growled into my neck, and began to suck and kiss my shoulder near my cardinal tattoo. "Pants, off.

Now," he whispered in my ear, undid my jeans and they fell to the ground revealing the matching black lacy panties. "You have me so hard, baby. Jesus Christ," he grabbed my face and kissed me with so much tenderness, I was putty in his hands. His kisses were so deep, I felt them to my core.

As I undid his uniform shirt, he continued kissing my neck and nibbling at that spot between my shoulder and my neck, and I was losing my mind. He dropped his pants, took off his uniform shirt hastily, and moved me over to the couch with him. He was completely naked now, and I was still in my bra and panties. As I was getting ready to take them off, he stopped me. "No, leave them on. It's so sexy," he whispered and pulled me onto his lap, straddling him. I was so wet with anticipation; I could hardly stand it anymore. Moving my panties to the side just a bit, he started circling my clit with his finger, causing me to moan involuntarily. I was going to come already. With his other hand, he pulled my bra down and latched on with his mouth sucking and lightly biting, flicking my hard nipple with his tongue.

"Brian, I'm going to come, oh, my God," I was panting as quietly as I could manage. He stuck two fingers inside of me, and began pumping them into me, while sucking on my nipple. I felt the waves coming, and I couldn't stop it.

"Come for me, Jo. Come on my hand right now, baby," he moved to the other nipple, and I began riding his hand to get my release. It came almost immediately, and I gasped for air as my orgasm washed over me and I grinded myself into his hand. He kept pumping me with his fingers until the waves had subsided, and then repositioned me so he had access to enter me fully. "Baby, that was so fucking hot, but I'm not nearly done with you." He positioned his rock hard cock at my entrance, and I pushed myself onto it letting out a gasp as he entered me. I was slowly riding up and down him, feeling the wave come again when he moved us quickly so I was on my back. Lifting one of my legs up on his shoulder he was so much deeper, I couldn't think straight all I could do was feel his length filling me up causing a buzz over my whole body. Thrusting harder and harder, I couldn't control my release and I felt him getting close too.

"Baby, come with me, I can't wait. It's so fucking good, come inside me now!" I willed him to fuck me harder, and grabbed him, pulling him as tight as I could. As I fell over the edge into ecstasy, he cried out my name, and pumped me harder, filling me up and getting his release with me. We laid there for a few minutes, catching our breath in silence. We started to get up, and when I grabbed for my clothes, he pulled me back to him for a kiss.

"Baby, that was fucking amazing," he smiled, making me smile back like a teenager again. He was right, that was amazing.

"It was alright," I jokingly smiled and winked at him, hopping up to get dressed, I mean we're in a public place. Looking shocked, he smacked my ass and laughed too.

"Alright, my ass. You know that was the best sex you've ever had." He gave me a sideways look.

"It was pretty good. We'll have to do it again for me to be totally sure I think," I kidded with him some more. I was having some fun with him, and he looked a little perturbed, making it that much more fun to mess with him.

"Well I'm all for more, lets get to it, Jo," he started to try undressing me again.

"No, no, no...not here. We're pushing our luck as it is, we shouldn't be doing this in here and you know it. It was amazing, Brian, I promise." I got up on my tiptoes to give him a tender kiss. "You know I like messing with you." We both laughed and we finished getting dressed quickly. This sneaking around was hot, and we were having fun, and being playful, I was truly enjoying it.

BRIAN

We got ourselves dressed and were joking around in my office. It's never been like this for me, so hot and then so comfortable and fun. I loved being around her, she was intoxicating, and when she smiled, it just lit me up inside and made me feel warm, like home. We opened the door to my office in case anyone had any notion of swinging by, although unlikely, it was still work and I knew we shouldn't do things like that, but honestly, I wasn't officially the Chief yet, and who could help themselves in my position really?

I actually did want to talk to her about some things and she probably wasn't going to love it but too bad. I cared about her, and it was important. I went around my desk and sat on the other side, and she settled into one of the visitor chairs and put her feet up on my desk. I smirked at her because that was kind of ballsy, but I was guessing she used to put her feet up there from that side her whole life when she was in here talking to her dad. All of his plaques and awards were still on the wall, I wasn't ready to take them down, and I thought that was something she should be here doing with me. That wasn't what I wanted to talk to her about though.

"So, how was your shift over at 19 today? Did you have any problems?" She knew exactly what I meant by the scrunched up face she made at me.

"If you're referring to Danny, he tried to talk to me this morning but I was busy, and then in the afternoon, we got called to your fire, so my day was uneventful from a professional standpoint," she was fairly terse with me about it and started looking around the room when her eyes landed on the pile of gear next to my desk. "Is that my gear?" she asked me looking surprised.

"Actually, yes, it is. I wanted to talk to you about that today..." I had practiced this in my head a few times, and now I felt like a teenager all over again for some reason. Before I could continue, she interrupted my thoughts.

"I can clean it out and decommission it if you want. It's been here for quite a while, I'm sure you'd like to be able to reissue it. I'm sorry I've left it here for so long..." she trailed off, seeming to be unsure of what to say, and then she sighed.

"Jo, I actually had your gear brought out, because I'd like you to start riding here again. I don't have a full time spot open yet, however we've been rotating per diems regularly, and honestly, no one that's passed through here knows the guys, the station or the town like you do, and you're working like ten different shift jobs all over the county, and that seems like a pain in the ass, and—"

"Wait, you want me to quit taking shifts at other places and come here essentially *full-time*?" her eyes got huge and I honestly couldn't tell if she was mad, happy or in shock at the suggestion.

"Yes, that's what I want. Actually, it's what your dad wanted, and its certainly what Matt wants. And yes, it's definitely what I want." I repeated myself because it was worth repeating.

"My dad?" She tilted her head quizzically at me and softened her expression.

"Okay, I'm gonna be straight with you, Jo. Your dad and I were tight, we ran this station together, and we discussed staffing regularly. He was planning to ask you to come back to 23 and quit working all these different jobs, he was just waiting for the right moment to approach you. He didn't want you to feel like he was pressuring you into coming back to work for him, he was hoping you would have approached him yourself." I sat back and waited for her response. She was completely still and just looking at me with those steely gray eyes.

She sighed again. "Why did he want me to come back?" Her eyes dropped to the floor and she seemed hopeful for an answer that she must have been looking for.

"We don't have any other women at this station, there aren't that many in the department that do both fire and EMS to begin with. He trusted you, we all trust you, and he called it 'getting the band back together'," I laughed a little thinking about that conversation with him. "He and I agreed for the record, that you're good for the department, and you bring a lot to the table. And on a personal note, we like having you around, and being honest here, nobody wants to juggle shifts like you have been, we thought it would be perfect." I was being honest. Jack and I had agreed not to approach her about this, but to maybe plant some seeds so she would think of it herself, we even got Matt in on the plan, but then Jack died. And now, with things going on between us, I wanted her near me, where I knew she was safe, where her family could look after her, where I could look after her. She can take care of herself on the job, I didn't worry about that, but we are her people. It's like her dad said, we're like a band, and it was time to get the band back together, he was totally right.

She wasn't saying anything, she took her feet off the desk, and put her head in her hands, looking down at the floor. I wanted to come around the desk and comfort her, do something, but I was frozen. I didn't want to do the wrong thing and I honestly couldn't tell if she was mad, sad, confused, or what. Uncertain, I asked her what she was thinking.

She moved to look up at me, and rested her chin on her hands, and took a deep breath. "I don't know. It's something I've been thinking about actually, but don't you think that what's been going on between us complicates that? I don't want to keep doing all this shift work all over the county either, but coming back here? I just don't know," she leaned back in the chair and looked up at the ceiling.

"Look at me, Jo. It's me. At the end of the day, we both know that we can work together, so that can't be the issue. We're your family, and you belong here with us. It's a good team, and as far as you and me..." I paused, looking for the right words and leaned forward putting my hands on my desk. I needed to say the right thing here and I wasn't sure what that was, I didn't know how she felt yet. *Fuck it, I have to be honest, I've dicked around for way too long*, "As for you and me, I only see this getting more serious between us regardless of where you work. I told you that first night that you were mine, and I meant it, and I don't intend for that to change in the foreseeable future." There. I said it.

"Are you serious? We couldn't keep seeing each other if I work here. You'd be my boss!" That was not the reaction I was hoping for. Shit shit shit.

"For now, nothing has to change. Work is work, and personal is personal, and we can keep them separate. Do you want to work here, Jo? Do you want to keep seeing me? I think you do, and I damn sure know I want to keep seeing you outside of work," I was starting to get freaked out that this was about not wanting to continue what we have before it gets a chance to go where I want it to.

"I do. I do, both. I need to think about it though. I don't know if we'll be able to keep us a secret if I'm working here, and I don't want to get a reputation, or for people to think there's some kind of favoritism going on," she seemed really conflicted. This was kind of a lot of information all at once.

"First of all, there is favoritism. You're definitely the only firefighter, or person for that matter, that I'm sharing my bed with. That being said, we're professionals. You and I know how to behave, we've fought fire and been on tons of calls together in our lifetime. So, how about this, how about you take a day or two and think it over, and maybe pick up a couple shifts here so you can see exactly how it would work?" Man, I pulled that out of my ass. Hopefully that worked.

"Okay, I'll think about it. I'm just not sure that we should keep—"

And then the tones dropped. We had a goddamn call.

JO

"Rescue 23, Engine 23, two car MVA at the intersection of I4 and Colonial Drive. Number of injuries unknown."

I've actually never been so relieved to be interrupted by the tones dropping. Brian hopped up of course, he's on duty.

"Jo, grab your shit. You're coming." He commanded.

"What the fuck are you talking about?" I snapped at him.

"Grab your gear. It's late, it's a rescue, more hands are better and it sounds like it could be bad at that intersection. Just grab your shit, you can ride with me, and we'll see what we have on scene." He was walking out the door as he demanded my presence at the scene.

Fuck it. I grabbed the pile of gear and followed him to his Chief's vehicle. The other guys were already hopping in the trucks and Matt looked over and grinned at me as I trailed

147

after Brian. I made the shoulder shrug, I don't know what I'm doing face, and just kept on moving. I hopped in the passenger side of the truck, and started donning my gear over my jeans, and checking my pockets to see if my tools were still there.

"Central, 2300 en route," he got on his radio.

"2300," they acknowledged.

"Central, is there an update on victims?"

"No, Chief, no update. Two cars, head on collision, one car into the guardwall. That's all we've got."

"Thanks, Central." He put his radio down and looked over at me rifling through my pockets. "Everything should be there, I checked it earlier today. I don't know everything you keep in it, but you sure are prepared with all your pink duct taped tools," he chuckled.

Yeah, the handles of all my shit was wrapped in pink duct tape. That's thanks to the fact that people "accidently" take your shit all the time, and none of those motherfuckers would dare keep my wire cutters, knife, or anything else if it was wrapped in pink duct tape. I've been doing it for years.

"Shut up. You know why I do that." I glared at him. "My safety glasses are missing. I need safety glasses for a wreck."

He leaned over me while driving lights and sirens to a call, opened the glove box and pointed. "Take mine, I shouldn't need them." Then he smiled and I couldn't help it, I smiled back. I didn't really know what I was feeling, but the rush of going to a call and helping people was getting me fired up. Car accidents and rescue, that was my wheelhouse, and I guess I was going to hop right back in it with my guys.

He switched channels on his radio so he could talk to the rescue truck. "Rescue 23, it's 2300."

"2300 go ahead," I recognized Scotty's reply. He was driving.

"I brought Meadows as extra personnel for this one. You've got an extra crew member tonight," he looked over at me and smiled again.

"No shit, Chief. You brought JoJo?? Sweet. We'll see you there." Brian started laughing and I just glared at him.

"JoJo? Nobody calls me JoJo. Good Lord," I rolled my eyes even though it was kind of funny. We arrived on scene first, and I grabbed a radio and hopped out and ran over to the SUV that had flipped upside down. I could hear the rescue and the engine in the distance coming up soon.

"Chief! I've got one victim here, still buckled in, and fluids leaking!" I yelled across the intersection to him where he was evaluating the second vehicle which appeared to be pinned up against the guardrail wall. "Fuck, this is a mess," I muttered under my breath, and got down on the ground to check on the victim in the SUV who was seatbelted in, upside down and basically dangling.

"Jo! My guy is stuck, his leg is under the dash, and he's got a serious head wound!"

"Are there any other victims?"

"It doesn't look like it!" he yelled back. The rescue and the engine both pulled up and staged so that we could get tools off the trucks, and get to work. I squished myself as flat as I could and shouted into the vehicle to the patient. "Ma'am! Ma'am! I'm with the Fire Department, can you hear me?"

She opened her eyes and turned her head to look at me. "Yes," she whispered and tears started to roll down her face. She was scared, hell if I were strapped upside down in my car I'd be scared too. She didn't look too banged up which was a good sign.

"Ma'am, my name is Jo. I'm here to help you. I need to you to look straight ahead, I don't want you to move your neck, I don't want you to move at all in case you've hurt your spine, okay?"

She looked straight ahead. "I don't know what happened. He came out of nowhere," she replied. She was definitely in shock. A paramedic rig rolled up, and two medics that I actually knew came running over, Mark tossed himself to the ground next to me.

"Ma'am, we can worry about that later, we need to ask you some questions, and then we're gonna get you out of here." I told her. Now that the medics were here, I could go get some tools to free her from the vehicle. She was going to need to be cut out of that seatbelt and it was going to take a few people to make sure she didn't just come crashing down. "Mark, I'm gonna go get some tools, I'll be right back," and I jogged back to the rescue, leaving him to assess and treat the patient.

"Jo! Chief needs you over at the other vehicle. The space is too small for anyone to secure the patient, and you're the smallest. I'll take over for you at the SUV," Scotty had come running to meet me.

"Okay, no problem, the lady seems alright, but she's gonna need to be cut out of her seatbelt, so take another guy with you so she doesn't come falling down, she's suspended upside down." I took off toward the other car, about fifty yards away. When I got to the other car, more or less all of the heavy rescue tools were out and Brian and Matt were discussing next steps with one of the medics from the second rig that had arrived. "What's the situation?" I asked as I assessed it for myself.

The victim appeared to be a young man, unconscious but breathing, who was trapped in the driver's seat, up against the guardrail wall. The dashboard had been crushed enough to trap one of his legs under it, and his spine wasn't stabilized due to the passenger seat getting shoved in the way. This made him out of reach without crawling into the vehicle, which they were all too large to do without jostling the patient too much. If I wasn't here, they would have had to, but I was there, and I knew what to do.

"We can't get in to stabilize the patient before we cut out this dash to free him, I need you to get in there," Brian said.

"Absolutely. Give me that blanket to cover the patient up, so when you pull the tools out, I can cover him up." I made my way into the passenger side of the vehicle, over the damaged passenger seat, and then over the console into the back seat. It was a sedan of some kind, but only had two doors, so it was definitely a tight squeeze. I took the blanket and covered up the chest and torso of the victim, so any more broken glass or debris wouldn't fall on him. As I looked him over, I could see an extremely deep head wound, as well as a better view of his left leg, which looked like a broken femur, thankfully not through the skin, but still nasty. "Anybody know this kid's name?" I yelled out as I positioned myself behind the driver's seat so that I could stabilize the kid's spine as best as possible without moving him too much.

"Kid's name is Marshall, it's on the insurance card from the glove box. Be careful in there, Jo," Brian leaned in. "What can you see over there?" he asked me.

"Okay, the only way to get this kid out is gonna be through the passenger side, but you're gonna need to cut that whole passenger seat out for us to get him out on a board properly. Get me a collar, I'm gonna stabilize his neck while you get set up." I demanded, and Matt took off to get it for me.

Brian leaned into the vehicle and lowered his voice. "Be careful in there. Glad you're here to help, we'll try to get you both out as fast as possible." We locked eyes, and I nodded. This is what we did, we put ourselves in precarious situations like climbing into crushed cars to help others get out. Matt came back with the collar, and I carefully manipulated it around the patient's neck, trying to not move him at all, you simply had no idea what kind of internal damage was done after a wreck like this.

The heavy rescue work was beginning. Most people think the Jaws of Life and the other large hydraulic tools they see on TV or hear about just come in and rip machinery apart like a hot knife through butter. It really doesn't work that way. In order for this to go smoothly, it had to be done in steps.

First, they had to pop the door off the passenger side. It was open, but the hinge was damaged, and the whole thing was just in the way and was going to make getting the patient out smoothly tricky. The whole point of this operation was to get the patient out to safety without any further injury. Matt got to work on that with the spreaders, which are actually commonly known as the Jaws of Life, because it looked like a huge set of jaws that open and close. What he needed to do, was position the points of the jaws into the door hinge and then open the jaws up, making the hinge pop. We called it a door pop. Once you heard that pop on both hinges, it meant that it was broken off from the main part of the car, and you could remove the door by just a quick yank. Some were easier than others, generally newer cars have a lot of plastic bullshit and wires that control window and locks that you can easily snip, or just pull away. Matt was able to remove the door in just a few moments, and it didn't even jostle the car a bit. I was crouched in the backseat, sweating my ass off, holding the patients head still and monitoring his vitals. I kept asking if he could hear me, and he would audibly grunt from time to time, which was a good sign.

The next step was to remove the passenger seat. It would probably be a real pain in the ass. It would require using the cutters, which look just like handheld cutters, but they're huge, and they're powered by hydraulics and attached to the truck from a hose, just like the Jaws. Because it was a bucket seat, it really was the best option for getting the patient out smoothly, and I knew it sucked, but this kid was in bad shape, the less he was moved around the better off he'd be. Matt stuck his head in the car before he started cutting the seat out. "You alright in there?" he asked with a smile. We'd always made great partners.

"Yep, all good. Hurry up though, it's uncomfortable and I'm sweating my ass off," I smiled at him.

"Your wish is my command. Let me know if anything changes," and with that he pulled his safety glasses back down, and crouched down to start cutting the seat out. It was going to require at least four cuts to get it loose enough to actually remove it. Car seats were definitely not designed to come back out. I looked around, and it appeared there were a lot of people on scene now, and traffic, while light at this time of night, needed to be diverted. I didn't see Brian anywhere, I'm sure he was bossing people around, I mused to myself.

I could see Scotty was back at the truck operating the other end of the tools where the power was, and there were other people helping that lady out of her SUV. I sighed with relief that she appeared to have minimal injuries. Seriously, a seatbelt will absolutely save your damn life. She had her window down, and without her seatbelt, she could have been ejected right out of that SUV.

After about ten minutes, Matt had two of the posts cut and then stopped to check on me and the patient again. "We're halfway there. When I get to the final one, if you could push it with your foot, I'll have Joe back here pulling while I cut, and we should be able to yank it out pretty smoothly, okay?" He was dripping sweat now too. It was stifling hot in the gear, shoved in the backseat, however I was just holding onto the victim, Matt was maneuvering a giant tool, and it was heavy.

"You got it, chop chop," I said. I saw the third little post snap, and connected eyes with Matt signifying I was ready. The medics were waiting right behind him with a board, ready to help get the patient out. As Matt started to cut the final post holding the seat in place, the metal twisted, and the seat snapped backwards, knocking right into my ribs.

"Aww fuck!" I winced, and fell backwards, letting go of the patient for just a moment. "Dude, get someone to hold the fucking seat man!" I yelled at Matt. Joe rushed forward, he had been standing right there, and grabbed the seat, pulling it toward them, instead of me and the patient, and within a few moments, the seat was out.

"Sorry, Jo, didn't see that coming. I thought you were gonna kick it back in my direction," Matt said and put the tool back on the ground where they were all set up.

"It's alright. I just wasn't ready. Hey, I have an idea, I think we can get away without rolling the dash, if I can reach the seat adjustment, and lean this driver's seat back, we should be able to slide him out onto a board without fucking around with this dash." It was going to require me to crawl down and seriously reach, but it could save a lot of time if it worked.

"Works for me, what do you need me to do?" Matt asked.

"Get in here and hold the patient's head still. I need to crawl down on the floor and see if I can reach between the door and grab the lever without smooshing myself with the seat."

Matt immediately got in, and took over securing the patient, and a little crowd formed around the vehicle while we tried to make this happen. I was never going to reach it with my turnout coat on, so I took it off, and took off my helmet so I could get my head low, and sprawled my lower body across the back seat. I immediately felt cooler, I was completely soaked with sweat. I scrunched way down below the driver's seat, and managed to stretch my fingers out just enough to reach the lever. When I pulled it, nothing happened. Fuck. It needed more weight to actually push the seat back.

"Okay, I need you to push *gently* back on the seat, he's not enough weight to move it. But I might get stuck down here, so get someone over here to pull me out too." I sighed. Maybe this wasn't the greatest idea, but it was still faster for the patient than getting out any more tools and cutting the car apart more. "Okay, on three," I yelled.

"One, two, THREE!" I grabbed the lever, the seat came back on me, and I was definitely now stuck. Fucking hell.

"Jo, the patient is almost flat on top of you and his leg is free, are you okay?" Matt yelled down at me.

I was pinned down underneath the seat now, not in pain, but extremely uncomfortable. "Get the patient out on a board now, then I can get out!" I couldn't see a damn thing except for the floor of the car, and I could hear scrambling above me.

Then I could hear Brian yelling, *oh fuck*.

BRIAN

"What the fuck is going on? Is she stuck under there?" I yelled. I knew the answer to my own question, and I was pissed off.

"Uh, sort of, she'll be out in one sec," Matt yelled at me while he was helping the medics get the patient onto the board. "Jo, one more minute alright?" he called down to her. All I could see was her lower half kicked out onto the back seat of the car, and her entire torso and head were covered by the flattened out driver's seat.

"Yea, hurry the fuck up," she said from underneath the goddamn driver's seat, sounding muffled. Seriously? I bet this was her idea. It was definitely faster for the patient, but now my girlfriend is stuck under the seat. *Crew member. She's a member of my crew.* At least I didn't say that out loud. I rubbed my temple and shook my head.

The medics had the patient out, and rushed him to their rig and took off. Matt jumped back in the car to get the seat off Jo. She lifted her head up and laughed at him then lightly punched him in the chest. Her face was bright red, probably from being mostly upside down for however long this was going down.

"Ow! What was that for, I just freed you!" he grabbed at his chest where she hit him.

"That was for hitting me with the passenger seat. What the fuck, man?" she laughed and rubbed her ribs. Was she hurt?

"If you two are done, both patients are now on their way to the hospital, we can clean up and get home. You okay, Jo?" I asked in all seriousness.

"Yeah, Chief, I'm great now. Let me know how that kid makes out." She smiled, grabbed her coat and helmet from the backseat and climbed out of the car. I got a good look at her. Her shirt was completely soaked, and you could see right through it, that sexy black bra that was for my eyes only, was now visible for everyone to see. Matt noticed right away too.

"Oh, hey now, putting on a show for us out here?" He laughed, and the guys around the truck started whistling. I was pissed. Nobody needed to be looking at her like that; nobody but me.

"Oh, shit! Well I wasn't exactly planning to be out here tonight," she turned bright red, and put her coat back on right away, but didn't buckle it up, left it hanging open. I was going to lose my shit.

Matt walked off to grab a water, and Jo followed him until I stepped in her way, stopping her. "Buckle your goddamn coat up. You don't need to be showing everyone out here what's mine," I growled quietly.

She stopped, stunned, and gave me a fierce look, "Listen, *Chief*, it's hot as fuck. I'm not wearing a uniform, because I hadn't planned to be out here, so how about you just back off," I think she actually hissed at me.

"You could have gotten hurt today, *Meadows*. Next time you're going to try a stunt like that get me over here." Okay, she really didn't need me to make that call, I was being a dick now because I was pissed everyone got a burlesque show here on the street.

She softened her expression, and responded as sweetly as ever. "I didn't realize that your leadership style was micromanagement, *Chief.* I'll keep that in mind when considering our earlier discussion about my employment. I did what I felt was best for the patient, and the rest of the crew on scene, the medics agreed, and I stand by that decision. It would have taken another ten minutes or more to roll that dash. Now if you'll excuse me, I need a drink of water. As I mentioned, and you can clearly see, it's hot as fuck." And with that, she walked off to the truck, grabbed a bottle of water, and drank the entire thing down, with her coat hanging wide open in my direction.

I was going to have to have it out with her later; we needed to establish some kind of understanding, and seriously, she needed to buckle the fucking coat up. I was so pissed off and totally turned on right now. Her little sarcastic commentary was hot. I loved it when she used the f word. Good thing my uniform pants are so heavy, or everyone out here would see I'm hard every time she's near me. I guess me being pissed at her isn't really her fault, but I didn't care. She was at the truck talking to the other guys, presumably telling them about her antics, which actually did give that guy valuable time, and the rest of the crews on scene were cleaning up. Once the tow truck took the vehicles off the road we were able to leave.

It was good to see her with the crew, smiling, and she and Matt totally worked so well together. It was like seeing twins. Knowing your partner since the time you were a baby gives you a sixth sense kind of thing. Because of the age difference, even Matt and I weren't able to read each other as well as Jo and Matt do. Drama, hearts and my dick aside, I really hoped she would take me up on my offer to come work with us full time. I think she'd be good for all of us. I knew already that she was good for me.

JO

That motherfucker. Check with him? Before making a call that gives a critical patient extra time? *Oh, fuck you, pal. Fuuuuuuuuck you.* That vehicle was perfectly safe, and Matt would never in a million years let me put myself in a precarious situation on a scene. So fuck him, fuck his micromanagement, and sure as fuck, fuck his attitude about my outfit. I was wearing jeans and a t-shirt, because that's what I wore to come and fuck him in his office. I knew this fling was a bad idea. I couldn't work here, and keep this up with him.

It was time to go, and I decided I'd ride back in the duty truck with the rest of the guys, not in the Chief's vehicle. I wasn't going to ask permission to do it either. I was expected to be part of the crew today, and I was going to ride back to the station with them. And I didn't want to talk to Brian even though I knew I'd have to back at the station.

"Hey, I'm riding back with you guys," I said to Scotty and Matt who were standing with me next to the rescue truck.

"So, are you gonna join us permanently, or what, Jojo?" Scotty asked.

"Uhhhhh when did you decide calling me Jojo was cool," I gave him the fish eye and raised an eyebrow in his direction. I didn't even hate it, it was just so ridiculous.

"Today," he laughed and went around the truck to get in the driver's seat. I actually started laughing too. Of course he decided today, probably at the moment he said it on the radio.

I looked over in Brian's direction, and we connected eyes. I wasn't going to ask him if I could ride the truck back, I was just doing it. And to be truthful, that's the right thing to do anyway. He acknowledged me with a nod, and actually didn't even look mad that I was riding back with them, so that's good.

Matt opened the door to the back for me. "Your chariot awaits, madam," he chuckled. I hopped in, I was just short enough, that I always have to kind of launch myself into a fire truck by grabbing the 'oh shit' handle and propelling myself up the first stair.

"Thank you, kind sir," I laughed back. Jax and Taylor were already in the back as well as a young guy I wasn't acquainted with, and after I hopped in, Matt got in the front right seat, the officers seat. We all put our headphones on so we could talk to each other; fire trucks are just loud in general, and we were lucky enough to have each seat wired with a set of headphones and a microphone so we could communicate with each other, or with Central dispatch if we needed to.

Matt asked from the front seat. "So, Jo, what was that little chat with the Chief about back there? He mad about something?" He was laughing.

"Oh, he was just giving me his thoughts on me squishing myself under that seat. He was somewhere between thrilled and ecstatic about it," I laughed.

Scotty chimed in from the driver's seat. "Eh, whatever. He needs to get his panties out of a bunch. So seriously, Jojo, you going to come back full-time or what? It feels like we got the band back together tonight."

I wasn't sure how I felt about it after getting yelled at. "I'm not sure. There's a tentative offer on the table, but I've got some other commitments I need to work out. Why, you guys need a den mother?" I teased.

"We need some better eye candy around here than these clowns, that's for sure," Jax spoke up, sitting across from me, he winked.

"Watch yourself, Jax, she'll kick your ass and not even feel bad about it," Matt joked.

I smiled. That is what it was like. I fell right back into a groove with them. It was nice. The kid I didn't know giggled but didn't say anything.

"Hey, what's your name, kid?" I covered my mic up and leaned over to him.

"Jason. Jason Barrett," he reached over and shook my hand.

"Nice to meet ya. You old enough to ride a firetruck?" I had to give him a hard time, he looked twelve.

"Yes ma'am. I'm twenty-one. Been riding on this crew for a few months now. I came from Seminole county."

"Uh, yea. Don't ever call me ma'am again, or I'll have to kick your ass too. It's Jo. Jo Meadows." I gave him a dirty look. Ma'am? I'm thirty-two. Sheesh. He looked scared now that I threatened him, and Jax was laughing hysterically because he could see and hear the entire exchange.

"Yes ma'—uh, Jo. Sorry," he said quietly. I smiled at him, he meant well I could tell, and he smiled back. Maybe they do need a den mother, I thought.

We were just a few minutes away from the station and Matt turned the stereo on and started playing Kenny Loggins "Danger Zone." We all settled in, rocked out and not talking. We were lucky with this truck, it was pretty much equipped with everything you needed for

171

an accident, and it had a CD player and stereo which was just a nice treat.

I leaned back and thought about what I wanted to do. I wanted to come back. I loved this job, I loved this station; it was my dad's legacy. Getting involved with Brian was a bad idea. I needed to put an end to it when I got back and if the job offer was still available, I could get myself off of the District 19 rotation within about a week and come back full-time. Yeah, that's what I would do. Thinking about what we were doing in Brian's office before the call, made my body betray me as I started to feel myself get warm between my legs. Apparently, my pussy didn't understand what's best. I needed to shut that down immediately.

We pulled into the station, and everyone was getting out of their gear and putting it away in their gear bins. I didn't have a gear bin anymore so I was going to have to go ask Brian what to do with my stuff which I was absolutely dreading. I'm in no mood for his Neanderthal attitude right now. It's now been a long day, I'm dirty, I'm angry at him, and I need to go home and shower this day away. My shoes and my keys were in Brian's Chief truck though, because that's where I got dressed in my gear, so I was without other options.

"Meadows, a moment of your time?" Brian poked his head into the engine bay and summoned me. Nobody thought anything of it, and just kept doing what they were doing. I think after all the adrenaline of the call wore off, they were getting tired. I knew I sure was.

"Sure, Chief," I carried my coat and helmet with me, still dressed in bunker pants and not really sure what was going to happen.

BRIAN

She came back in my office, the office we
had sex in a few hours prior, sat her coat and
helmet down on my office couch and took a
seat in my visitor chair. I needed to do the
reports on the call, so my desk had fresh
paperwork all over, and after she sat down, I
shut the door and sat down at my chair on the
other side of the desk.

"Your shoes and stuff are in my truck,
you can grab them after we talk," I said. I felt
like I had a million things to say to her, but I
honestly wasn't quite sure where to start. We
were officially in that gray area where I wanted
to have a Chief to firefighter talk, but I also
wanted to ask how she felt about being back
with us, and I wanted to know why she was
rubbing her ribs earlier, and kiss whatever it
was that was making them sore.

"Okay," she replied.

The sweat from earlier had mostly
dried, but I could still faintly see her black bra

under her white t-shirt and it was distracting me and my cock. I stared at her, forgetting what I wanted to say altogether until she spoke up.

"What do you want me to do with my gear, Brian? I do want to come back, but I have other commitments as you're well aware, and I'll need to see them through. After that, I would like to get back on the schedule. And while I'm at it, let's just face it, we need to quit seeing each other, or sleeping together or whatever this is. This is work, and I need the job as you're well aware, and I don't think after our argument today that we should keep doing—" I cut her off right there.

"Whoa, wait a minute, you want to what? It was a disagreement and wasn't a big deal. Why would we stop seeing each other? You can't be serious," I was stunned, and certainly didn't expect that response. I understood that we'd had a small argument at the scene, but she shouldn't be letting everyone get a look, and no, just no, we can't stop now. She can't be serious. My face had to be bright red, I felt my entire body temperature rise like I had a fever.

"I'm serious. I can admit that this was just some fun, and maybe an escape for a bit, but if I'm going to come back here to work, I don't think either one of us needs the bullshit that happened today to happen every time we work together. When I'm here, I'm more or less one of the guys, and I've always been that way. You can't treat me differently because I've sucked your dick, Brian," she said matter -of-factly; as I balled my fists up at my sides.

"I don't consider this a fling at all, which I've said several times. Do you really think that's all that's going on here?" She had to feel something; I knew she did. An unfamiliar wave of desperation came over me, giving me a horrible sick feeling.

She looked me squarely in the eyes. "I do. I would like the rest of my firefighting career to be at the station my dad ran my whole life, but it's your station now, Brian, so you tell me if that's going to be a problem." She was cold and as my heart started racing, she just kept staring blankly at me waiting for a reply.

I took a deep breath, and thought of what to say. I needed her to be here, with us, with me. "Jo, if that's what you want, then I'm not going to beg you to keep things going. I think it's a huge mistake, but I want you as part of the crew here. That's what your dad wanted." I didn't know what else to say, I was feeling my heart sink that she was slipping away, but I didn't know what to do to stop it. I couldn't bring myself to say how I really felt; it was bubbling to the surface, but I just couldn't say the words to her. I wasn't ready. "There's an empty gear bin next to Matt's that we cleared out a while ago, and it's yours if you want it. It was all I could get out.

"Okay. I'll put my gear out there, and I'll work my schedule out at 19 tomorrow; then I can be on the schedule here. Should take a week to work it out, two tops. Will that work?" She was like a stone; I don't understand how everything changed so fast. I honestly didn't know what to do and I just couldn't be totally honest with her, even though I felt the stabbing pain in my chest of her leaving. I was losing her and it was the last thing I wanted.

"Yea, that's fine." That's all I could say. She stood up to leave, and I sat in my chair, frozen.

She grabbed her stuff, and got up to leave, stopping in the doorway. "I'm sorry, Brian, I'm not the girl for you, and it's better if we just try to be actual friends, or whatever. Last time we had a moment it was a huge mistake and we barely spoke for a year. We can't do that, you're my boss now. Thanks for the job offer. I'll let you know when my schedule is worked out; I'll try to have it handled tomorrow," and she walked out, shutting the door behind her.

"FUCK!" I stood up and yelled when I was pretty sure she was out of earshot. I threw my dirty coffee cup from this morning across the room, shattering it into a million pieces, and sat back down putting my face in my hands.

JO

I stopped outside the door after I left, and rested my hand there trying not to cry, and keeping myself from going back in and running into his arms. I loved him, and I couldn't let this keep going, knowing full well it was headed for a crash and burn. Working at the station, and remembering my dad was way too important; I needed to honor my dad, not fulfill a childhood crush. It hurt so badly; my heart actually ached. I heard him yell and throw something in his office after I left, and it ripped my heart in two. He'd get over it though, I knew he would, but I honestly wasn't sure I would. In my view, for him, it was pride. For me though, I had a taste of what I always wanted, and Brian didn't end up with anyone, especially not me. He'd never been the guy that was going to love me, be by my side for better or for worse. He's the guy that's a good time, with a brilliant smile, the charming guy that gets your panties wet, but you can't ever keep. It's better to just end it now, on my terms, before I got in any deeper, as if that were possible, and cut my losses before he did the inevitable himself.

I took a deep breath, went out to his truck; grabbing my shoes and keys from where I left them on the seat. I came back in to the engine bay where the gear racks were to find Matt standing there waiting for me.

"Hey girl, he super pissed at us or what?" he smiled. He had the same charming smile his brother had, no wonder he was a hit with the ladies too. He was leaned up against his gear bin, next to an empty one, which was apparently mine.

"Nah, he didn't even bring it up. He wanted to tell me there was a gear bin already here for me. How long have ya'll been planning this, and why were you so sure I'd say yes?" I tried to pretend nothing was wrong of course. Matt and I shared almost everything, but I obviously couldn't tell him how I was feeling or what was going on with Brian.

"We honestly weren't sure you'd say yes. I was pretty sure when your dad was here you might, but after he died, I wasn't sure. So you said yes?" he smiled at me, clearly realizing that I was going to be joining him back at the station.

"Of course I said yes," I gave him a smile. It really did feel so good to be there. "This is my home; you know that better than anyone. I just have to finish out my schedule at 19, and then I can be more or less full time here in about a week or so." It just occurred to me that the change would require a conversation with Danny. That was unfortunate. Whatever, this was what I really wanted in my heart, even if my heart was hurting over Brian. Nobody needed to know that part.

"Sweet! Well, here's your rack, next to mine. I kicked Travis, the C shift guy out of this spot because—well because I can," he laughed, and I joined in. He does his best to look out for me. I hung my coat up in the wire rack, and put my helmet on top and stared at my name already on it. J. Meadows FF/EMT. That was me; it was also my dad I thought. I reached up and traced the letters with my fingers softly.

"He'd be so happy right now, Jo," Matt put his hand on my shoulder and pulled me in for a hug. I grabbed onto him really tightly, more than I normally would and rested my head on his shoulder. "You okay? Is something else going on?" he asked, giving me a squeeze, then pushing me out so he could look at my face.

"No, no. Everything is great. I'm actually exhausted. I'm really happy," I lied. "I'm gonna head home and shower and call it a day. I picked up a short afternoon shift at 19 tomorrow; just covering for another guy, and it's been a long day. I'm so happy to be back though." I took a step back from him, and took off my bunker pants, situating them just right in my bin, the way I like them and put my regular shoes back on. We all have our own way of pushing the pants down around our boots, so we can step into them in a hurry.

"Alright, sounds good. Text me when you get home." People always thought we were dating over the way we looked out for each other, but it was never like that with us. Thankfully, neither of us ever felt anything more than friendship. We were just tight is all.

"Will do," I smiled and waved as I made my way out to my jeep. Meanwhile, I felt my heart beating out of my chest over the end of Brian and I. I loved him. There's just no denying it. That love is a drug, and my body was in withdrawal.

BRIAN

I don't know how long I was sitting there staring at the ceiling when my brother came to my office.

"Yo, what the fuck happened here?" He waved at the shattered ceramic that had spread across the floor.

"Nothing. It's nothing," I was completely aware that we both knew it wasn't nothing at all, but I wasn't sure telling Matt anything was a good idea.

"Uh, yeah, it's something. Spill it," he sat down in the chair Jo had just vacated. Fuck it, I'll just tell him a little bit, maybe he won't want to kill me.

"Had a small disagreement with Jo over some things, but it's fine now. No big deal," I knew he didn't believe me. He looked at me like I had two heads, and I knew I was going to have to tell him. "Okay, it was more than a small disagreement, but it's personal, so I don't want to talk about it," I said.

"This explains why she looked like someone kicked her fucking puppy on her way out of here tonight. What did you do man? Seriously, didn't we talk about this? Did you fuck her?" he yelled at me.

Technically, the answer was yes, but now I'm feeling protective and don't want to say that. What we had is more than that. It's more than sex, way more…it is..,it's just more than sex. I didn't say anything, I just looked at him in silence, choking inside trying to find the words I was too afraid to say.

"What the fuck is wrong with you, Brian!? She isn't one of those dumb whores you mess around with!" He was getting red, and really angry, and I was getting angrier by the minute too. "Seriously? You fucked her. Her dad—basically the only dad WE ever had just died—and you fucked her. I can't even fucking believe you would sink so low as to take advantage of her like that," he threw his hands in the air waiting for an explanation from me. I honestly wasn't sure that I had an explanation to give him, maybe he was right. Maybe this was all my fault for starting something and not coming clean as soon as I realized how I felt about her. Maybe she wouldn't have ended it if I told her the truth. How my heart ached right now, how making her smile was all I cared about now.

"It wasn't like that, Matt," was all I said.

"Oh? It wasn't like that? So tell me, what exactly was it like, man? You don't use up friends. You don't love 'em and leave 'em to family, dickhead. I can't believe she said she'd work here for you. What the fuck happened? I want the truth," he was pointing at me to drive his point home, and I blurted it out without even thinking.

"I love her, dude! I fucking love her. But she doesn't want anything to do with me other than working here, so that's how it's going to be. Now back the fuck off!" I screamed back. I said it out loud, and it felt so good. But it should have been her I was saying it to. With my lips on hers, touching her and confessing my feelings to her. But no, I just screamed it at my fucking brother.

"You what?" He leaned back in his chair and ran his hands through his hair, clearly stunned by my confession. "Oh, Jesus, dude. What the fuck," was all he muttered.

Yeah, what the fuck indeed.

"When did all of this happen? You need to come clean, because eventually I'm going to hear about it when she's ready to talk to me, and I'm your brother, and her best friend, and fucking dude— ugh. What a goddamn mess." He shook his head at me, and I leaned back in my chair, putting my hands behind my head and letting out a big sigh myself.

"I'm not sure when it happened exactly, but we've been sneaking around together for a little bit since the funeral, she didn't want anyone to know," I confessed, and actually felt hurt that she still didn't want anyone to know now, after the fact.

"Yeah, because she's smarter than you. You can't tell anyone else that you two had something going on. You think you're in love or whatever, and all you're going to do is make things hard for her. And I'm not letting you do that. She deserves better than to deal with your bullshit or firehouse gossip, especially now," he was lecturing me like a little kid now, and I'm not appreciating it.

"Hold on one minute. It takes two people to make a decision like this. I wasn't exactly in it on my own." I tried to defend myself.

"Yeah, I'm sure. While we're at it, why don't you tell me what happened last year that made you two stop speaking more than two words to each other. Is that how long this has actually been going on? Oh, God, it hasn't has it?" he looked sick, likely because he knew I had been with other women in the last year, that wasn't a secret. Thinking about Jo, and other women at the same time made me feel ashamed that I wasn't ready for something when she approached me last year. I just didn't know how I felt, and now I wished so badly that I had thought more of it. I thought back to my discussion with her dad.

"You wanna come in here, son?" Jack motioned for me to come to his office. I had been

staring at Jo, and I'm pretty sure I just got caught.

"Yes, sir, of course," I felt my face get hot and followed him into his office where he shut us both in.

"You know I love you and your brother like my own sons, right, Cavanaugh?" he sat down at his desk his stern expression letting me know he was about to give me shit. His lips curled up and the lines above his eyes furrowed.

"Yes, sir, we feel the same. You're the only father I've ever known, and I hope we make you proud," I meant that deeply.

"That there is my only daughter, Cavanaugh," he pointed out his door. "She's the single most important thing to me in the world."

"Yes sir, I understand," I nodded my head. I was deathly afraid of where this was going.

"I'd love nothing more than to see two of my favorite people end up happily ever after, Brian. But if you're not—ready shall we say—for more than what it takes to be serious, I'd like to warn you to keep it in your pants, son," he looked almost as uncomfortable as I felt. "Josephine is *my life, Brian, and I'm not going to allow a broken heart to keep her from her dreams in the fire service, here at this station. I expect you to be Chief after me and when I'm gone, I expect you to look after her."*

"Sir, I'd never do anything to hurt her. Jo is family. I'm sorry if I gave you the wrong impressi—" he interrupted me.

"I think I know exactly what's going on, Cavanaugh, and when you're really *ready, you have my blessing. You better be ready though and not one minute beforehand, are we clear?"*

"Yes, sir, we're clear," I was going to try to explain myself more, but wasn't really sure what to say, and opted to just shut up, sitting there looking at him.

"That'll be all," he pointed at the door, signifying it was time for me to get the fuck out and think about things.

"Yes, sir," I got up and made a hasty exit, with my tail between my legs wondering what he thought he saw. And giving me his blessing? What was that about? What did he think was going on, because nothing was going on except I

got caught staring at the hottest firefighter I've ever seen in my life.

It was about two weeks after that talk with Jack that we were all partying at Jax's house, celebrating something, I can't even remember what, when I went outside to get some fresh air and found Jo sitting on the front porch drinking her beer. She was pretty drunk and so was I, but I sat down next to her, admiring her beautiful tanned legs she had stretched out on the railing.

"What are you doing out here," I asked her. I looked around, expecting to see someone else, that she wasn't just sitting out here alone.

"Just enjoying the fresh air, I love it out here. It's such a beautiful night. Too nice to stay cooped up inside," she looked at me and smiled, those soft lips revealing her perfect smile. "What brings you out here, Cavanaugh? Lose something?" she laughed at me.

"Lose something? No. I just wanted to get some fresh air. What do you mean lose something?" I didn't get it.

"Oh, I saw you show up with some girl, I figured you were looking for her is all," she said.

I rolled my eyes. "Oh her, yeah no. I didn't lose her. She actually belongs to someone else as it turns out, and I don't play that game, so I sent her on her way awhile ago," I kicked my feet up on the railing too. This is a nice night, she's right.

"Ahh, I see, well better luck next time," she looked away and took a long sip of her beer. I don't know what about it was so hot, but I very suddenly wanted to be that beer bottle, with her lips around my cock like that.

"Eh, whatever. It wasn't going to go anywhere anyway," I wanted to change the subject desperately. She was still looking away, and I could feel myself staring at her profile, admiring her features. Her short hair, which I just loved on a chick, her pouty lips which always looked pink, and those legs. They're worth mentioning twice. She was wearing a fire department hoodie, cut offs, and Chuck Taylor's. She was so effortless, and so fucking pretty.

She turned and gave me a skeptical face, her eyes were all squinted at me. "Oh, you're looking for something to go somewhere?"

I froze a little, "Uh, well...I don't know. I'm not not looking for something to go somewhere?"

She took her legs off the railing and swung herself in my direction. She looked me dead in the eyes and asked me. "So you're telling me, Mr. Single Player Cavanaugh, is no longer just looking for his next lay? Enlighten me sir, I'm shocked and intrigued," she was totally mocking me.

"I didn't say that. I just said that I'm not opposed to it necessarily is all."

"And describe this woman you're not opposed to, will you? I'm fascinated," she leaned in, and I felt myself being pulled toward her.

I was whispering now. "I don't know, she understands what we do for a living and appreciates it. Not in a badge whore kind of way, but genuinely appreciates what it means to us. That's all." What I was describing didn't really exist. Women say they understand, and that

193

they're supportive, but deep down, they don't feel important enough if they've never been a firefighter, and to be honest, most female firefighters aren't like Jo. They're not smoking hot, they are masculine and act like they have something to prove. Whether or not Jo felt like that, she never acted that way.

"There's a handful of us out there, I guess you'll just have to keep looking," she whispered back.

"None like you," I said, and as I leaned in closer to whisper it to her, she leaned in to meet me halfway and our lips just barely touched.

"Like me, huh?" she smiled, still millimeters away when I reached up to touch caress her cheek and bring her in closer for a proper kiss that I now couldn't do without.

"No." I brought her in gently and kissed her more softly than I've ever kissed anyone in my life. It was full of passion; the kind of kiss everyone thinks their first kiss will be like but it isn't of course because you're a sloppy mess. It was the perfect kiss. She parted her mouth, and let me explore it with my tongue gently and I

brought my other hand up around the back of her neck, playing with the short hair back there. She brought her hand up to my chest, sending tingles all over my body. It was a kiss that made you forget you ever kissed anyone. I had butterflies; I was buzzing.

"Let's leave," she whispered, and I came to my senses, back to reality and what it would mean if we did leave, no matter how badly I wanted to. My back stiffened up and I pulled away, stopping the most amazing moment with a woman I've ever had in my life.

All I could think of was Jack. Her father. My Chief. 'I'm not going to allow a broken heart to keep her from her dreams in the fire service, here at this station. I expect you to be Chief after me and when I'm gone, I expect you to look after her'.

"We shouldn't be doing this, Jo, I'm sorry I did that," I stood up to leave. Really, I wanted to run away at top speed. She stood up too.

"Why not, Brian? This works," she gently waved at the air between us.

"No, no it doesn't. We've been drinking, and this just isn't going to happen. I'm sorry I let this happen Jo. I didn't mean—I don't—" I couldn't even think of the words to say. I wanted it to happen, but all I could think of was her dad, and I wasn't ready for that discussion. With her, with him, with myself.

She changed her demeanor; straightened her posture, rolling her eyes at me again, "Oh I get it, Brian. All of Orange County is good enough, but not me. It was a big mistake. Let me guess, 'you're drunk', 'we work together', 'you're like a sister'...I'll save you the trouble Cavanaugh," and she started to walk away when I grabbed her arm.

"Don't act like a baby, Jo, it was just a kiss. You're not my girlfriend and you're not going to be, nobody is," I immediately regretted saying that, it was mean and I knew it as the words escaped my lips.

She turned to stone. "Let me go. Now." I let go of her arm, and honestly thought she was going to punch me but she didn't. She inhaled. "Don't act like a baby? Are you serious? I was wrong about you, Brian. I've always thought you were someone you aren't, and you never will be. Enjoy the revolving door of women while the rest of us move the fuck on. You're right, it was just a kiss, it was a huge mistake." She walked off the porch out to her Jeep and I just stood there wishing that I'd said something, anything except what I said.

That day, I felt like something had changed, like I had lost something, but I didn't own it. She stopped speaking to me for anything other than business at the firehouse or cordial hellos after that, so I definitely lost something, I lost her once already back then. I felt incomplete, not whole every time I saw her after that and I felt like an asshole. I told my brother a much shorter version of all of this while he listened, completely speechless just looking at me like a wide-eyed cat shaking his head every once in a while. I didn't get into the details of the last week with Jo, Matt knew what he needed to, that we'd been sleeping together, and that I loved her and that was a lot. Anything more than that wasn't any of his fucking business; even if she wasn't speaking to me, again.

When I was done being as honest as I could allow myself to be, we sat there in silence for a minute that felt like an hour until finally he spoke. "You're a dick." He got up and walked out of my office.

He was right, I was a dick.

JO

Once I got home, I immediately got in the shower. Along with all the dirt and grime, I tried washing my heartbreak away, even if I sort of caused it myself. I had what I always wanted for a little bit and honestly now I don't know if having a real taste was better than nothing or not. I wept on the shower floor, letting everything I'd been holding in for who knows how long just swirl down the drain with my tears. Deep down, I thought maybe it could work with Brian, I mean we've been friends forever, and my dad absolutely loved the guy, but he didn't fight me on it, so my instinct to break it off must have been right.

I guess it didn't really matter anyway, my dad's not here, and Brian was going to be my boss. I spared myself the pain of more heartache by ending it,, and cutting my losses before things got any more serious. Being alone is probably what I needed anyway, right? Something about growing and whatever. I knew I was going to have to tell Matt what happened at some point, but for the moment I had planned to just focus on getting myself out of Station 19, and back to my home. Then I'd worry about my next move.

The next day I slept in late. Really late. I missed four text messages from Matt, two from Danny, but none from Brian. Even though I expected I wouldn't hear from him, it was still disappointing. Matt was just texting me because that's what he does; none of his were important, but Danny hasn't texted me in ages.

Can you come in early to cover a couple more hours?

Hello? Can you help me out or not, Jo? I'd appreciate a reply either way.

I rolled my eyes. The text messages were from about twenty minutes ago and they were about a minute apart. God he's so impatient—what did I ever see in him? Danny wasn't really my type, he never was. He was good looking, don't get me wrong, but he was Mr. Clean Cut, ass kissing, work his way to the top guy in a schmoozy kind of way. Not in the put in hard work and make it happen kind of way. I decided to go ahead and take the extra couple hours, it never hurts, and I was going in anyway, so I texted him back.

Just got your messages. Long day yesterday. Yes, I'll take the hours, I can be there at noon. Good?

Then I sent a second message, *I need to talk to you about my schedule as well.*

He replied immediately, *Long day? I see. I'm not in the station today, I have fire marshal inspections around the district. What's wrong with your schedule?*

I guessed he had inspections to do, he was always so vague with how he spent his time when he was out doing "fire marshal stuff". Generally, a fire marshal does inspections and investigations, as well as handling fire prevention week and activities like that, but it wasn't close to fire prevention week. He could never just be specific with me about what he was doing though, a major reason our relationship failed miserably.

We can talk about it later. I need to change my schedule.

I'll come by this afternoon.

Great, of course he's going to make a special trip. I didn't even bother replying. I'd been so nice to him, because I cared so much about him having a good reputation especially with my dad. When I found out that he was cheating on me, I didn't get upset. I talked shit to Matt about it, and let that be my outburst. Besides the fact that it was embarrassing to be cheated on, part of me was kind of relieved because our relationship was more out of a convenience than anything else. I also just didn't believe in creating a scene. I wouldn't get anything out of pitching a fit or getting over emotional; I definitely learned that trait from my dad who would be mad as hell at someone and talk calmly as if he were whispering to a baby.

I rolled my ass out of bed and put a uniform together. I honestly didn't like doing laundry or chores of any kind. I had plenty of uniforms to choose from so I didn't have to be washing them every day unless something really gross happened. I was riding the firetruck today, not the ambulance, but it was the same uniform either way. Since I showered the previous night, I just washed my face, brushed my teeth and fixed up my short hair. If I had to do any work today, I'd have a helmet on anyway, so it wasn't really worth getting too fussy, and I honestly didn't want to seem attractive to Danny. The last couple times I saw him, he gave me this awful dirty feeling when he looked at me, and he wasn't ever even that into me so I don't get it.

I had no energy, my limbs felt heavy, and I dragged myself around the house getting some coffee going, and changing my clothes. I couldn't stop thinking about Brian, and how I ended things last night. Part of me had really hoped there would be a message from him this morning, because I know I'd have gotten another taste if he had tried at all. He was so convincing even when he wasn't trying. One look at those eyes, and I forgot just about everything. Convictions? Out the window. Inhibitions? Please, they don't exist. But this was different. My feelings were so deep for

Brian Cavanaugh; I just couldn't let it be a fling. He says it's not, but I couldn't sacrifice what my dad always wanted for a few rolls in the hay. Fucking glorious rolls in the hay. I was getting turned on and wet just thinking about him growling in my ear, and fucking me; just the thought of his touch made me shudder. *Okay, Jo, get ready for work, fuckkkkk.* I rolled my eyes at myself, poured some coffee in a thermal mug and got on my way.

I worked at Station 19 a lot over the last year or so out of convenience. It's not a particularly busy station, but we were back up mutual aid on a lot of calls and that's more or less how Danny and I ended up dating. After Brian and I kissed last year, and it ended abruptly, and I was super pissed and hurt, Danny started flirting with me at work. He's a good looking guy, and had a lot of women that wanted him, and I decided that if he was into it, why shouldn't I go for it. I mean, I wasn't going to wait for Brian, and I had already put myself out there and got the proverbial smackdown on my heart anyway, so why not date someone new.

Danny and I started dating, and within months, it quickly escalated into me moving in with him. I think I did it so that I wasn't scraping by, and honestly, at the age of thirty-one, which I was at the time, who doesn't want to feel like they should be with someone? I figured that this was the guy I was supposed to be with mostly because we had the fire department in common and he was good looking, and that even though we didn't have the passion I had longed for in my life, maybe that was just a fantasy. My dad did not like me living with Danny at all. It was something we didn't see eye to eye on at all, and I pretty much knew he was right deep down.

After a few months, we were not working the same shift, which is where it turned out he was cheating on me. While I was at work. Funny how when we were dating we never ended up on the same shift, but now that we're apart, he kept showing up on my shift all of a sudden.

Now I was feeling the anger toward Danny, the loss of my dad and the loss of Brian; it hit deep. How I ended up in the situation was more than depressing, I felt an ache down to my bones. My body was hijacked by loss and there was no ransom that could fix it.

BRIAN

Matt wouldn't speak to me the rest of the night at the station, and I slept like shit. I couldn't get her out of my mind. I tried to rationalize what happened in my head, to make myself angry with her, to think of reasons why being with her was a bad idea, and all I could come up with was that I fucking missed her, and I had a huge pain in my chest. In my heart. She is mo chroí. My heart. Mo chuisle, My pulse, as my mom would say. I felt weak thinking about her leaving me. I knew that her happiness had to be first, not mine.

Our mom was born in Ireland and taught us the Gaelic. It was all bits and pieces, and sometimes when we were growing up and getting into trouble, she would yell at us in Gaelic phrases I still don't understand. She moved here when she was a young girl, maybe 10 I think, and so she didn't have much of an accent unless she was really fired up about something, then she would start talking fast, and you could hear it a little bit. It's funny, how when you feel like shit, you want your mom. I want my mom right now. She'd know what to do. I'm gonna have to tell her what I've done though. Fuck it. Jo's worth it; she belongs with me, and my mom will help me figure out how to get her back.

I basically moped around my house most of the morning, feeling like a big dick and an outsider since the people I give a shit about weren't really talking to me. My brother wasn't speaking to me, I obviously couldn't talk to Jo right now, this was a good idea, I'm gonna go see my mom. I'm way overdue for a visit; I hadn't seen her since Jack's funeral anyway.

I'd been sitting around sipping my coffee all morning which was just leaving an awful bitter taste in my mouth like everything around me. Literally, everything was making me sad or annoyed. Mom lives about 20 minutes away, so I showered and shaved and got my shit together, tail between my legs, knowing that my Irish ass reaming would be a big part of my begging for her help.

"Mamai," I said when she opened the door. She looked surprised to see me. I guess I needed to come by more often. We used to do regular dinners, but the fire department schedule didn't make that super easy, and once we were getting called away all the time, she just kind of gave up on us boys showing up on a regular schedule.

"How are you, my love? Get in here, come come!" she exclaimed when she opened the door, clutching me into her arms in the best hug ever. Seriously, there's nothing like a mom hug. It just warms you all over.

"I'm alright, Ma. I'm sorry I haven't seen you since the funeral," I knew my mama had a fondness for Jack and I left it at that. If it were any other man on earth, I may have—no I would have—had an issue.

"So sad, my love. I know how busy you are helping people. Get in here and give mama some love and let me put some coffee or tea on. Which are we having today love?" she was always so welcoming.

"Let's have coffee, Mama, unless you've decided it's whiskey time?" I loved teasing her. She only drank when things were really bad, or really good.

"It's one in the afternoon, Brian Patrick. We Cavanaugh's don't do that unless times are tough. Are times tough?" she gave me a furrowed brow and a concerned look as she led me to her sitting room which was super traditional old school old lady. I loved my mama, however this room was the room you weren't allowed in until you were an adult, the furniture looked so comfortable when I was younger, and then when you finally were allowed in as an adult, you wanted to go back to the kids' room where you could actually get comfortable on the furniture. She had flowered chairs, and *the* most uncomfortable couch on earth in this room, but you were an adult in this room. She led me to the sitting room, and then rushed herself off to the kitchen to make coffee.

"Mama, you don't have to do that, I'm a grown man, I can get coffee. I came to visit with you." She was getting older, and with Jack's passing, it made me think of my lineage, and how my mama was no spring chicken. I don't want her fussing over me of all people. I did however, know better, so I sat my ass on the old fashioned flowered couch where I knew she wanted to sit across from me and I waited for her to come back with coffee.

A few minutes later, she returned, probably because Matt and I bought her a fancy automatic coffee machine with pods so she wouldn't get out the ancient multi person brew pot she used to. She handed me a cup and I took a sip and pursed my lips from the fire that the whiskey sent chasing down my throat.

"Holy cow, Mama, what he hel—heck?" I tried not to curse in front of her unless it was the holidays and we were all drunk. She laughed at me.

"I know you need it, my love. Something must be happening in your life for you to come by unannounced. If it makes you feel better, I have a splash in my tea, in case it's too much for me to handle," she winked at me and sat down on the same couch as me, turning herself to me.

"Mama, I can't just come to see you and check in?" I asked. She was onto me. I didn't swing by as often as I should.

"Don't play a game you did not invent, my child. I know you are here searching for something, so let's get to it. I have plenty to keep me busy in my grief over my dear friend," she was referring to Jack, and I felt like I knew something had happened there. "How is my dear dear, Josephine?" she asked me. My heart sank even further, which I didn't think was possible.

"Uh, she's okay?" I made it a question. "I've talked to her a lot the last week or so. I got her to come back to our station sort of full-time," I again, said it like a question I was asking for approval.

"Your feelings are no secret, my love. What happened that made you come here for comfort? I know you, love, and I know your ways…Has something happened? Talk to your mama…" she patted the couch between us. My mom's voice was so soft and soothing, with that faint Irish accent. The sweetness in her voice always made everyone want to spill their guts to her. She was everyone's mama.

"Mama, everything is fuc—messed up, and I don't know what to do about it. Jo is going to come back to Station 23, so me and Jack's plan worked, but..." I just didn't really know how to say it.

"But you're in love with her," she finished my sentence for me and smiled. I let out a huge sigh that I'd been holding in since the day before when I talked to Jo last. I didn't say anything at all and she continued. "Why does this leave you exasperated, Brian? Does she know how you feel?"

I looked up at her, how did she know? "Not really, no, I don't think she knows how I feel, but I do know she doesn't want anything to do with me except for working together I guess. I don't know what to do and I thought I could just let it go, but Mama, I'm sick over it. I've never felt this way about a woman before, and it's like my brain doesn't even work right now." It's true. I couldn't see straight without knowing she was mine. "She is *grá mo chroí*". I admitted to my mom.

"Ah, she is your eternal love." Now mama was smiling so big she looked like she would laugh.

"Why do you look like you're going to laugh? This isn't funny. This is terrible." I poured the rest of my coffee down, feeling the burn of the whiskey all the way down to my stomach.

She grinned and got up and went to the liquor cabinet. She pulled out two tumblers and poured us both a healthy amount of Jamison's. "Well my dear," she said as she passed one to me, then clinked my glass with hers, "Jack and I always knew this would happen eventually," she giggled and took a sip of her whiskey.

"What are you talking about? Jack told me to stay away from her," I recalled that conversation in my head again.

"I know exactly what Jack said to you. He didn't tell you to stay away from her. He told you not to lust after her like a conquest. I also know that he told you that you would have his blessing when you were really ready for what that sweet girl deserves," she said matter-of-factly, and sat back down on the couch looking pretty satisfied with herself. "It seems you are now ready, so tell me, why doesn't she want to be with you?"

"How do you know all of this, Mama?" I was now very sure she had a relationship with Jack and I was kind of mad about it.

"Jack and I had a very special friendship, Brian. You and Matt were like sons to him, and he was a wonderful person to us especially in our time of need. Jack and I were very close and he often came by to check in on us, and we talked. You don't get an opinion on this, your mama is a grown woman you know." She looked away and I could see the hurt and sadness of his passing in her teary eyes.

"I'm sorry." I really was sorry. If she loved Jack half as much as I loved Jo, her sadness breaks my heart too.

"It's fine, we all go eventually. Jack and I often talked of the dangers of the job for him, and for you boys, and for Jo of course. Now, tell me why you think she doesn't want to be with you, and why you are so sure this cannot be fixed." My mama thought everything could be fixed. With whiskey and hugs mostly, which was actually mostly true if you really think about it.

"Well, we started seeing each other...secretly," I waited for a reply or judgment, but she just motioned for me to continue. "After a little bit, I told her about how Jack and I wanted her to come back to our station and work with us, and the old crew, and she seemed to like the idea. Then we got a call, and we went out to handle it, basically like old times, great teamwork, everyone got saved, the whole thing. But..." I really didn't want to tell my mom what a dickhead caveman I was at the scene, but I had to come clean.

"Go on, Brian, you may as well tell me, because you know if you don't I will just call Matty and ask him later," she winked at me. I gave a little sarcastic laugh. When she wanted answers, she got them, so I drank the rest of the whiskey in my glass and told her.

"Honestly, I didn't treat her like one of the guys on my crew. I was overprotective, and unprofessional about it and gave her a hard time because I wanted to protect her. And she was mad. Mama, really really mad. I was a jerk. I thought it was just a little argument, and that we'd talk about it later, and she didn't want any part of it. She said that she wanted to come back to the station full-time, but we couldn't see each other anymore. I had to decide if it was going to work for me or not. I wanted her to be happy, and I knew that being at Jack's station is what she wants in her heart, so I let her go. I didn't fight for her," I hung my head. Getting the full story off my chest was a relief, but didn't take away the pain in my chest that her absence had left.

"Oh my dear, I'm quite certain this can be fixed. But I'm going to give you the hard truth, as you do to your boys down at the firehouse," she lowered her eyes at me, and looked at me over her glasses. Oh shit.

"Okay, Mama, shoot," I said and took in a big breath.

"Man up," she said. She took her whiskey down, and put her glass on the coffee table and looked at me.

"What?" I almost choked. That was her advice?

"You heard me, son. Man up. You love this girl? Go fight for her. Go get her. Don't sulk and whine like a little baby. You go tell her the truth, and you tell her how you feel. She'll see you're serious. A serious man fights for his woman. This I know." And with that, she folded her arms; was clearly done with her advice.

I thought about it for a moment, and realized she was right. I was a total pussy not to stop her in my office. We were tired, she was mad and I just let her go. What the fuck kind of way is that to show a woman you love her? I needed to get a plan together for getting her back, for good.

"Mama, you're right. I'm gonna get her back. Thank you," I scooped her into a big hug and wouldn't let go.

"You're welcome, sweetheart, sometimes we need someone to point out the obvious to us because we cannot see what's right in front of us."

I got up to leave, and then decided I better tell her that Matt and I weren't speaking before she heard about it.

"I forgot to tell you that Matty knows about this, at least some of it, and he's pretty pissed off at me right now too," I started to put my hand over my mouth for saying pissed.

She waved her hand at me and laughed a bit, "Oh I know. He called me this morning and told me everything." She already knew everything I had come to tell her. She's a wily woman; I couldn't even be mad. I needed the kick in the pants, we all do sometimes.

"I'm not even mad," I laughed.

"You have no reason to be. You need to set things right with your brother though. He loves Josephine too in his own way. Those two have always been very close, and he feels like you betrayed a trust, a sacred bond. He doesn't understand true love yet, but he will someday, and you can teach him once you get your affairs in order. But until then, he wants to protect her from getting hurt too, just in a different way. Go see him, he will talk to you, I made sure of it," she instructed me.

"Okay, Mama I will. I'll go talk to him later tonight," I gave her another hug and a kiss on the cheek. "Thank you, Mama. I'm gonna make her my wife, you'll see."

"I have no doubt that you will, my love. I have something for you, hold on a moment," She walked back to her bedroom and came back with a small box, and put it in my hand.

"What's this?" It looked like a ring box.

"This is a gift that Jack gave to me a long time ago, and I think that it's the perfect thing for you to give Josephine when you set things right. Now go," she shooed me out of the house. I didn't open the box, I needed to go home and formulate my plan and talk to Matt. Time to make Jo mine. For good. Operation MJM, "Make Jo Mine". Yeah, it was game on.

JO

I had about four days to get my shit together, and be okay seeing Brian at work on a regular basis. I had managed to get a couple other guys to take some of my shifts at 19. Towards the end of the time frame, I was looking to leave, so I should only have to put in another two, maybe three shifts here before getting on the schedule over at Station 23 more or less full time.

It had been a slow afternoon at the station, and I was only here for a quick six-hour shift. I was covering for another guy that had kids, and there was some kind of event at his kid's school. Matt and I had been texting since I woke up, and he wanted me to come out for beers tonight, which I really didn't want to do, but I had no reasonable excuse not to. It would be better than sitting at home feeling sorry for myself, but I wasn't convinced it was the best idea. I did want to talk to him about how uncomfortable Danny had been making me with his comments and looks lately. I'd been avoiding him like the plague and I just felt like something was up with that. Hopefully tonight wasn't a "gathering" and it won't be all the guys, and Brian of course. I'd love a night to chill out and talk to Matt. I just didn't want to see Brian, until I figured out how to cope with the situation. I was going to have to pretend that I'm perfectly okay with the things that I said, which honestly I wasn't. I regretted it. In my panties I regretted it, and in my heart I regretted it, but my brain came out on top this time.

Matt filled me in about some new girl he met that sounded about as interesting as watching cement dry, when our tones dropped for a car accident. I was actually covering for the first officer that afternoon, so I shoved my phone in my shirt pocket, and headed for the truck. Stepping into my gear, I got that same rush I always do from emergency response.

As we were pulling out of the station, Danny was pulling in and gave me what I'd call a death stare. He glared at me in such a way that pierced me with his glassy eyes. Hey, it's not my fault we got a call, and I never told him to come here to talk to me in the first place. Station 19 does not have a heavy rescue truck like Station 23 does, and so often we called for them to join us on a car accident because they have some of the tools for a bigger job. This was a tractor trailer accident, sounds like it flipped on it's side and no one was hurt, but we called for them to join us anyway, just in case. It wasn't my shift that would be working, they all got off at 7am this morning, so at least I wouldn't see Brian there. And it was 19's scene anyway, even if he were there, he wouldn't be in charge of this one.

We got to the scene, and it was more of a big mess than anything else. The driver of the vehicle had "lost control", hit the guard wall, and flipped his semi on its side. He was standing around yelling about some mystery car that cut him off and caused the accident. The semi was filled with citrus. Lemons, oranges, limes and grapefruits were everywhere. Literally all over the road, and a whole bunch of them had gotten smooshed into the road already from passers by, and it smelled delightful. We were all chuckling about it, and working on cleaning up the mess so the truck could be hauled away and become someone else's problem when I saw Brian's Chief truck pull up.

Come on, seriously? What's he doing here? It's not even his day to work. I tried not to stare, and to just do my job, but I wanted to see what he was doing there. My heart started racing as he got out of his truck and walked over to the on scene commander for a minute, then went over to see his crew. It wasn't station 23's mess to clear up and they would probably be released from the scene as soon as enough of the mess was cleaned up to open the roadway back up. I looked away, but I swear I could feel him looking at me. I was wearing my bunker pants, t-shirt and helmet, but no coat because there was really no danger, and as usual it was pretty hot out. I thought about our argument the last time we were on scene together and chuckled to myself; today I'm wearing a uniform shirt which is navy blue with the fire department insignia on the chest.

There would be no public sweaty show today, *so there, Chief.*

I couldn't help myself, I looked over his way and he was staring in my direction, wearing jeans and a t-shirt that accentuated those beautiful muscles of his. His visible tattoos on his arms were so sexy, and he was standing with the officer of the 23 truck, with his arms folded in front of him, and his sunglasses on. He must have been on his way somewhere, or on his way back from somewhere because he lives on my side of town. It was none of my business what he was doing, but I couldn't help myself. I felt desire rising within me just from seeing him, and I think I was staring, because he smiled right at me. *Oh shit, I got caught staring. Fuck me.*

I shook myself from my Brian trance, and helped my crew finish up what we were doing. I tried not to look in his direction again. I saw him leave out of the corner of my eye, as we were winding up, and his guys got sent home. It took a little longer than expected to wrap up; citrus can be a little unruly—who knew? I had about an hour left in my shift by the time we got back to the station, and Danny was in the day room, presumably, waiting to talk to me.

After I put my gear back, I went over to talk to him. "Did you want to talk about my schedule?"

He looked up from the paperwork he was reviewing. "Yeah, that's why I'm sitting here waiting for you." He was curt with me.

"I can't help when there's a call, Danny, so lose the attitude," I didn't know what his problem was, but I didn't need his shit today.

"Yea, I get it. What's the deal with your schedule?"

"I'm going to take myself out of the per diem rotation for awhile. Well indefinitely actually. I've been offered a more steady gig, and I've decided that it would suit me better to have a more normal schedule, so I'm going to take it. I have two more shifts here this week; I got the rest covered." That pretty much summed it up. I waited for a response and got a smirk.

"Going back to daddy's old station I assume?" he asked smugly.

I was pissed. "Yes, I am. It's closer to my house, I grew up there, and they're offering me a full-time spot, so yes." *Fuck you, Danny, fuck you, fuck you, fuck you.*

"Fucking the Chief over there now?" he demanded, his anger beginning to show.

I didn't even know I was going to do it until it happened, but I slapped him right across the face. I could've gotten in a lot of trouble for that, and honestly I didn't care, even if I didn't plan it, he deserved it.

"Wow," he said as he rubbed his cheek where I hit him. "Sensitive subject, eh?" he laughed at me. He *laughed* at me.

"No, Danny it's not," I lied. "It's actually none of your fucking business, this was about a job opportunity. And you don't get to talk to me like that. What the fuck is your problem?"

"No problem, Jo. No problem at all." That smug look of his was infuriating me. "I'm sorry if I offended you. How's going through your dad's stuff? Have you gone through all of those notebooks of his yet?"

Now he wanted to make nice? The guy was a dick; I honestly have no idea what I ever saw in him. I did just hit him though, so I figured I would make a little bit nice. "No, I haven't gone through them yet, probably this weekend. I need to make sure there's nothing in the notebooks that needs to be sorted." Who knows what's in all of those notebooks, my dad journaled in addition to keeping meticulous call notes. I definitely wanted to read his journals, but I didn't even know if they're all in the same place. I hadn't really gone in his room yet to poke around.

"Ah, I see. Well good luck. If there's nothing else, then I guess that's it. Your shift is about over, I can cover the last half hour if you want to leave now," he offered.

"Uh, alright, cool. Thanks." I was a little confused, but getting away from him sooner rather than later sounded ideal to me at this point. I started to walk away.

"Oh, Jo?" he called after me.

"Yeah?" I turned around to see what he wanted.

"Looking sexy today," he laughed. "Really sexy." He narrowed his eyes at me.

A chill setttled all over me. That was completely out of the blue, and totally creepy. *Looking sexy? What the hell is that about?* I didn't reply.

I got out of there as quick as possible. There was something seriously wrong with him, and the way he'd been glaring at me the last few times I've seen him disturbs me. And why would he care about my dad's notebooks? I made a note to schedule time to go through them this weekend, I felt like something in those notebooks intrigued Danny, and if that was true, I needed to find out why.

BRIAN

I showed up on that scene to see her. I knew she'd be there. I was on my way to go see my brother straight from my mom's when the call went out. I had hoped to have beers with Matt tonight, but he told me he was meeting up with Jo, and frankly, I needed to make things right with Matt before he saw her so he would help me get her back. The plan would start as soon as possible.

I thanked the Lord above when I saw her she was wearing a dark blue uniform shirt, her uniform looking like everyone else's. Except that no one else on that scene makes my cock hard. No one anywhere, actually. I'd been getting a few texts here and there this week from girls I had gone out with recently, and I told every single one of them that I was off the market and wished them well. Even if Jo didn't know yet, there's no other woman for me and she will find out soon enough. I honestly couldn't stand the thought of touching anyone but her and I cringed at the thought.

As I headed over to my brother's house, I thought about how different life felt since I tasted her. Like I was carrying a weight around before I realized how I felt about her. I was so excited about my future with Jo, I wanted to call her and talk to her about it like she was my best friend. She wasn't really speaking to me, but that would change soon enough. I was absolutely going to man up, and be the man she deserved in her life. I'd protect her and love her forever. The sappy shit made me so happy I could burst, I didn't even care, I could shout it from the rooftops.

I pulled into my brother's driveway, he lived with Jax in a house that belonged to Jax. It was their bachelor pad more or less. I preferred my house being my sanctuary, and I kept most of my partying outside of my place. Jax was probably down at the station tinkering with things or researching stuff, I didn't see his truck there and you could find him there most of the time, even on his time off.

It was a nice afternoon, and I was pretty sure my brother was out back in his back yard, so I walked around instead of coming to the front door. Sure enough, there he was, lounging in a chair beer in one hand, phone in the other.

"Hey, Matt." I approached the beast carefully. I really did need his help, and since we've both already talked to our mom, I wasn't quite sure where to start and I was hoping he would actually.

"Oh, hey dickhead. How was your visit with mom?" he laughed sarcastically in my direction, not really making eye contact with me. Obviously he wasn't going to make this easy for me.

"It was...you know, enlightening. Apparently she already knew everything. Nice mouth," I got a beer for myself out of the cooler next to him and grabbed myself a seat.

We sat in silence drinking our beers for a couple minutes, when Matt did finally speak up first. Thank God.

"Look. I have to just ask you, because I don't even get it right now, but mom told me to listen to you. So, are you serious? Like really serious about this? Because this changes everything, man, you can't be kinda sure, or whatever. You have to be honest with me, do you really love her?" He looked over at me and waited for my response.

I turned myself to face him and took in a deep breath. "Matty, I've never been so sure of anything in my life. She's my heart. Like Mama used to talk about love. My life is empty without her in it. I'm in physical pain without her right now and I don't know what to do to get her back, but I have to. I was put on this earth to take care of her and to love her. I need you to help me." I meant every word, and I hoped it was enough for Matt to understand the depth of my feelings for her. I didn't really know what else to say.

Matt was looking at me intently, and then he finally spoke up., "Okay, I get it. If she's the one for you, then I'll talk to her tonight when I see her. I'm not making any promises because she doesn't even know I know anything yet, but I had already planned to bring it up tonight. She is meeting me out for drinks later. Okay?"

"Yeah, absolutely. Seriously, man, I owe you one. I'm telling you I've never felt like this before and I swear to you it's the real deal."

"Do you think she feels the same way about you?" He asked me.

"I think she does. I think she's afraid of what people will say, but I don't care. I'd give up being Chief to be with her," I'd have given up whatever it took to make that empty feeling go away.

"Okay, settle down. Let's not go resigning from our jobs. I'm pretty sure you can make this work one way or another if she really feels the same way. She's squirrely though, and you know that about her. She starts on Sunday with us, so don't do anything before then. I'll talk to her tonight, but that's so she can tell me what's going on from her perspective. The only way to win this game is patience. You're gonna have to take it slow or you're gonna piss her off, and you know what that means," he laughed.

I laughed too, when Jo was pissed off, she'd go to the end of the earth to make sure you knew she was right and you were wrong out of principle alone. And she would win. Every time. "Yeah, I definitely do. I'll try to keep myself in check, but you gotta tell me how she is after you talk to her. I haven't seen or heard from her, and I can't stand her working at 19 this week with that Danny Russell wrapping up her shifts."

"Yeah, something about that guy really gives me the creeps lately. I used to just think he was a dick, but I feel like something else is up and he's actually been showing up on Jo's shifts this week when he's not scheduled," Matt confessed.

I stood up and clenched my fists, "What? Is he giving her a hard time? What's going on?" I was consumed with rage, if he was harassing her or even sneezing in her direction, I'd fucking kill him.

"Relax for right now, she says it's under control, and in less than a week, she'll be full-time with us. Let her play this out her way so she feels like she did the right thing. I don't like it any more than you do, I feel like that guy needs a swift punch in the dick myself."

"Alright, it's only a couple days, but you need to check in with her about it. A lot. I don't like it one bit. We're her family regardless of anything else, we have to take care of her." I don't like feeling helpless, but Matt was right. I needed to let Jo have her space to work this out her way. I couldn't control everything in her life, but one thing was for damn sure, after she was done at 19, I wasn't letting her out of my sight, and if I had any say in the matter her beautiful face would be the first thing I saw in the mornings, and the last thing I saw every night.

JO

I really needed to start going through my dad's stuff, and organizing his notebooks and stuff. I wonder if maybe I can just give the notebooks to Brian to hold onto in case he needed them for anything. I made a note to ask Matt to talk to Brian about it. I was trying to avoid initiating a conversation with Brian until we were working together, because it hurts. I've got a pit in my stomach, and every time I've thought about him, I felt my face getting warm, and my eyes becoming full of tears. I knew the feeling would pass, it had to eventually.

I was meeting Matt tonight, just the two of us, to catch up and hang out and have a couple drinks. We hadn't really spent any time together since I left the bar with Brian that night. That night, that sealed my feelings, and makes me weak in the knees. I started to get a tingle just thinking about how hot it was. *Stop it, stop it, stop it.* Oh, but it was so good. It could never be that good with anyone else, ever. I actually rolled my eyes at myself and finished getting ready.

Matt and I had decided to meet up at a place across town for some food and drinks, and we didn't really feel like running into everyone we know, so it was worth the extra fifteen minutes on the road to get there. It was actually a little Irish place kind of close to Station 19 that I had discovered one night after a shift there with some of the guys that lived on that side of town.

I wasn't an especially high maintenance girl, I was definitely a t-shirt and jeans chick, but I still liked to feel pretty when I wasn't riding a firetruck. I had messy short hair that I thought looks pretty cute when I put some makeup on, so since I was feeling so shitty, I decided that I would definitely do my face tonight. It wasn't a date, but I was leaving the house and trying to put on a brave face, so it was a bit like painting on confidence.

I absolutely needed to tell Matt what happened. I couldn't keep this secret from him, and I was so afraid he was going to be angry with me about it. Scotty and I had been texting, and he said something was going on with Matt and Brian at work and they were barely speaking the other day. I was really hoping that it had nothing to do with me. I was sure it didn't, but I couldn't help the thought. I felt so fucking guilty for being dishonest in the first place. Really, this was probably never a good idea, since we couldn't be together publicly, I couldn't help but think that I set us up for failure by trying to keep him in secret. Well in true Jo fashion, it is what it is. Now it's time to clear the air, confess to Matt, and talk about what's next.

I pulled in to the parking lot of Erin's Pub, parking next to Matt. He obviously beat me here. I checked myself in the mirror real quick, freshened up my lipstick, and got my ass in gear. When I walked in, he was sitting at the bar with his back to the door, wearing his usual beat up fire department baseball hat, t-shirt and jeans. I could have spotted him a mile away.

"Excuse me, is this seat taken," I whispered in his ear trying to sound as sexy as possible. Hey, why not have a little fun with him.

He turned around quickly, and then looked shocked to see me, and I couldn't help laughing hysterically. He definitely thought I was a strange new possibility. Mission accomplished.

"What the fuck, Jo?! You can't do that to a guy! I'm in a dry spell! That's so not fair!" he pretended to be mad at me and it was making me laugh that much harder.

"Aww come on, Matty, that was funny. *Is this seat taken*?" I mocked him further.

"Yeah, yeah, hilarious. Come on, let's get a table," he stood up, still pretending to be mad, leaving a few bucks on the bar for his beer.

I followed him over to a booth where he sat facing the door, and I sat across from him, my back to the door. Something a lot of emergency personnel do is evaluate a room—anywhere they go—for the different exits. It's called a means of egress. We're always calculating how we would get out, if there was an emergency. Normally, we all like having our eyes on the door for some reason, it was just instinctive, but in this situation, I was fine letting Matt have eyes on the door, as long as one of us did. If I were here with someone who wasn't a partner, or in emergency services, I would have insisted sitting on the other side, just to have eyes on the exit. It's just an instinctive thing we all do and you don't even realize you do it until you are out and about with people who don't do it.

"Are you hungry?" he asked, and grabbed a menu from the little metal tray holding them, handing it to me.

"I can always eat," I grinned. "But I'm definitely thirsty more than anything," I poked my head up and around like it was on a swivel, looking for a waitress. Before I even sat myself right, an adorable little blonde girl popped up in front of us to take our order.

"Hi, I'm Summer, what can I getcha, hunny?" she asked me with the sweetest little southern accent.

"Hi, Summer, I'll take a Jameson's and ginger please," I smiled. She seemed really young, but she sure was perky. Matt was definitely enjoying the view himself.

"I'll have another one of these," he showed her his beer bottle and she smiled.

"Do you two need a few minutes with the menu?"

"I do actually, thanks," I said, and she smiled again and took off like a little fairy. "She's pretty cute, you should talk to her," I said to Matt.

"She's cute, but she's not my type. Looks a little young. Anyway, I'm here to hang out with you. How's it going? I feel like it's been the longest week ever, and we haven't really had time to catch up much. How are you doing?" He asked me a bunch of questions.

"I'm alright, it's still weird being in that house without him if we're being honest. And now, I really just can't wait to be done with 19," I didn't really want to tell Matt exactly how creeped out I was becoming by Danny, but I think he could tell.

"Is that motherfucker giving you a hard time?" he asked.

"I wouldn't call it a hard time exactly," I scrunched my face up trying to figure out how to describe it. Matt was waiting for me to clarify. "He just keeps showing up, and he's made a few kind of inappropriate comments, but I don't think it's a big deal. He knows I'm moving on and taking up residence at 23, so it is what it is. It's only a few more days, then I won't really ever have to see him."

Matt looked at me sternly before he replied. "It's important that you tell me if he's doing anything that you know is over the line." He awaited my response.

I sighed, knowing he was totally right. "I promise I will. I think he's pushing his luck with me for some reason, I don't know why now, but whatever. I don't think it's that bad. I promise I'll tell you if it's otherwise."

"Okay. I'm serious though. There's something about him that's really been bothering me lately and the sooner you get out of there the better."

"Yeah, I agree. I have a shift on Sunday overnight before I start with 23 on Monday morning that I'm trying to get someone to just cover for me. If that works out, I'll only have to see him one more time maybe, if he shows up on Saturday when I'm working in the morning." I had actually decided that the money this week wasn't worth seeing him, and instead of switching shifts with other guys, I offered mine up to people that just wanted to work a little extra this week.

"Uh huh," he prompted me to continue. He knew something was up. "So, how about you 'fess up and tell me what's clearly going on in that head of yours, because it's totally obvious you have something to tell me. What's really going on with Danny at work?" he fucking knew me and although that wasn't bothering me like the Brian situation weighed me down, he knew something was up, and he knew me better than I could ever pretend to hide.

"Eh, he's just hanging around all the time now like I said, and he made some 'you're looking sexy' comment that was fairly awkward and definitely uncalled for. Other than that, I'm just riding out the rest of the week, and trying to find someone to take my shift there Sunday so I can just be done with it already." The Danny thing nagged at me a little bit, but I really don't think he's up to anything weird or nefarious, I think he's just a dick and is using his last bit of time to make me uncomfortable.

"Did you report him to 19's Chief?" Matt asked.

"Of course not. It's not that big of a deal, and let's be honest, I've heard way worse at 23, than 'you're looking sexy' and you know it," I gave him a sideways glance. Firefighters can be raunchy at times, and while there's obviously a sexual harassment policy, more often than not, the intent was not to harass, it was just messing around.

"I don't like that guy, Jo, and I especially don't like that he's left you alone all these months since you broke up, and now he's showing up all the time, making comments. Something isn't right about it." He looked genuinely concerned.

"So far, it was one comment, and he's just 'around' all the time," I waved my hands around, "I don't think it's anything to be worried about, however I promise you that I will report in immediately if anything changes, okay?" I put my hand over my heart, and promised sarcastically. I honestly deep down was a little creeped out by Danny, but I'm sure that it's nothing. I decided not to tell Matt that I'd slapped Danny earlier.

"Alright, you better," he ordered me, then changed the subject. "So what else is on your mind, we've barely talked, and that's unusual to begin with, but you seem really distracted about something. If it's not Danny, then what is it?"

I guessed it was the time for me to confess my sins to my best friend. Just then, Summer walked up with our drinks, and took our order. We were more snackers than anything else, so we got a bunch of appetizers to share which was pretty much our standard.

"Uh, everything is alright I guess," I was definitely stalling and he looked down at me indicating that he knew there was more.

I took a deep breath, I mean I did want to 'fess up, "Okay, okay, you're right. I need to tell you something, and I really don't know where to begin, because I really don't want you to be pissed off at me, and I need your advice, but I'm one hundred percent putting you in the middle of what I would consider a situation." My eyes got big and I waited for the go ahead.

He leaned in over the table. "I know. And you're my best friend, Jo, so let's get to it, and solve whatever the problem is now. There's literally nothing you could say that would make me not love you, you're my family. So just spill it and let's fix it," he reached over, giving my hand a squeeze, signaling the go ahead.

"Alright, fuck it. Here's the deal, I slept with your brother. Okay? More than once. I did it, I'm sorry, please don't fucking hate me, it was a thing, and now it's not a thing, and I'm sorry, and I probably wasn't thinking, but now it's kind of fucked up, and I'm sorry—" I was rambling when he cut me off.

"Okay! Okay! You're sorry, I get it. Relax, Jo. *Relax.*" He laughed a little. Okay, that was a good sign right? Wait, was this funny?

"This isn't funny," I scrunched my face at him. My face was hot, and I wasn't sure if I wanted to cry, or run away.

"You're right, it's not. Obviously you've been thinking about all of this a *lot*, so tell me what's going on before I even consider giving you my opinion on the matter. And before you even ask, I'm not mad exactly," now he looked stern.

I needed to just spill it, all of it. "Look, I've had a crush on your brother since I started liking boys. He was so mean to us, but I didn't care. I always had a thing for him," I started. "We kissed and had kind of a moment, and he blew me off bad last year. I'm sure that's what you're wondering about, right?" I asked. Matt never ever pressured me about what made me stop talking to Brian regularly last year. He knew something happened, but we never talked about it.

"Okay, so something happened last year, that's not a shocker since you barely spoke for a year, but what the fuck happened now?" I was borderline mortified; I couldn't even believe I was saying it out loud. I felt like Matt deserved to know, and I want his advice, but I also feel like I cheapen my 'moments' with Brian by bringing them up for discussion to his brother.

"Well what do you want to know exactly?" I was dodging for sure, but I also didn't really want to discuss the exploits in detail. I felt like he knew something and was coaxing confirmation out of me or something. "Do you know something? Did you talk to Brian about this, Matt?" I know I was sounding defensive. They were brothers, they very well may talk about this stuff, I actually have no idea. Oh, God, I hope they didn't talk about me in bed. Oh, God.

"Alright, in the interest of full disclosure, Brian told me a *little* bit of what happened. Not really any details though. And don't *you* tell me any details either, dear God, that's all I need is a visual I can't get out of my head," he rolled his eyes dramatically. "I'm more interested in where your head is at, and what is going on with you," he said.

I sighed and rolled my eyes too. So, he already knew. Ugh. "Ugh, okay great. Wonderful in fact," I put my head down, let out a huge sigh, looked back up and let it roll out, "Ok, so Brian and I had ourselves a fling if you will over the last week or so. I thought it might be something more, but it's not. And now, I'm coming back to work full-time at the station, and so that's it more or less."

"So, is it more, or is it less exactly?" he questioned me.

"Uh, it is what it was? I mean look, we can't be together. I haven't talked to him, and I'm gonna pretend that it's back to normal except for you know, that he's gonna be my boss for real now," I took a huge gulp of my drink. Maybe this going back to the station was a bad idea. I didn't know if I could look at either of them that often after this.

"So, explain to me...why can't you be together? Do you *want* to be together?"

I hesitated. The answer was yes. But it felt more complicated than that. We couldn't have a fling, and then go back to working together like nothing happened, and if he started seeing someone after me, I might die of the heartbreak.

"What did he tell you, Matt?" I was dodging the question.

"Honestly, he told me he didn't want to stop seeing you, that you ended it, not him."

"That's true. I thought it was for the best. You know that I want to stay at 23 for the foreseeable future, maybe the rest of my career, and I don't think that having a relationship with the Chief is a very professional way to do that, do you?" I asked.

"I don't really think you answered my question, Jo. I think you're dodging me," he tilted his head at me like a puppy.

"Did I want to break it off?

"Yea, that is the question on the table."

"No. No I didn't. I've loved Brian my whole life Matt. Not like me and you, that's

251

weird," I nervously laughed. "You and I both know how he is, and I care about working at 23 more than anything," I paused. "Look, honestly, I've been in love with Brian from the beginning; since as long as I can remember. But I know I did the right thing," I got serious, and sad. It felt so sad and so wrong to tell Matt, and not tell Brian what my real feelings were.

"So, you're in love with a man, who wanted to be with you, possibly loved you back, but since you have no idea how he felt, you think you did the right thing because of *work*? That's where we are, correct me if I've missed anything," He summed it up about right.

"Yeah, pretty much. Sounds about right," I just stared at him blankly. I didn't know what to say. I felt empty after telling him everything. He sat there in silence, making me super uncomfortable and I shifted in my seat. "What?" I finally said, frustrated. "What do you want to say? It's obvious you have something to say about all of this."

"You're both so fucking stupid." He put his face in his hands and groaned.

BRIAN

Basically, I spent that whole evening trying not to text Matt and ask him how she really felt about me, or if she said anything about me. Like a damn teenager, I paced around. I went to the gym for a little while, but I felt like shit. I spent the whole night fretting, sick to my stomach, nervous and anxious, hoping and wishing that Matt could help me fix what I should have never let get broken.

I had to work in the morning, so I thought I'd go to my office and do a little paperwork, to maybe take my mind off things for awhile. If I texted Matt, he'd be pissed at me, and while patience isn't really my thing, I thought better of irritating him, since he was technically trying to help me. I had some reports to write, and I was still going through a lot of things that Jack was working on that he hadn't finished. I needed to work on grant proposals soon, and thank God, Jack had started to teach me how to do a lot of these things over the last year or so or I'd be totally fucking lost.

It's really a lot of bullshit sometimes, and often I miss actually fighting fire. I'm not that old, and the idea of spending the rest of my career not actually getting to go in and 'do work' was frustrating. I cared very much about being a leader, but this whole thing with Jo has me thinking a lot more about what I really want in my life. If this job is the real reason she won't be with me, I'll go back to being a black hat firefighter right now, I don't need to be in charge of shit at the station if that's what it takes.

I didn't have the attention span right now to do any of this paperwork, I was just shuffling things around on my desk. I decided to just save it for tomorrow, so I wandered around the station shooting the breeze with a couple of the guys on shift before making my way out. Finally, I got a text from Matt, he was on his way home.

Yo, I just left.

And? I replied.

You're both so fucking stupid.

Fuck you.

Are you going to tell me what happened or not?

Yea, what are you doing now?

I was just heading home

I'll meet you at your place so we can talk

Is it bad

I don't know, I'll meet you at your place and tell you what's up

Ugh, I didn't know what that meant, but it didn't seem that great. We weren't really phone talkers, and Matt only lived about five blocks away, so it was usually just as easy for us to meet up in person to talk, but I didn't like the sound of this. I got in my truck and headed home. Contemplating my future without her in it just wasn't feasible. Regardless of what Matt had to tell me, I knew she had feelings for me and I was going to do whatever it took to bring us together.

It was only a ten-minute drive to my house from the station, and I had to pass Jo's house to get there. I stared at her jeep in the driveway as I rolled by, she was home now too and the light in her bedroom was on as well as the one in the living room. I wondered what she was doing, what her and Matt talked about. My mind wandered to what she might be wearing too. She was so fucking sexy, especially when she wasn't trying. She was probably wearing little shorts and a fire department t-shirt like she usually did. *Fuck, I've gotta make this right.* I flipped open the glove box to make sure the box from my mom was still in there. Safe and sound, right where I left it.

Matt was parked on the street in front of my house, he knew it irritated the shit out of me when he parked in my driveway. It was only big enough for my giant truck. I thought about how I'd either make the driveway bigger or let Jo park her Jeep there if she wanted. My God, I was so fucked for her. He hopped out of his truck as soon as I pulled in.

"So, what did she say?" I cut right to the chase. The suspense was killing me, literally.

Matt laughed. "Geez, bro, calm down."

"Honestly, dude? I can't." And really, I couldn't. I was obsessed. We walked to my front porch and sat on the steps, both of us staring out to the street. "Okay, let me have it. What's the deal?"

"Well, first of all, we need to look into this Danny more. He's making comments to her, and I think something is up."

"What do you mean, comments?" I was furious in an instant. I'll kill the motherfucker.

"She didn't really get into it and kind of blew it off, but I think something else is going on. He honestly didn't give a shit about her for months, now he's showing up on her shifts, making inappropriate remarks and shit. Something doesn't add up. She has a thick skin and all, but I think something is just off about the whole thing," he said. He looked like he was trying to figure out what it could be, and so was I. Whatever it was, I'd put a fucking end to it. An end to him. Nobody will mess with my Jo, even if she won't have me back.

"Okay, we'll pay this dickhead a visit ASAP," I said. "So, let's get to it, did she talk to you about me?"

"Yeah, Romeo, she did. Settle yourself. She fucking loves you, so calm the fuck down." The heavens opened up and released some of my pain immediately. *She loves me!* I could do a fucking Irish jig in my own front yard. I tried to restrain myself from the dancing and attempted to be cool like a cucumber, but inside, seriously, I was bursting with fucking hearts and flowers.

"Oh yeah?" Was literally all I could say. I didn't want to sound like a fucking pussy, I'd already poured my heart out twice today, once to mama and once to Matt. That's more than enough to revoke my man card as it is.

"Yeah. But here's the deal. There's two obstacles here," he held two fingers up at me.

"Okay shoot," I wanted to get a goddamn notebook out and take notes so I got it all and could formulate my plan, but I sat still.

"One, she's afraid of ruining her career, which you already knew." He held up finger number one.

"Yeah, well I already told you my thoughts on that. If she marries me it doesn't ruin her career you know," I was dead serious.

Matt rolled his eyes at me. "Oh, God, whatever, man. Two, she honestly doesn't think you have what it takes to be serious."

"What? I don't get it. What do you mean she doesn't think I have what it takes to be serious?" That one hurt.

"Well, let's just call it like it is. None of us, especially you, has a reputation as a guy looking for a girl to settle down with. This really shouldn't come as a shock to you." He gave me a sarcastic smirk. I didn't think it was funny at all, but unfortunately, I totally get it.

"Okay, so I need to prove it somehow," I said.

"Yes, you do. But I would recommend that you first prove that you can work together without it being uncomfortable or weird."

I mulled that one over for a moment. I didn't really want to wait. I wanted to take action, now. That's what I did. I fixed things, I solved problems, I did things now. But I also didn't want to lose the opportunity to make this work by being pushy about it, knowing how she feels. She's impulsive, much like me, and she'd just quit and walk out. That would be just like her, and that's the last thing I wanted. I needed her to be happy, with me of course, whatever that takes.

"Okay, so what are you saying? I should wait until she's working with us, and show her that I can be friends as a way to win her back? That seems counter productive to me. I don't want to be friends," I honestly needed better advice than this. I wanted to just go to her house, and demand that she speak with me to sort this shit out immediately.

"I'm saying that once she gets back on our shift, you should then make your move. Nobody gives a shit that you're the boss except her. You need to prove that you can work together normally, because guess what, pal? If you end up together, she isn't gonna quit the department, so you'll have to work together anyway. So you need to warm her up to that because *that* my friend, will make her happy. And none of that bullshit from the scene the other day. Yeah we all saw her bra. Big fucking deal, man. She didn't do a strip tease on the roadway, and you made her feel bad about something she shouldn't have to fucking worry about. You have to put your fucking dick away sometimes."

I audibly groaned. He was right, I was a first class asshole that day. But waiting until she's working with us? She doesn't even start working with us full time for a couple more days.

"Dude, we're talking days, not months, not years. When did you become such a pussy? Jesus Christ." Matt was definitely not one hundred percent comfortable with this whole thing, I could tell.

"I gotta ask, man, do you have a problem with this? You seem like you do." If he did have a problem with it, I'd have to figure out how to fix that, because it didn't change my plan.

"I don't have a problem with it really, it's just weird. If you two want to be together, you should. I'm not a total heartless douchebag you know," he rolled his eyes at me. "Jo is like a sister to me, and I don't want her getting her heart fucking broken by anybody, including you. I want to protect her too, you know? And it hasn't exactly been her year."

"Alright, man, I just wanted to make sure there wasn't something else there, like maybe you had hoped things between you…" he cut me off.

"Ahhhh no. I don't feel that way about her. At all. I never did. She's basically always been one of the guys to me, and just as tough as any of them too. So you should probably watch your ass too or she'll punch you just like ol' horsey face back in third grade," he laughed at me.

I couldn't help but to laugh. When we were little, Matt was kind of scrawny, and Jo was a tomboy. Some kid was giving Matt a hard time, and little pigtailed Jo punched him right in the lip. The kid ran home to his mom, who went straight to Jack's house to confront them, it was hilarious. When Jack asked Jo why she did it, because of course she didn't deny it, she told her dad right in front of the kid and his mom that the kid was a horse-faced bully, and so she punched him in his big horse teeth to teach him a lesson. I was a little older, so I wasn't around for it, but all the other kids talked about it for years, and nobody ever messed with either one of them after that. Jack told me the whole story one day when we were shooting the breeze down at the station during a random shift. I couldn't catch my breath I was laughing so hard. Jack told me that it took everything he had in him not to laugh when it happened too. That was Jo, tough as nails, a protector, and a fighter.

Matt grew up to be tall and athletic like me, and had his own good luck with the ladies. Since he and Jo really were like two peas in a pod; it never occurred to me that he might have a thing for her until this moment. I was fucking glad he doesn't.

"Alright, as long as you know she's mine," I laughed.

"Yeah, yeah, Tarzan, I get it. Just don't fuck it up. Give her a tiny bit of space to get her bearings, and I think you might actually end up the white knight on the horse and all that shit," he started laughing at the horse reference, and then we both couldn't stop laughing like little kids again rolling around on my porch.

JO

So, after Matt told me how stupid both Brian and I are, he proceeded to tell me that he thought that I was being a real asshole for not giving Brian a chance when it seemed like it was more than a fling to begin with. He said that I put Brian in a losing situation by making our relationship about his becoming Chief of the department instead of owning up to my own feelings. While that may be somewhat true, I sure didn't appreciate hearing it.

I admitted that I may have reacted too quickly, but that for now it was for the best because I didn't want to mix work and my personal life anymore. He didn't buy it, but said he'd leave me be about it for now, whatever that means. In any event, we basically agreed to disagree, and agreed to get together the day after tomorrow to go shooting. Another hobby we have in common is target practice. It's fun, and the local range lets all firefighters, EMTs and police officers shoot for free.

He was right. I didn't give Brian a chance, I basically made an excuse for him, his promotion, and bailed out after that. He didn't try to fight me though, and if he really loved me, he would have argued or fought back or something. He just let me go, and that's all the proof I need that his feelings aren't the same as mine. Matt didn't really know what he was talking about, he wasn't there, and frankly, he had no room to talk about feelings anyway. He was a bit of a playboy himself, running around with every blonde in town that has a thing for *hoses*. He didn't have any response for the other women comments that I made about Brian other than that I didn't give Brian a fair shake, and that was all he had to say about it.

Matt made it really clear that he didn't want to be in the middle of it, that he would not tell me exactly what Brian said, and that if I wanted to know, I had to ask him myself. That's just not happening.

When I left the bar, I told Matt I'd think about it and I apologized for putting him in the middle. I didn't want to do that, it was not my intent, but he was glad that I shared with him what was going on; at least the PG rated stuff. Now, I have two days off if Jonah, the guy that always wants extra hours takes my last shift at 19. Then, we'll see what happens. After all of this, maybe it's just better to stay friends with Brian anyway. Who was I kidding? I couldn't be friends with a man who fulfills every fantasy I've ever had in my life. *Fuck. This sucks.*

I sat at my dad's desk for a while going through his stuff when I got home. These notebooks are everywhere. My dad had some journals in his bedroom as well, but I wasn't ready to go through those, and he kept them hidden, I knew they were personal. I was tired. I was tired of thinking about Brian, tired of being angry at Danny, tired of being sad in general.

I happened upon a shoebox in my dad's bottom desk drawer and pulled it out. It looked like he was in and out of it a lot because it had worn corners, but I don't ever remember seeing it. I pulled it out and sat it on the desk, taking the lid off carefully. Inside, was a stack of envelopes, mostly a soft pink color. As I looked through them gingerly, they all had my dad's name written on them, "Jack" in lovely cursive, definitely a woman's handwriting.

Suddenly, I felt like I was snooping, and I even looked around to make sure nobody was watching. I took the box over to the couch, and opened the letter on top that was dated two weeks ago.

My Dearest Jack,

I so love that after all these years, we continue to write these beautiful letters to each other. Even though I see your sweet face grace my home often, it still tickles me each time I receive one of your letters. I look forward to seeing you on Wednesday, I've been thinking about what you said regarding telling the kids about our relationship, and you've worn me down. We'll tell them next week, and then you must get Jo to come back to the firehouse. Then the family will all be together. See you soon, sweetheart.

Love Always,

Your Catherine

I looked around again. Is this real life? It *is* real life. Brian and Matt's mom, and my dad were in a relationship? I'm not even mad, but man, am I shocked. I think we all kind of suspected it, but this was actual proof. My heart was racing, and I wanted to tell someone about this, but I didn't even know where to begin. I couldn't call Matt, this is just too crazy and it's been a rough night of talking to him. I immediately picked up my phone to call my dad, then realized I couldn't. I slumped over and felt tears forming.

My dad and I were so close; I still wasn't sure what I was going to do without him. He used to let me tag along with him no matter what he was doing my whole life. I never felt like I was in his way, and I could talk to him about anything. When I found out what was going on with Danny behind my back, I was so embarrassed, and so angry. I went to talk to my dad at his office about it and he never made me feel bad or stupid about it ever.

Jo, some people will never deserve the love that's in your heart. Don't let it stop you from loving again, he said to me.

I feel so stupid, Dad. I know it moved too quickly, and I just think I wanted to find someone. I was ready, ya know?

I had been crying and he just handed me some tissues from across his desk and kept going. *The man that deserves your heart is out there, hell you might already know him. You just keep being you. The strong, stubborn, hard worker that you are. You're just like your mother, Jo, and she'd be just as proud of you as I am. Don't let the actions of one fool change who you are.*

We lived together, Dad. What do I do now?

That seems like a silly question. You come back home.

Dad, I'm too old to come back home. I rolled my eyes at him.

You're not too old to take care of your old father. We both know I eat like shit, so you can help keep me on track while you regroup. You work too many different places, and could use some stability Jo. Maybe this is the man upstairs' way of telling you to take a breather and rethink your strategy. It's no different than on a fire sweetheart. Sometimes if something isn't working, we need to back out and figure out a new plan. So, come home and figure out a new plan.

He was kind of right. Who was I kidding, he was totally right. *Okay, Dad, thank you. It's just temporary though, while I regroup.*

Of course, just temporary. He winked at me.

No, seriously. I rolled my eyes at him again.

Oh settle down, he laughed. *Stay as long as you want. It'll be nice having you around, I absolutely hate texting you, now I can actually just talk to you.*

Seriously, Dad, you have got to get with the technology.

Yeah yeah, that's what you say. I like pen and paper best of all and I always will.

He sure did like pen and paper best of all. Between his notebooks, the journals I found in his room that I hadn't read yet, and these

271

letters, he was a true old fashioned guy. It was actually one of the things I always loved about him, was his sense of tradition, coupled with his progressive attitude about me pursuing my goals. He was one of a kind.

I brushed my fingers over the date on the soft pink paper. This letter was sent two weeks ago. They were going to discuss telling the kids, who must be me, Brian and Matt, on Wednesday. That means that...my dad died the day before they were going to talk about all of this. Tears started rolling down my face. Over the next several hours, I sat on the floor in the living room, reading all of the letters, dated as far back as fifteen years ago, when they started writing.

There were letters that detailed their feelings, apologies for misunderstandings. These were genuine, old fashioned love letters. They were brief reminders of occasions and moments that they shared. It seemed that they had dinner together once a week, and they sometimes did other things. They enjoyed walking together out by the lake. I felt even closer to my dad after reading them.

After reading for hours, I gathered that they had been in love for years. They'd been intimate in every way. There were no details thankfully, but it was implied that they shared several overnights together over the years, and it was also clear that my dad had initiated this old fashioned tradition between them several years after my mom died, which was the sweetest thing I'd ever heard in my life.

I cried for them. I cried for their secret love that they didn't share with the world. I cried over the guilt I felt that they kept their love a secret from us kids. We'd been adults for so long, I felt ashamed that they were afraid of our reaction to it.

Then, I realized the loss that Catherine must have been feeling. I felt so terrible that she had to keep this secret that I was almost ashamed of myself. I assumed that I must have done or said something somewhere that made them feel like they had to keep a secret from me, and this brought the weight of guilt upon me. I truly would have loved for my father to find love, no matter who it was with. I've always been in love with love. The daydream of

273

being in love always brought a smile to my face. Even just the fantasy of it as a teenager used to make me feel so enthusiastic about finding the boy I was going to marry. I didn't really remember my mom. My dad talked about her a lot, it was important to him that I knew who she was, so I knew where I came from, but I didn't miss her like I missed my dad. It was just different.

I needed to take these letters to Catherine; they belonged to her. I decided that I'd go see her the next day, I hadn't seen her since my dad's funeral, and she was the closest thing to a mom I'd ever had. She was always making us snacks, and letting us climb the trees in her yard. She used to yell at us for getting into trouble, and said we'd give her a heart attack one day with our shenanigans. Oh, man, if only she knew the shenanigans of the last week or so. I'd skip the confessions this trip, and give her the letters, she deserved to have them.

I went to bed that night feeling like I knew a part of my dad now that I didn't know even existed. But, I was also so empty inside.

Sad that I didn't have someone I could talk to. Sad they felt they had to keep a secret from us. Brian would have loved to see these letters, maybe his mom will show him and Matt. That would be up to her, I feel like I've spied on something very private, and it's not my secret to reveal. And it's not like we're speaking anyway. I'd give her the letters and apologize for reading them all. Until then, I was praying for just one decent night's sleep where I didn't have the same nightmare I'd been having for days. I didn't understand it, but I'd been dreaming of Brian rescuing me from a fire. It's the same dream over and over again, and I wake up sweating and crying in the middle of the night every time.

BRIAN

Today I'm just aggravated. I'm spending my entire day trying not to think about Jo, and she's the only thing on my mind. I feel sick and weak, I kind of want to cry, and it's all because of her. How the fuck did I get here? To the place where I'm now just a pussy that couldn't have the girl. I knew she was worth it, but the waiting to take action was literally killing me.

I was driving around doing bullshit errands on my day off. I reminded myself of the plan; reaching down to my glovebox and taking out the box my mom gave me. I held it in my hands, and thought about my future. How I didn't want one without her, how every image I have of myself in the future includes her now. I also thought about how this ring, was given to my mother from Jack. It was a silver Claddagh ring, very simple, no stones. The Claddagh is a traditional Irish ring which represents love, loyalty, and friendship. It is two hands representing friendship, holding a heart for love, topped by a crown symbolizing loyalty.

I didn't ask her for details, I knew it was none of my business, but for my mom to encourage me to give it to Jo, says so much about how close she and Jack were. They were in love. I wondered why they didn't just tell us; we were all adults so it's not like we were going to be angry little kids. I'd have to ask my mom about it eventually; it really makes me sad that she felt she had to keep it from us. Jack too, he was a good man, he deserved to be happy. He was the kind of guy you would be okay with dating your mom.

As I drove around thinking about not thinking, I decided to go to the firehouse. I had an absolute shitload of paperwork to do. Normally when someone becomes Chief, there's a transition, a period of time where you work together on things and kind of do a handoff of responsibilities. That obviously didn't happen here, and it didn't seem like the district was in any big hurry to make things official one way or the other. It was frustrating to me that there had been no talk of any official announcement yet, even though they had appointed me to the position immediately two weeks ago.

Being the Chief was a lot of work, and I wasn't even sure that I really wanted the job right now. I always knew that I would eventually become Chief, it was my goal to be Chief *someday*, but it's a little early in my career to not fight fire anymore. I wasn't totally in love with being the Deputy Chief before any of this happened. The higher your rank in a mid to large sized department, the less actual fire you got to fight. The fewer accidents you worked on. You became the white hat dick at the top of the chain, and it wasn't as glamorous as many would think. People become firefighters because they want to fight fire, they want to save lives and make a difference. Nobody ever said, I can't wait to be a Fire Chief and sit behind a desk listening to other people's shit and doing budgets and schedules all day.

That didn't stop the need to submit the budget which would be due soon, and was extremely critical in terms of getting the gear and tools we needed replaced, as well as funding for some advanced training we were hoping to attend this year.

Jack had his own system, he had been the Chief for so long, I knew some of it, but certainly didn't comprehend his personal filing system, and I'm not sure what he kept electronically or not. Jack wasn't a lover of his smartphone or his computer for that matter, however he did believe that a progressive department technologically, as well as training wise was a sustainable model for a fire department, and he was committed to transitioning us to things like electronic maps in the trucks on tablets, and other 21st century treats for a department. The only way to have those things though was to include them in your budget requests, nothing is free, and budgets were consistently getting cut year over year, even though it was getting more and more expensive to maintain equipment and keep up with the ever evolving technologies.

When I pulled into the station, I saw that Jax was there. It was his day off too, so I went looking for him to see what he was up to. Jax was kind of a quiet guy, he went to high school with us, he was actually in my graduating class, but he didn't join the department until he got back from two tours with the marines. He was infantry, so he probably saw some shit, but he really never talked about it with any of us. Always cool, he never got mad at the dumb petty shit that can happen when you spend twenty-four hour clips together.

I found him in the computer room reading some stuff on the internet, not unusual for him. "Hey, man, what's happening?" I asked.

He looked up from the screen at me. "I was just reading about these new flat airpacks that allow you 'theoretically' to get in and out of a confined space more easily. I'm not convinced they're any better than what we have, and you know how I love new shit." He smiled. He really did love to ask for the newest and hottest thing in fire suppression, and it was usually really expensive too.

I laughed. "Why theoretically?"

"Well, in order to have the same amount of air that a firefighter is used to, while making the pack flat, it seems that they have elongated the whole setup. This means that anyone that isn't five foot ten or taller is going to have mobility issues with it. So, it's crap if you ask me. It looks cool though," he pointed to the screen. It did look pretty cool, but his point was valid.

"So don't ask me for it in your next wild request then, eh?" I laughed.

"No worries. I was thinking we should get a boat though," he grinned at me.

"Oh I'm sure you were. None of us even knows how to operate a boat," I rolled my eyes.

"Scotty knows how to work on anything. Just sayin', a sweet boat would be nice," he laughed at me. Thank God, he was only half serious.

"Yeah, he sure does, however the only thing we'd do with a boat is tow it in parades, so we're gonna pass on that for this year. Besides, I need to see where we stand with our current requests, and the budget for next year. That's what I'm doing here today. What brings you in on your day off besides free internet?" I questioned.

"Basically free internet. Matt and I are going to hit the gym in a little bit, then maybe go out for some drinks and look for some ladies. You should join us. You've been kind of crabby lately, man. Maybe you should get some ass," he chuckled.

The thought of any ass except Jo's turned my stomach. The last thing I wanted to do was go to the local bar and pick up hose whores. All I wanted to do was to come home to her, kiss her, talk about our days, and make love—yes, make love—to her every night.

"I'm gonna pass, you two have your fun, may the odds be in your favor. I'm actually going to try to get through some of Jack's stuff and figure out what we can afford for next year before they decide to bring in some new asshole as Chief and tell all of us what they're going to give us from behind a desk," I replied.

The real fact of the matter is that the district could be taking their time because they're screening other potential Chiefs. They could decide to move someone from another station to be our Chief leaving all of us with a new boss. That would suck, mostly because we have such a great team, and a great camaraderie, a stranger would really put a kink in that. Even if I wasn't sure what I wanted to do in terms of my own career advancement, it was better for my guys, and our team if I did the work now without ruffling feathers, and then figured out what I wanted to do myself along the way.

"Your loss. It's ladies' night at the Yard." He went back to reading.

"Have a good time. I'll catch you later," I left and went back to my office.

I sat down at Jack's desk, my desk I guess, and turned the computer on. I hadn't really had much of a chance to get into the meat and potatoes of the job with everything that had been going on the last two weeks. I started looking through the budget requests for the upcoming year, as well as the expenditures from last year. I already wanted a drink.

Jax needed new gear, his was old and worn, so that was a must in the budget. We already purchased the tablets last year, so we were going to have to get the software that goes on them. It basically told you all of the hydrants and other pertinent information in a location when a call comes in. It's synced to the paging system, so it already knows the address of the call you're going to, and this enables the officer in the truck to assist the driver in proper truck placement by hydrants or whatever they may need for a particular call. In the old days, you either had to know already, or you had to look for it when you got there, which takes time. Maybe a few minutes, but a few minutes could save lives. That was definitely going to go in for the upcoming year.

I mulled over some call reports that needed a signature on them. It was our policy to have a senior officer or the Chief review all call reports to ensure they were accurate. After about an hour of that, I was done reviewing the ones that still needed a signature. I closed them up, and decided to poke around on the computer to see what kind of electronic filing system Jack had, if any.

An icon in the lower left corner lit up awhile ago, it was a message that looked like it was synced from someplace else. I opened it, and it was Jack's text messages, they started popping up from the last two weeks. As I watched it load, I saw messages from myself, from Jo and from several others all pop up. Most of them were over two weeks old of course, but there were several from one number that wasn't programmed in as a contact, and it seemed like they didn't know that Jack had died.

I read through the messages from the unknown number.

Jack—I think you're right, there is definitely racketeering going on, we need to get a file on this with the evidence you have and then build a case

Where are you? We need to get together.

Are you getting my messages?

Shit, why aren't you replying, is everything okay?

Then they stopped. They were all from about a week ago, one week after Jack died.

Jack found out there was some type of racketeering? He had evidence to support this too? Who was he talking to about this? I stared at the screen for awhile before deciding that I had to get in touch with the person on the other end.

JO

Nobody ever thinks of their parents as anything other than parents until they're confronted with it. I knew for me, my dad was my dad, and he was the fire Chief. He was my friend and my confidant and advisor too, but I didn't really remember him as a husband to my mother. He was a friend to a lot of people, but since they were all mostly fire and emergency services people, it almost didn't even count, because it was still kind of work related.

Realizing that my dad had a relationship with Mrs. Cavanaugh, Catherine, was a real revelation for me. I decided not to call before making my way over to her place, I didn't really know what to say I thought that swinging by would be better. I grabbed the box of letters, looked at them one more time quickly, and packed them and myself up for the short trip over to her place.

She still lived in the same house the boys grew up in, and I'd always loved it there.

They had a huge climbing tree in their front yard just like my dad's, and Matt and I used to basically just sit in the tree planning out our lives. We didn't need a tree house, just a good solid branch. Brian would join us once in a while when we were really young, but when we became teenagers, he was off doing his own thing. God, I missed him. I missed his touch. I missed the way he took control. He made me feel like I didn't have to worry about anything; he was so strong and assured. He felt like home.

I needed to get a move on, it was already noon. I had spent most of my morning lazily re-reading the letters I was about to give over, and thinking about what I'd say to Mrs. Cavanaugh. It was time to get to it. She deserved these letters.

I pulled up in her driveway, and her front door was opened, leaving the screen door to the porch open. My Jeep isn't exactly super quiet, so she probably heard me coming, since she came out to the porch when I pulled into the driveway. She started waving immediately, and looked happy to see me. She was so pretty, she had her red hair, which had started to gray over the years, up in a cute loose bun, and she always wore a dress. Always. She was no nonsense, but she was also very feminine.

"Well, Josephine! How lovely to see you!" she called out.

"Hi, Mrs. Cavanaugh, I hope this is an alright time to just show up?"

"I've told you one hundred times, love, it's Catherine," she scolded me.

"I'm sorry, Catherine. I hope it's okay I just showed up without calling?" I asked.

"Of course it is, love. Come on in, let me put on some tea for us and you can tell me what brings you by, sweetheart." She was so warm and inviting all the time. I really loved her as much as I would my own mom.

"Thank you," I made my way into her sitting room, which was just for adults and looked around, waiting to see where she wanted me to go.

She looked at me standing there, holding the box and laughed. "Sit, sit, my dear.

You're a grown up now, you can sit in here," she chuckled on her way to the kitchen to make us tea. I wasn't a huge fan of tea unless it's iced tea, but whatever she wants. The visit was feeling pretty awkward. I sat on the flowered sofa and looked around at the pictures of Matt and Brian, and a few of all of us doing a variety of things through our adolescence. We were some real goofballs back in the day. There was one picture of all of us making smiles with orange peels in our mouths that made me laugh out loud. That was definitely taken when we were playing soccer together on the Police Athletic League team. Since Brian was three years older than us, it was one of the rare times that our age difference put us all on the same team which was so much fun. Matt and Brian were always close, they never fought as brothers at all, and actually played really well together, much like they did at work as well. My dad and Catherine would come to our games and yell from the sidelines. I don't know if it's the Irish in her, but Catherine got yellow carded for screaming from the sidelines more than once. You'd never know that about her because she's so soft spoken usually, but man did she love some soccer, and she loved calling out the referees on what she felt were bad calls. I would have been so embarrassed, but the boys loved it, they always thought it was the funniest thing, and she'd have to go wait in the car for the rest of those games

"Oh, that picture makes me smile every single day, Josephine," she smiled at me and handed me an iced tea. She knew me.

"Thank you so much," I took the tea. "We were so silly back then," I said, drifting off into memories of what felt like one hundred years ago.

"It wasn't all that long ago you three were getting into trouble all the time," she laughed. "So what brings you by, dear? What's in the box?" She gestured to the shoebox I had placed on the coffee table in front of me.

I took a deep breath. "Well, I was going through some of my dad's things last night, and I found something that I think belongs to you." She was watching me, small lines forming around her lips and eyes as she smiled. I suspected she knew exactly what was in the box.

"I knew you'd come eventually, I just didn't think it would be so soon." She took my hand in hers. "I loved your father very much, Josephine, he was a very good man." She smiled sweetly, tears filling her bright green eyes. She and Brian had the same beautiful green eyes, I couldn't take my eyes off of them. "I'm sure you knew that already though, love." She paused. "Before you begin, let me tell you a little bit about your parents, and the side of your father that I came to know, and then you can share with me, okay?"

"Okay, yes please," I started to sniffle a little bit. I had a tendency normally to simply just not be soft, I'm not sure why. Maybe it was spending so much time with boys my whole life, but I didn't talk about my feelings much, and I didn't like acknowledging them, but being here with Catherine, about to hear about a side of my dad I didn't really know, gave me butterflies.

"I know you didn't know your mother very well, you were so young when she got sick, and you stayed with us quite a bit when your father was trying to take care of her, do you remember that?" she asked me.

"I remember that a little bit. I mostly just remember hanging out here with you and the boys a lot more than anything. I don't remember very much about my mom to be totally honest. My dad told me about her sometimes. He said he wanted me to know who she was, and said that I reminded him of her sometimes."

"Well, he was right, dear. You certainly look just like your mom, she was beautiful and you two have the same smile. You know that she was my friend, and she was a very loving person. She and I became good friends after we met in the hospital when we had you and Matt. She became sick soon after you were born though, and spent several years trying to get well again before the doctors realized what was wrong, and by then it was just too late to help her. Your father's job became to make her comfortable more than anything else. At the same time, my husband left me and the boys, and I developed a friendship with your father as we joined forces to take care of your mom and you little ones.

Your mother asked me to look after you and your father when she knew that her time on this earth was coming to an end. It was heartbreaking for all of us, but she knew that you would be raised in that firehouse, and she wanted you to have a woman in your life that you could come to when you needed, and I gladly offered to do whatever I could before she ever asked. It was shortly after your mom passed away that your father and I became closer. First, we shared our grief together, and then the challenges of raising you kids." She smiled as she was thinking about some memory. I'm sure the three of us were a handful back then, hell we were kind of a handful as adults too. I stayed quiet and hung on every word as she recalled the past I knew nothing about.

"One day, when you and Matt were about four years old, and Brian was seven, your father stopped by to see me, and he didn't have you with him, but he had flowers that he had clearly picked somewhere. When I asked him where you were, he said that you were at your Aunt Molly's house for the weekend, and that he had come just to see me. It was at that moment, that I fell in love with your father. He had come just to visit with me, and brought me those beautiful flowers. The boys were out back playing, and we sat on my front porch talking about where our lives had ended up and what we wanted for you kids, and for ourselves.

After that day, we began to have a romantic relationship. Don't worry, I won't go into details with you, but I want you to know that I never felt a love for anyone in my life like I did for Jack. He was my soulmate. He gave me a scanner so that I could listen to calls because I worried about all of you, and he taught me about what you do. Your father was a gentleman, Josephine, he was everything I hoped for my boys to become; kind and gentle, but tough when he needed to be. He showed me a love I never thought truly existed, and we shared our lives together quietly, because that's what felt right for us. When your father died, I too lost a piece of my heart, sweetheart."

Those beautiful green eyes of hers started to fill with tears, tearing me up inside.

I felt my chest tighten, and tears started to fall from my eyes. "I'm sorry, I read all of them, Mrs. Cavanaugh. I feel like there's a whole part of my dad I didn't even know and I feel so awful you had this wonderful love between you and that you felt like you had to keep it a secret..." I trailed off and started really crying.

She leaned over and scooped me into a huge hug. "First of all, you call me, Catherine. And second of all, don't you dare feel bad. It was a choice that we made as adults, and we were quite comfortable with it over the years. Our relationship was unique, and we liked it that way, so don't for one minute feel like you kept us from anything." She comforted me like only a mother could, stroking my back and squeezing me in that hug. Some people give weak hugs like they can't wait for it to be over, not Catherine, she was all about a good hug, and I loved every moment of it.

I pulled away to wipe the tears from my face, and she smiled at me. "Shall we have a real drink and talk, Miss Josephine? I want to answer any questions that you have," she stood up and walked across the room to grab some tissues for me.

I laughed a little through my tears. "Okay, that sounds good." I took the tissues from her, and she turned back to go to the liquor cabinet, and poured us both some whiskey. She handed me one, and then walked over to a curio cabinet in the sitting room, and opened a drawer. She pulled out a beautiful round hat box with flowers all over it, and brought it, and her drink over to the couch.

Setting the large hatbox down next to the shoe box I brought, she said, "These are the letters your father wrote to me over the years, Jo. You are more than welcome to read them if you'd like. It may give you an understanding of who your father was besides the Chief, and your dad of course. He was a deep and loving man, who loved you more than anything in the world, and was always so worried whether or not he was doing what was best for you."

I dabbed at my eyes and my runny nose and looked up at her. "Are you sure? These are private, you don't have to let me read them," I felt like I was ten years old suddenly, and I didn't want to hurt her feelings or intrude any further than I already had.

"I'm quite sure. Now you sit and read, and I'm going to make us some lunch and then we can talk about anything you would like, okay?" She stood up.

"Okay, thank you so much." She smiled at me and reached over to squeeze my shoulder gently, and then made her way into the kitchen.

I opened the box and looked at the stack of letters, and took the one off of the top, touching the corners of it. You could tell it wasn't that old, the paper was bright white, and I recognized the handwriting on it as my dad's. I'd seen him write a million reports, and he was always writing in his notebooks or journals, so I'd know it anywhere. On the outside of the envelope, it simply said "Catherine" in his unmistakable penmanship.

I opened the envelope and pulled out the small piece of folded paper. It was dated about two and a half weeks ago.

Dearest Catherine,

I'm so excited to tell the children, I hope they won't be angry we've kept this secret for so long. At the time it seemed like the right thing to do, and then it was our special thing that was just for us, like a vacation from the craziness of everyday life. I love those boys of yours as if they were my own, and Josephine already looks to you as a mother figure, and for that I cannot ever express my gratitude.

You've meant so much to me all of these years, and shouting it from the rooftops doesn't begin to be a big enough celebration of our future together.

Love you always,

Jack

I smiled and put the letter back in the envelope and sighed. It was really sweet that he had someone, and in all honesty, I loved Catherine. You had to love her, she was the sweetest lady on earth, and she was also a good mother. She was always laughing with us, but also didn't take our shit either.

I pulled another letter out and opened it. They all looked pretty much the same, plain white envelopes, with Catherine's name on the outside, and the notes were written on plain white, unruled paper.

Dearest Catherine,

I know we talked about it, but I still wanted to send a note apologizing for canceling our dinner plans the other night. I look forward to seeing you always, and I don't like it when work interferes with seeing you. Soon, I'll be able to retire, and we can sit on the porch together and not worry about these things. You are my heart, my mo chroi (I Googled it to make sure I got the spelling right, are you impressed?) I love that you teach me so much, my heart is full.

I'll see you soon

Love you always,

Jack

I giggled at that one. My dad really had a love hate relationship with technology. I considered it a big deal for him to Google something for a love letter. I read the rest of the letters, which were mostly summaries of how he felt about different things they did together, and about future plans. He talked about going to the beach with Catherine, she went with him fishing one time which shocks me, but apparently they had a lovely time not catching anything at all.

Another one detailed how much my dad loved going to a flower show with her. My dad at a flower show, now that's a sight I would liked to have seen. Apparently, they had a fantastic time smelling the roses, and they picked up a bunch of things that he planted for her here at her house. I saw Catherine peek out at me from the kitchen a couple of times to see how I was. When I was finished reading all of them, I relaxed and smiled. I felt happy, and relieved that my father had love in his life.

I got up and walked into the kitchen and without saying a word just hugged her from behind. She had been at the kitchen counter doing something, and I just couldn't hold back. She turned around and hugged me back.

"Are you okay, dear?" she asked me while we stayed in each other's embrace.

"I'm better than okay, Catherine. It makes me so happy to know how happy my dad was," I released her and stepped back. "I used to worry so much about him, and thought he spent way too much time worrying about what I was doing, or making his whole life about the fire department. I'm honestly bursting with joy that he had all of these wonderful experiences with you over the years. I just wish that we could have shared it together, that part makes me sad."

"Don't be sad, Josephine, to be honest, we talked about that a lot over the years, as I'm sure you gathered from the letters. At first, we just didn't want to complicate your lives, and then later on we kind of enjoyed our little secret. It was an escape for us. I'm sorry that you had to find out the way that you did, you know your father was going to tell you but then..." she trailed off.

She turned around to finish making us sandwiches, and continued talking while I sat down at the kitchen table to listen. "We can't change the past, but we can certainly make the most of the days that we have here with our loved ones. Your father knew that, and he knew that you would eventually find your way as well."

"Did he talk to you about me?"

"Of course he did! He would have been so happy that you are returning to the station, even though he's not here to see it." She said as she put a plate down in front of me. She set one down for herself as well, and sat across from me.

I smiled. "Did Matt tell you I was coming back?"

"Actually, no," she smirked at me. "Brian was here the other day, and he told me all about it."

"Oh he did?" I tried not to look as guilty or annoyed as I felt.

"Yes, he did. I understand you two had a bit of a falling out the other day. He was quite upset about it," she was definitely egging me on now. I didn't want to take the bait, but I was dying to know what he said. *So, he was upset?*

"Hmm, well you could say that. He asked me to come back to the station, but then he was kind of a jerk to me when we went out on a call together the same day. I'm still going to come back though, I belong there. I wish my dad was here to see it." I didn't want to say anything bad about her son to her, and honestly, I wished things were different anyway. If I could be with him, I would.

"Yes, he said that you two had become close and that his behavior pushed you away. Does that sound about right?" She leaned back in her seat looking at me over her glasses now, and I was getting anxious. Did he tell her what we were doing? Oh, my God, this is getting embarrassing.

"Uh, yeah sort of," I hesitated. I really didn't want to talk about this with her or anyone else.

She could sense I was in flight mode. "Jo, those boys of mine both love you like their own family. Sometimes they don't know how to tell us women how they really feel, but what they lack in communication, they make up for in their loyalty. I'm sure you two will sort it out just fine," she smiled at me again. She totally knew.

"Well Matt and I have always been tight. It's always been a different situation with Brian. It'll be fine though, we're all working together day after tomorrow. I don't know what he told you, but I'm not mad or anything. We just clash a lot, we kind of always have, we don't see eye to eye on a lot of things," I sighed a little bit. That was the best way that I could think of to summarize the situation without being blunt. I was still mad at him, and missed him at the same damn time.

"Well my dear, Irish boys are very strong willed, often to a fault. My boys, all of them," she smiled, she was including my dad in that statement, "have always wanted to protect you, whether you needed it or not. And us strong Irish lassies, just kind of have to remind them who they're dealing with," she smirked at me and had a fire in her eyes reminding me of how tough she could be if she wanted to, she just rarely needed to. Catherine had many layers, and it was so easy to see why my father fell for her.

"I'm so glad I came to see you today, Catherine. I hope this doesn't sound out of place, but you know I'm always one of the guys, and generally, I totally like it that way, but lately, I've really felt like I needed a mom, and you've always been the next best thing and I don't think I ever really expressed how much it has meant to me. I can't thank you enough," I reached across the table to take her hand in mine.

She squeezed my hand. "I'm always here for you," she rose and picked up our dishes, taking them over to the sink. I stood up, as it was time for me to go. I needed to take care of a few things and truthfully, this was an emotional afternoon.

"Thank you for lunch today. And thank you for letting me see your letters, I know how personal they are."

"You are most welcome, dear. You deserve to know the whole man that your father was, and I loved him very much, just as I love you. Those boys of mine both love you too you know. We're all family in our own special way." She hugged me tight again. I would definitely be coming back here for hug fixes when I needed them.

"I know they do. Hopefully, after we've been working together again for awhile, Brian and I will be able to get along better," I said as I moved toward the door.

"Josephine," she stopped me as I was walking out. "I'm not one to interfere..."

I laughed. "Why do I feel a but is coming?"

"Because you're a smart girl. I promise you that I don't know everything, but I know that Brian feels awful about how things transpired this week with you. I think he cares for you far more than you know, perhaps you'll give him a chance to explain himself when you're ready," she gave me a pleading smile with that sweet face of hers.

"I will, I promise," and I hugged her again and made my way out.

I thought about what she said; give him a chance to explain. He had a chance, it's not like I denied him the opportunity; he never took it. He still hasn't taken it. There's a shelf life on everything, and I'm not going to pine away for him, even though just the thought of him near me gives me chills, in a very naughty way.

BRIAN

I decided to text the phone number back from Jack's computer so that I'd get a reply.

I wasn't sure what to say, so I started with: *Jack passed away, I'm a friend that can help.* And I waited for a reply.

Almost immediately a reply came through.

I know about Jack. Who is this?

A friend of Jack's. I think I can help you.

Can you meet in person? I'll decide if you can help.

Yes, where?

Meet me at the Brewhouse downtown in one hour. Ask for Izzy. Someone will let me know.

Okay, one hour.

This was extremely strange. But I felt like if Jack was helping with some kind of an investigation, it was my duty to help see it through if I could. I wrapped up a few things, and made my way out to my truck. I was familiar with the Brewhouse downtown; it was someplace I've been to several times. A lot of cops hang out there, which in this moment, I was very grateful for since I didn't know what I was getting into exactly.

I drove past the Brewhouse, it didn't have it's own parking lot, so I had to park about three blocks away in a garage. There just wasn't any parking closer that would accommodate my truck. I didn't take the Chief's truck, in fact, I tried not to drive it on my days off anyway, it was just so conspicuous. I really didn't want anyone thinking I was out and about doing personal business in a department vehicle. Sometimes it was a pain in the ass to switch out, but integrity still mattered, and I really didn't know what I was getting myself into.

I walked into the place, it was actually pretty crowded, it was a Friday night, so I'm not really that surprised. I walked over to the bar and waited for a bartender to come my way.

A young guy, probably in his twenties came over. "What can I get you, man?"

"I'm actually looking for Izzy," I gave him a questioning look. He took a step back, looked me up and down and laughed. I don't know what that was about, but I don't like this.

"She's over there in that booth drinking a martini, watch yourself," he said.

"I'll take a Guinness with me," I said. He nodded and walked away to get it for me. I couldn't see this Izzy from where I was standing, the booth was in the back corner of the joint. The bartender brought me my beer, I paid, and made my way to the back of the bar.

"You Izzy?" I asked upon arrival.

A little tan-skinned girl with light eyes pointed to the seat across from her. "Yes, have a seat."

I sat down across from her, with my back to the door, which I absolutely hate. It made me feel trapped to not be able to see an exit wherever I'm at, so I was immediately uncomfortable.

"So, you knew Jack?" I wanted to disrupt the silence hanging over us.

"I did. And I suspect you did as well, since you texted me from his phone?" she asked.

"I actually texted you from his computer, he must have had it synced to his phone."

"Interesting. I wasn't aware that was possible, I'll have to keep that in mind. So you are?" she asked.

"I'm Deputy—eh Chief Brian Cavanaugh, of Fire District 23. I've known Jack most of my life, he was like a father to me. I was appointed to his position after his passing, which is how I happened upon your number," I was going to just be straight here. I didn't have anything to lose.

"Well, I'm Detective Isabel Cruise. You may know my sister, June, she's a paramedic," she held her hand out for me to shake.

Taking her hand, I took note of how petite she was. She was awfully pretty and tiny to be a detective. Not my type, because I'm still heartsick over Jo, however she's really pretty for a cop. "Nice to meet you," I said. "I do know your sister, she's a good medic, and often partners with a good friend of mine," I added.

"Yes, Josephine Meadows. I know who she is." That made me uncomfortable, and I started to feel defensive.

"So, let's cut to the chase here. You were working with Jack on something, and he was gathering evidence for you to build a case against someone who was clearly bribing or doing something dirty, correct?" I wanted to get to the point.

"Okay, sure, let's get to it. You seem like you have the best interests of the department in mind. Jack figured out that someone freelancing was essentially strong arming businesses into paying a little extra for a passing fire inspections when they didn't have passing standards."

I stared at her. So, basically someone was giving passing inspections to people who didn't deserve them. That puts lives at risk, and I felt my blood boiling about it. If someone was extorting money from businesses, they were unlikely to stop there.

"Okay, so how can I help?" I asked and took a sip of my beer.

She ran her fingers through her long dark hair and looked me in the eye. "Jack had evidence somewhere, but he died before he could get it to me. Someone has been extorting money from businesses all across town for at least two years. I need access to Jack's files, or I need you to look through his files and find the evidence so I can build a case against this guy."

"Do you know who it is?" I asked.

"Yes. You familiar with a Danny Russell?"

I immediately rolled my eyes and clenched my fists. That motherfucker was probably using Jo all along. I was gonna kill that fucking guy.

"So that's a yes," she glared at me.

"Yeah, I know him. He's a piece of shit. I'm not even a little bit surprised he had something to do with anything unsavory." I was furious at the revelation he might have been playing Jo.

"Jack said the same thing," she replied, and took a small sip of her clear martini. She was awfully small and good-looking for a detective. If I wasn't so into Jo, I'd definitely have some inappropriate thoughts about her, but right now all I could think about was pounding this motherfucker's face in. Anything I could do to ruin him, and I'm in.

"Yeah, that doesn't surprise me. Apparently, he was dating Jack's daughter for awhile. I've been watching her to see if she's involved," she said.

"Yea, she's not," I said curtly.

"Are you here for the greater good, or do you have some kind of thing for this girl?"

"That's none of your business, *detective*," Who does she think she is?

"If she was involved it is my business," she gave me a nasty challenging glare.

"If you were working with Jack, you already know she has nothing to do with this.

Do you want my help to bring this dickhead down, or are we just going to banter all night, because I have plenty of other shit to do besides sit in this dive wasting my time with a cop," I wasn't going to take this chick's shit.

"Settle down, Romeo, you're right. I already know she has nothing to do with it, but I wanted to test you a little bit," she waved her hands for me to chill out.

"Okay, so where did you stand when Jack died? I have access to most of his folders, and shit. The rest of his information he kept in notebooks, he was always writing stuff down in them, but they're at Jo's house and I don't have easy access to them without saying something to her about it if she hasn't already read it for herself," which worried me. Jo could be a loose cannon, and was definitely not the first person who would reach out for help if she knew some kind of shit like this was going on. God, I hoped she hadn't figured this out for herself.

"I'm not sure where he kept his files to be honest, he said that he had gathered some witnesses that would testify that Russell had coerced them into paying him to sign bullshit documents giving them shortcuts. I gave him permission to promise immunity for their testimony, per my DA, however now I don't know who they are because he hadn't turned the evidence over to me yet, he kept saying he could get more, and he wanted to see if he could get Russell to confess first."

I ran my hands through my hair, sighing, and taking it all in. I can't believe that Jack kept all of this from me, but I also totally understand it too. He would never put any of us in a situation like this if he could avoid it, and clearly he thought he had this under control.

"Okay, well I can tell you that dickhead won't confess to me, even if he might have to Jack. He might tell Jo something, but I doubt it, and if Jack didn't want her involved, I want her involved even less. I don't get along with him at all and I want him as far away from her as possible," I was just going to put it out there before it ever became a question.

"Yeah, I know all about you. I heard about you grabbing him at Jack's funeral," she smirked at me. The sassy little detective had some balls.

"He fucking grabbed her at her own father's funeral, so yeah, I manhandled him, and I'd do it again," I was getting pissed off just thinking about it, and I waved for the waitress to bring us two more drinks. "What else is it that you *know*?"

"I know that Jack assumed you were going to look after his daughter," she said.

"He told you that?" I was shocked, but filled with pride and also feeling a little defensive and vulnerable. Jack told her all of this?

"Yes, he did actually. He said that you and your brother would look after Jo no matter what happened, and he was not going to let Danny continue to get away with the extortion." She was very matter-of-fact, and almost expressionless. She was a hard one to read, maybe it came with the job. She seemed awfully young to be a detective.

"Interesting. Well, that's true. Jack knew us, and he was like a father to us our whole lives basically," I wanted to change the subject. It was all still too raw, and I just wanted to be with Jo now that we were discussing her dad like this. "So, you need me to go through Jack's shit basically?"

"Yea, more or less, he was certain he had the evidence, so I need you to find whatever that is. I didn't know that he passed away until a few days after it happened and I'd been trying to reach him. Do you think by any chance that his death was anything other than an unfortunate situation?" she asked me seriously.

I felt like the wind got knocked out of me. "Are you asking me if I think Russell killed Jack?"

"I'm asking you if you think it's possible," her brown eyes were like lasers right now.

"It never occurred to me, but I don't think so, I just don't know. He wasn't a young guy, and he'd been on the job a long time. I think the stress may have gotten to him, but he died on scene, I tried giving him CPR myself. There didn't seem to be any foul play, it was more like thirty years of being a firefighter and dealing with that than anything else," I thought back over the last several months and wondered if I was right. Honestly, I think that it was natural causes, but really, what do I know. It would kill Jo if something more sinister had happened to her dad, especially if that douchebag was behind it. I silently prayed I was right, and that it was natural causes and years of working a stressful job that took him from us.

"I didn't really think so either, but it's something to keep in the back of your mind while you look for whatever he had found. I don't know how he kept it, we had talked about files, but I don't know if they were electronic, or paper, or what. So what I need is for you to find that out. And you cannot tell *anyone* until this gets blown open." She was very serious now.

"Are you sure nobody was helping Jack get the evidence?" I asked.

"I'm very sure. In fact, he's the one that reached out to me when he figured out what was going on. I'm not even sure that this Russell character is on to it yet. Which is good, because then I have the element of surprise when it's time to take him down," her eyes were even more serious now.

"I'll get on his computer tomorrow and see what I can find. He was getting better and better at technology, even though he hated it, so maybe something is stored there. If it's paper, I'm going to have to talk to Jo, because all of his notebooks are at home, he didn't keep them at work," I told her. I really didn't like the idea of involving Jo in this. She was going to be so upset no matter what, and if I asked for the notebooks without telling her what's going on, and before I get the chance to implement Operation MJM, I'd never be able to explain it.

Isabel and I were leaned in across from each other in the booth when I saw Jax and my brother walk into the bar out of the corner of my eye. Fuck. I don't want them seeing me with her, and I can't explain what I'm doing here yet. Hopefully they didn't see me.

Awww fuck. Matt walked up with Jax by his side. "Well hello, big brother, whatcha doing over here in the corner of a bar with this lovely young lady," he motioned to Cruise. "I thought you had some other things you were *sorting out.*" he said nastily.

"I'm actually here discussing business if you must know," I tried to explain without saying too much. Detective Cruise just watched the exchange and smirked.

"Oh business, that's what they're calling it now?" Matt gave a sarcastic chuckle. "Well this isn't going to get you what you say you're looking for." I sighed and dropped my head, when Cruise stepped in.

"Hi boys, I'm Detective Cruise, with the 23rd precinct. I was just discussing an ongoing investigation that I need some help from the fire department with," she smiled kindly at them both, and Matt wasn't buying it.

"Oh, a detective eh? What do they have a junior program now?" He was being an asshole, and I couldn't stop it.

"I'm older than I look, sunshine, and I don't have to explain anything to you," she stood up to leave, and looked over at me. "You know what I need, I'll wait to hear from you." She walked out of the bar, leaving me with an angry Matt and a completely clueless Jax standing there staring at me.

"Well she was fucking hot, dude," Jax chimed in. I buried my face in my hands, this was the last thing I needed right now.

"Yeah, she sure was. Not at all what I'd expect you to go after these days," Matt glared at me.

"It's not what it looked like Matt, you know how I feel," was all I could say.

"Oh really, do I? Because it looked like you were out in secret with some hot little Latina chick when you told me you had eyes for someone else," he said right in front of Jax.

"Are we talking about Jojo? We're talking about Jojo, aren't we...?" Jax asked the question with a childish grin. *Fuck, of course he asked.*

"I'm not explaining myself to either one of you right now," I got up to leave. "Matt, I need you to trust me, I cannot tell you what's going on, but I promise in a couple days I will. Nothing has changed from our previous discussion. You have to trust me." I repeated. I couldn't get him and Jax involved in this, there's just no way. Until I found out more information, I didn't want anyone else involved.

"I feel really out of the loop, but that chick was fucking hot. So, if you're not doing her, is she up for grabs?" Jax asked. I rolled my eyes.

"Dude, whatever you want. I gotta go," I was still standing there trying to leave, but I really needed Matt to acknowledge that he trusts me. "Matt, can you just trust me here?" I was pleading to him.

"Yeah whatever. You know where I stand, and if you're fucking around, I'm not going to stand for it and I'm definitely not going to help you," he said. Jax had to know what he was talking about but he didn't say anything else, and thankfully we just ignored his Jo comment earlier and he didn't press on it.

"I get it, bro. Look, I need to leave, I have to take care of some things tonight. You two have fun, and please for the love of God, stay out of trouble," I wasn't even kidding. The two of them often found themselves in some precarious situations when they went out. "And both of you," I motioned to Jax who was pretending not to be there by looking everywhere except Matt and I. "Need to keep this exchange to yourselves. It's important, and I can't tell you why, so don't fucking ask."

"Fine, whatever, settle yourself, Chief," Jax put his hands up in defense.

"Yea, fine. I'll call you tomorrow," Matt said.

"Ok cool. Are you still hanging out with Jo tomorrow?" I asked.

"Yea, we're going shooting. So, you should stay away," he laughed.

I rolled my eyes. "Just don't tell her about seeing me here tonight." I leaned in so Jax wouldn't hear. "It's important, I'm serious." I gripped his shoulder and looked him in the eyes. "This is really serious, Matt.

He stopped the smirk and laughing, and acknowledged my seriousness. "Are you sure everything is okay?" I sighed.

"It will be. I promise I'll fill you in as soon as I can. A couple days, tops."

"Okay." He looked concerned, but I honestly couldn't tell him what was going on.

"Alright, I'll catch you guys later, I really gotta roll," I tossed some money on the table and made my way out of the bar.

I couldn't believe that motherfucker, Danny Russell was taking bribes to pass inspections, and God knows what else. I wondered how Jack figured it out; how long he knew? Was Jo still dating that piece of shit when he uncovered this? She was going to be so fucking pissed off when she found all of this out.

It was too late to go back to the station tonight. I'd go through his computer the next day with a fine-toothed comb. I felt like if he was texting Detective Cruise, he was more comfortable with technology than he let on to us. There had so be something in his files that would bring this guy down, and I was going to find it.

JO

I woke up the next morning with mixed emotions. I was happy I'd spent the day with Catherine, and that we'd talked, but I was still missing Brian so much. She obviously knew something was up, I wondered what he told her. Clearly he told her enough that she wanted me to give him a chance to explain himself. Honestly, there wasn't much to explain. He didn't fight for me, and that's probably because he doesn't want to be exclusive, like he said a year ago. And of course the working together thing, and him being my boss can't be explained away either. It happened, and we can't go back now, so the only thing to do is just put my mind on the job and hope that the longing for him subsides someday.

I had plans with Matt for the day, but I honestly didn't feel like doing anything at all. All this talk of love was just making me cranky. I wanted to avoid seeing any of them until work, but that's not how big girls deal with real life I guess. I decided that I'd try to get myself motivated by going for a run. I grabbed my phone and some ear buds, and made my way out of the house.

As I rocked out to some of my favorite music, I let the thoughts of my suffering heart float away for awhile. I was going to need to let go of all of this at some point, before I turned into some kind of a spinster. Once I'm on a normal schedule at 23 I can start thinking about how to move on and what my next moves are. While ending up at my dad's station again is important to me, it can't be my whole life either. I need to figure out what I'm doing.

I ran through town, and decided to stop at the station to get a drink of water before running back home. It was only a couple miles, and it made for a great halfway point so I didn't have to carry a water with me. As I approached, I saw that Brian's truck was there. *It's his day off. Maybe he won't see me.* Maybe I'd say hi and just show that we can be friends and that it's no big deal. Yeah, who was I kidding? I'm standing here in front of the firehouse getting turned on at the thought of saying hello to him. My body betrays me at just the thought of him.

I wanted to be close to him and I couldn't stop myself from walking toward his office, after I grabbed myself a water from the fridge in the kitchen. I held the cool bottle to the side of my face in an attempt to lower my body temperature from the run, and from the anxiety of seeing him. His office door was open, and he was intently staring at the computer screen. As I scanned him quickly, I couldn't help but get distracted by his delicious biceps and broad shoulders. I quietly knocked on the open door and his beautiful green eyes met mine instantly.

I forgot to speak, I was lost in his gaze.

"Jo, is everything okay?" he asked.

"Oh yeah. Yeah. I saw your truck was here, so I thought I would stop in and say hello. I'm sorry, I didn't mean to interrupt you," I started to retreat and he stood up immediately.

"You're not interrupting me, stop. Come in and sit down for a minute," he motioned to the couch and came out from behind his desk.

The couch he'd ravaged me on just a few days ago. He was wearing jeans and a white t-shirt that was tight in all the right places, showcasing his muscles, and highlighting the colorful tattoos on his arms. My heart was beating out of my chest, I was certain he could see it.

"I, uh, I can't stay long, I'm on a run and was just stopping for a drink," my words say one thing, but my body still walked over to the couch, where he met me and we both sat down. I felt a magnetic pull to him that I simply couldn't control or explain anymore.

"You look amazing, Jo," he said softly.

I felt myself blushing and looked down to break our locked stare. "Thank you," I whispered. I was sweaty, dirty, and in the middle of a workout, he's crazy and I loved it. I can feel myself getting pulled into him, fighting it is impossible, it's magnetic. I was literally quivering, and the feelings I was having were so carnal. I wanted to crawl all over him right now.

He reached over and raised my face up to meet his. "Look at me." His touch was still like lightening rushing through my veins, nothing had changed. I met his eyes with mine, I still couldn't speak, I was in a trance. His eyes were scanning my face, he was looking for something and I gave him a shy smile.

I felt myself leaning in closer, as he moved his hand to my face, brushing my cheek with his thumb. He pulled me to him, with both hands and his lips were now barely touching mine.

"I'm going to kiss you, Jo," he whispered just before pressing his soft lips to mine. I melted into him, raising a hand and placing it on his rock hard chest. I could feel his heart beating, the same rhythm as mine. I let him part my lips gently with his tongue, causing me to forget all sense of right and wrong. This was against everything I said I wanted but it didn't matter in that moment. I slid my hand down his chest, feeling his abs tighten as I ran my fingers across them. He pulled me in closer, deepening the kiss and I didn't stop it, I relish in his touch. He brings me to life.

Suddenly, he grabbed me, pulling me up with him and moving us across the room by the office door. His hands ran all over my body as he kicked his door shut slamming me against it. He lifted both my arms above me with just one hand, pinning me to the door, kissing me savagely, desperately. I gave in to him, softly moaning at his touch. My brain told me to stop, but my body wasn't listening.

"Brian...we can't do this..." I caught myself saying as I lowered my hands, pulling him into me by the waistband of his jeans.

He grabbed the hem of my tank top, yanking it over my head. "I need you. Now," he growled into my neck, biting me gently and sending my brain into overdrive.

"This doesn't change anything," I breathed out, barely able to speak as I kicked my shoes off.

Grabbing both of my hands, pinning them out to my sides, he leaned back and looked at me hungrily. "Shut the fuck up, Jo."

BRIAN

I yearned for her. I was hungry for her.
She tried to say something and I told her to
shut the fuck up. I didn't want to talk. I didn't
want anything but her sweet pussy wrapped
around my cock. I was going to fuck her in my
office again, and she'd feel me for days. I didn't
give a fuck who was around either. The minute
she touched me, my dick was straining against
my jeans, aching for her.

I had her pinned to my office door
panting, wearing just her sports bra and tiny
little shorts she was out running in. Her tight
little body was hot to the touch, and I couldn't
keep my mouth off of it. As I kissed her roughly
and moved my hands down the front of her, I
grabbed her heaving breasts, pinching her stiff
little nipples causing her to cry out in need. I
roughly grabbed the bottom of the bra, yanking
it over her head and taking a mouthful of her
delicious tit in my mouth, rolling my tongue
over her nipple and gently biting down on it. I

moved over to the other one, sucking and kneading it, while she pressed her hips into mine.

She wanted me as bad as I wanted her, she unzipped my jeans and freed my cock from it's restraints; meeting my eyes. Those gray stormy eyes looked at with me the need I felt as well, and I was consumed by her. I was angry and frustrated with her for pushing me away, but I desperate to have her. I yanked my shirt off over my head, and she immediately started licking and kissing my chest, leaving my skin burning wherever she touched it. I fisted her hair in my hand roughly, yanking her head back, exposing her neck to me.

Her chest was heaving and I ravaged her neck roughly before I dropped to my knees, taking her tight little shorts and panties down with me. I rolled my shoulder between her legs and tossed her leg over me, opening her sex to me, inhaling her scent. I knew I was gripping her hips hard, but I didn't care. I almost wanted to leave marks on her, she was mine, she just didn't see it yet. I took a lick of that sweet pussy of hers, and she grabbed my hair roughly, pulling me into her folds. As I sucked and flicked at her hard little nub, she cried out, thrashing around and knocking a picture off the wall. She's moaned loudly, and I knew she was going to cum soon so I stuck two fingers deep inside her, pumping them to meet her unbridled desire. She couldn't stop this now, she didn't want to stop, and I loved every second of it.

"Yes," I growled into her pussy.

"Fuck me, Brian," she tried to breathe out quietly.

"You'll come for me first, then I'm going to fuck you so hard you'll never be the same," I told her with a mouthful of that sweet pussy. She was writhing with me, grabbing at the wall around her. It was exactly how I wanted her. Begging for it.

"Please! Oh God!" She started convulsing and I could immediately taste her juices. I slowed the pace while she climaxed. Looking up at her, I could see her eyes closed while she was lost in the moment. As she came down from her high, I stood up and kissed her roughly. I wanted her to taste herself on me.

"You taste so fucking good," I said as I dropped my pants and boxer briefs to my ankles, not even taking them off. "I'm not done with you yet," I pushed her back up against the wall.

"Brian, I..." she began.

"I said no fucking talking today, Jo," I didn't want to talk. I wanted to fuck her into next week. The corners of her mouth turned up into a devilish little smirk, she knew what was coming. I picked her up by her naked ass, she wrapped her legs around me, and I lowered her onto my throbbing cock.

She moaned again loudly, and I fucking loved it. I didn't care who could hear us. Once I was balls deep in her, I started pounding at her pussy, holding her up against the wall. She held onto my neck, panting and biting at my shoulder while I took all of my frustrations out on that delicious, wet pussy I just had in my mouth. She was bouncing up and down on my cock and I wasn't ready for it to end. I set her down and turned her around.

"Turn around," I growled at her.

"I can't... take..." she panted out, still obeying my command to turn around, and even spreading her little legs apart, knowing what was coming.

"Oh yes you can," I pumped my cock in my hand a couple times, and smoothed my other hand over that juicy ass of hers, right before I smacked it. She jumped, startled.

"Brian!" she cried out. She didn't move though; she actually backed her ass up closer to me, showing me she wanted more. So fucking hot. I lined my dick up to her slit and thrust it in all at once and smacked her ass again lightly. I knew I filled her up, and I could get so much deeper this way. I pumped into her hard, pushing her up against the wall, knocking more pictures and crap onto the floor. It made me even harder that she was moaning in pleasure, trying to quiet her own yells of ecstasy while pictures literally fell off the walls from our fucking. I reached around, and pulled her as tight to me as I could. I was so close, and I knew she was too, she was practically breathless, and I could feel her heart pounding against her chest.

My lips rested against her neck, while I continued to thrust into her, on a mission to ruin her. She's mine. "Brian, I'm going to come, I can't..." she whispered.

I felt her channel start to squeeze my cock with her release, and I pumped harder, wanting to come with her. She cried out, and I groaned as I emptied myself into her. She felt so good, and although I may have punished her pussy, she's covered in a slick sheen of perspiration, looking sated as well. I slowly pulled out with a groan, and released her from my grip, her skin was glowing pink where I smacked her ass and grabbed at her. Nipping at her shoulder before reaching down to pull my pants back up, I noticed she was quivering. I wanted to stroke her hair, hold her, but that's not what that moment was about. It was a reminder of what animal passion we have.

Walking to my desk to grab tissues for her to clean up with, I watched her gather her clothes up and start to get dressed. She was still out of breath.

"Brian, that was…I…" she looked for the words, but couldn't seem to figure out what to say. *Good*.

"Today isn't for talking, Jo." I reminded her in a gruff whisper as I reached down to gently clean up the mess dripping down her leg. She stared at me, mouth slightly open, clearly in shock.

I grabbed my shirt off the floor, putting it back on and then leaned up against my desk, arms folded, just watching her finish dressing. She put those tiny little shorts back on, and my dick started to twitch again. She had the sweetest ass I've ever seen. She opened her mouth to say something, and I held up a hand making the stopping motion.

"Don't, Jo. Just go home. We aren't talking about this today. I just can't." I went back around the other side of my desk and sat in my chair, pretending like I was going to get back to work, which was total bullshit. Her mouth was still open, and she was flushed all over, so fucking sexy. I wanted to kiss her so badly. I was so frustrated, but I couldn't talk to her, I just couldn't. With a stunned look on her face, she turned around and walked out. I watched that ass as she left. I laid my head on my desk letting out all the air I had sucked in while I was holding my breath to stop myself from saying more.

JO

My legs were shaking from the fucking I had just taken, and my brain was in an overloaded electrical storm trying to process what had just happened. I attempted to jog back home, but basically trotted along or walked most of the way in a state of complete and utter shock. My legs were really not working anymore. Certainly not from running. Did I want that to happen? I certainly acted like I wanted it to happen. Holy shit. He devoured me, like he *needed* me. It was so fucking hot and he wouldn't even let me speak. It's a good thing too, because I would've done something stupid like stop it from happening.

I knew he was angry with me for pushing him away, but he was so turned on, so hard. It wasn't like before. He was even more demanding and controlling, and now I'm insanely turned on again just thinking about it. What he did to me is unreal, I was consumed and couldn't shake him loose. *Do I even really want to?*

Once I finally got home, I got in the shower and stood under the hot water for what seemed like an eternity. I was sore and my muscles were quivering. Definitely not from the run. He was right, I was feeling him. I felt him everywhere. Clearly, things are unfinished with us. *Today isn't for talking.* I kept repeating those words to myself.

After the water ran cold, I got out, got dressed, and gathered myself together. I was supposed to meet Matt at the range in about an hour, and needed to get my two guns and other stuff together. Similarly, to my pink wrapped tools, I have a handful of gun accessories that are pink as well, like my ear protection, and my eye protection for the range. It was hot out today, but I wore jeans and a fire department t-shirt anyway, I don't like to underdress for the range.

Matt was already there when I pulled up, setting up his guns. He had quite a collection including a couple rifles, three standard handguns, but then he also had a couple cool ones that he always let me shoot too. Jax was also there, setting up some of his guns. None of us had as many as Matt, he had become a bit of a collector over the last few years. Jax was a Marine, so he had a couple of pretty standard handguns as well as an AR-15, which was so goddamn fun to shoot. It made me giggle and laugh every time for some reason, it was so powerful.

"Hey, hope you don't mind I tagged along, Jojo," Jax quipped.

"Nah, I don't mind, as long as I get to shoot the AR," I laughed. "And why does everyone keep calling me Jojo all of a sudden?"

Matt and Jax both laughed. "I have no idea actually, but I'm pretty sure it's gonna stick, so better get used to it," Jax proclaimed.

"So what were you up to this morning?" Matt asked casually while we were all loading our magazines and getting our targets organized.

"Nothing, why?" I asked defensively.

"Uh, it's a pretty standard question actually," he gave me a confused look.

"Oh, yeah. I went for a run this morning, stopped at the station real quick to get a drink like usual. Well you know, when I run," I chuckled a little. I was a totally inconsistent runner. I usually only did it when I was feeling fat, or I was stressed out. But when I did do it, I generally always took the same route through town, stopped at the station for a drink and to pee, and then ran back home. I did this off and on through the years, which of course Matt already knew.

"Ah, stressing out? Or feeling fat?" he teased me.

"Go fuck yourself, Matty," I actually did laugh, he was a jerk, but he was my jerk and obvioulsy knew me well.

"Run into the Chief while you were there?" Jax asked.

"Yeah...I uh, saw him for a few minutes. He was working on something in his office and I stopped by to say hello." I tried not to sound like I was hiding something. I felt like I sounded suspicious, and that's probably because my sex was tingling at the flashback to my morning.

"He's trying to get caught up on paperwork and stuff I guess. He's got some side project going on too apparently," Matt said.

Jax laughed. "Yeah, side project." Matt gave him a nasty look.

"What's funny, Jax?" I looked at Jax, then at Matt and they both looked guilty as hell.

"Oh nothing, sorry, nothing." He was trying to cover something up.

"Oh something is funny, what's going on? What's this side project?" I was getting angry, surely it had something to do with me if they're both acting this way.

"I honestly don't know what it is, Jo. We ran into him the other night having a meeting with a detective at the bar. I don't know anything else, and we weren't supposed to say anything about it, *were we, Jax*?" He gave Jax a hard stare.

"You weren't supposed to say anything? To me? Or in general?"

"In general, I don't think it has anything to do with you if that's what you're wondering," Matt replied.

"Why would I think it has to do with me? You guys are the ones that brought up the big secret meeting with some detective, not me," I was actually curious. Why would he be meeting with a detective, at a bar in secret?

"Yea, she was some detective alright," Jax cooed. I felt my face get hot and I met Matt's stare with my own.

"Oh, she was hot?" I asked coyly.

"Oh, she was smoking hot," Jax daydreamed about it while we watched.

"Enough, Jax," Matt snipped. "Jo, it was a meeting, that's all we know. We went on about our business after we saw them," he explained.

"Why would I care?" I lied. Matt knew I was lying. He knew how I felt. My heart sank all over again.

"I don't know, why would you?" He asked me sarcastically.

346

"I don't, so anyway...let's shoot, I'm ready," and I walked off to install my targets.

I pretended that I didn't care, but I cared. I cared a lot. I was fucked six ways to Sunday raw by him this morning, and he was out at the bar with some hot cop the other night? This is exactly why I ended things with him. *Motherfucker*. What happened this morning will never happen again. Ever.

Jonah texted me to let me know he'd take the half shift I was supposed to have tonight, so I spent the rest of the afternoon shooting paper with the boys, pretending my heart wasn't completely broken again, and that I didn't feel completely used up by him. *Fucker*.

BRIAN

That, was the hottest thing I've ever experienced in my life. *Fuck me.* After she left, speechless, and I regained composure myself, I picked up the mess we made in my office. Four pictures, two trophies, and a flag all fell or got ripped off the wall while we went at it this morning. Nice work if I do say so myself.

I was so frustrated by the whole situation with her, it was tearing me apart inside. She obviously felt the pull we have. When she was near me, I could actually sense it. My brain didn't even know what to do with this except be grateful for her touch today. I know I probably seemed cold to her, but I couldn't tell her how I feel, it would just complicate things even more. She wanted me physically, and I knew she had feelings for me, I just needed to keep myself close to her and if amazing sex is how to do it, that's how it had to be.

I didn't expect for that to happen, but fuck if I'm not happy it did. I knew her. She'd be reeling right now, wondering what the fuck was going on because I wouldn't talk. She may have tried ending this, but after that mind-blowing sex, I'm going to be on her mind. And I really didn't want to talk right now, I knew that stunned her. I was frustrated and it's not the right time to talk. But I couldn't keep my hands off of her. If she thought about me half as much as I think about her, it would be a fucking lot. That was the plan all along, whether that particular delightful moment was planned or not. I'd see her tomorrow at work and we could keep this little game going until I win her back. I'd give her some space for to think about what we did.

I needed to get my head back in the game here with this investigation. I told Detective Cruise I would rummage through Jack's electronic files to see what I could find and that's actually what I was doing when Jo showed up. I had been going through folders on Jack's desktop, and had come up empty-handed so far. Where would he keep evidence? I'm not even sure what I'm looking for, and part of me thinks the cops should be sitting around doing this which is also frustrating.

Leave it to the cops to have me do their legwork. Fuckers. I clicked for hours, coming up with nothing. I tried accessing his Cloud, but frankly I don't understand the fucking Cloud, and it had a password on it that was probably synced to his home computer or something. I tried Jo's name, her birthday, her mom's name, I even tried *my* mom's name, and couldn't get in. Hell, it could be anything.

I got up to go get a cup of coffee, then it occurred to me, that if Jack had his text messages synced from his phone to his computer, maybe what I was looking for was actually on his phone. He had to be using that damn thing way more than we thought he was. I needed to get my hands on Jack's phone. Jo had to have it at the house, *fuck*. I'm going to have to tell her what's going on or find another way to get that phone to Detective Cruise.

I decided to give Cruise an update, and sent her a text.

Hey, it's Cavanaugh. I'm coming up empty handed, but I have a thought.

Okay what's that?

She replied right away.

I think what you're looking for might be on Jack's phone.

Why do you say that?

He's got synced files I can't get into, but he was texting you through his computer, so I think maybe he was using his phone more than we knew

The more I thought about it; the more sure I was.

He not a phone guy?

Wasn't a technology guy, but the more I dig, the more I think he was and just didn't tell anyone

Ok, so where's his phone

At his daughter's house I think

Can you get it from her?

I hesitated. I wasn't sure how to answer that one after the events of today.

I'll figure it out. I finally replied.

I don't have enough evidence, circumstantial or otherwise, and no witnesses are coming forward, so without it, we have no case. Make it happen so we can bring this guy down.

Will do. I'll be in touch tomorrow.

This was going to be a little more complicated than I thought. I'd have to think about the best way to get my hands on that phone without involving Jo in what's going on. I didn't want that motherfucker anywhere near her, and I'd like her to stay away from the investigation for that reason alone.

It was getting late so I decided to go home, and come up with a plan when I see her tomorrow. We have a twenty-four hour shift together starting at seven a.m. and I was sure I could find some way to make it seem like I needed to poke through the phone for work or something. It could wait though, I was exhausted physically, and emotionally, and needed to get some sleep. Maybe I would have one night where I didn't wake up wishing she was there. Probably not, but hopefully soon she will be.

JO

I was so aggravated the remainder of the afternoon, and so relieved I didn't have to go in to work. After we were done shooting, we went out for a few beers and I was tired. The topic of the hot detective did not come up again while we were out, but it was definitely lingering in the air. Matt kept watching me, he knew I was mad because he knows how I feel. I wished I hadn't said anything to him in the first place.

I went home tired and cranky. Brian didn't actually owe me anything, but I had started to think that our romp in the office was his way of reconnecting with me. He didn't want me to end it after all. I guess that was all bullshit and out of convenience anyway. None of it really added up to me but at this point, I needed to get some sleep before working a twenty-four hour shift with him the next day. It was my first day back at 23 full-time, and I did smile to myself about that. My dad would have been really happy.

I walked into my house, and immediately dropped my keys in shock. I looked across the room, and Danny was in my living room at my dad's desk going through his notebooks. As I scanned the room, I realized there was a gun on the desk next to him. *What the fuck is going on here? Shit, my guns are still in my car and I just went shooting!*

"What are you doing in my house?!" I screamed at him. He rushed over to me, grabbed me by the neck, and shoved me against the wall by the front door, I had trouble breathing immediately. *Oh shit, what's happening right now?* I was terrified, and my heart started to thump against my chest.

"Shut the fuck up, bitch," his eyes were empty as he stared into mine. "You were supposed to be on crew tonight at 19," he looked around the room while still holding me against the wall.

"Someone is covering my shift," I whispered, grabbing at his hand around my neck. He had the gun in his other hand up against the wall, and I really didn't want to struggle with him until I could get my bearings. He was a lot bigger than me.

"Well, this wasn't part of my plan, but I can improvise. Sit down on the couch and do not move." He moved me slowly over to the couch where I sat, and he shoved the gun in the back of his jeans. He skulked over to an end table and grabbed a lamp, then pulled his multi tool out of his front pocket and cut the cord off of it. Putting the knife back in his pocket he walked back over to me with the cord, demanding I stand up and turn around. *Seriously, he was tying me up? What the fuck is happening?*

I did what he said, but pleaded with him. "Danny, what are you *doing* here? What are you looking for? I'm sure I could have helped you find what you need. What is this about?" He tied my hands up behind my back roughly and swung me back around and shoved me back down on the couch. Then he raised his right arm and backhanded me across the face, knocking me down hard. It hurt so badly that I cried out.

"I told you to shut the fuck up. And that, was for slapping me at the station. Someone should have beat the fucking sass out of you a long time ago," he menacingly stood over me. "I'll deal with you when I find what I'm looking for. Your father had information in his notebooks that I need, and I'm going to find it. Until then you will sit there and be quiet, or I'll fucking gag you next." I was reeling from being hit, he didn't hold back at all, he intended to hurt me. I was so confused, and scared. No one would stop by, no one would stop this. I needed a plan; the anxiety of the situation was making me nauseous. I kept scanning the room, looking for something that would help me formulate a plan to get out of this.

I continued to check the clock on the wall. For the next several hours, I silently watched him read my dad's notebooks with frustration, tossing each of them across the room when he didn't find whatever he was looking for. My face was throbbing from where he hit me; it had to have left a mark.

I couldn't figure out what would be in those notebooks that Danny would even care about. They were mostly notes from calls and things like that. They didn't have any personal information in them, because he wanted to be able to use them as testimony if he ever needed to be reminded of an incident. It was just his quirky thing. I was starting to get the feeling that what Danny was looking for was in my dad's personal journals, that were in his room, in the closet.

Whatever he was looking for, he wasn't finding and he looked angrier by the second. The sun was going to be up soon. He'd been at this all night long, and my body was stiff and fighting the fatigue of being awake for so long and left in such an uncomfortable position. I was dying to pee but didn't want to risk asking him; he wasn't in a stable frame of mind from the way he had reacted to me.

As the sun came up, I looked over at the clock and realized that I was supposed to be at my first day at work in about thirty minutes. My phone, which was in my back pocket, dinged with an incoming text message, snapping Danny out of his reading.

"What the fuck was that?" he demanded.

"It was my phone. It's in my pocket," I replied.

He stormed over to me, grabbing me roughly by the arm and pulling me up. "What pocket?" he growled in my face.

"My back pocket," I was trying to sound strong and angry, but I was fucking scared. This is not the guy I thought I knew, hell if I really knew him at all I wouldn't have stayed with him. He reached into my back pocket taking the phone. He looked at it and said, "Oh of course, its Matt. You fucking him yet?"

I didn't reply and the phone dinged two more times. "Jesus Christ, what a little bitch. He has to check in with you nonstop?" he retorted. "Are there any more notebooks, Jo? I need to know right now." He grabbed me by my hair and got in my face, making me wince. He was getting anxious. Beads of sweat were forming at his temples, and the veins in his neck were visibly bulging.

"Only what's there! What are you looking for?" I cried out. The fucking guy was off the rails and I wasn't sure what he was going to do to me, but I wasn't going to give up my dad's journals. He could go fuck himself.

He tossed me back to the couch and sat down on the coffee table in front of it looking at me intently, just a foot away from me. "Jo, your dad had evidence of some things I need to destroy."

"What are you talking about, Danny? What evidence?" Now I was getting really scared. Hopefully Matt would realize that me not answering would not make any sense since I was supposed to be at work soon. I prayed intently that Matt would pick up the vibe and come over, or better yet, send someone else over.

"Well I guess I may as well tell you since you're not going to be able to tell anyone," he gave a sinister chuckle that didn't bode well for me clearly. *Please Matt, swing by to find out why I'm not at work yet.* I didn't say anything at all, I wanted this story to take as long as possible to buy me some time to figure out how to get out of this or to have someone show up and save the day. In this state, I just couldn't see how I could get myself out of this alone.

"I've been making some extra money on inspections and some other side services for years, and your dad somehow figured out what I was doing before he died," suddenly I was hot all over envisioning him doing something to my dad.

"What do you mean, extra money?" I asked. Any of us that were inspectors made a certain amount per inspection, but that can't be what he's talking about. It was a regulated set amount, so the only way to get extra would be to extort it.

"There are some businesses that are willing to pay a little extra if you look the other way on a few of the fire codes is all. It's not a big deal. Well it wasn't until your dad found out about it and confronted me about it," he looked off angrily like a crazy man in a soap opera staring off camera. This is bad, he's crazy as fuck. Did he kill my dad?

"Danny, did you kill my dad?" I was trembling, afraid of the answer.

"No, I didn't. Thankfully the asshole died before I needed to do anything drastic. But it looks like I'll have to do something about you now," he looked down at me. I was relieved knowing my dad hadn't been murdered. Then the rest of his words sunk in and he looked at me with those dark empty eyes, sending real terror into me while he then paced around the room. He meant to kill me. My phone rang again, making us both jump.

"Jesus Christ!" he yelled, looking at my phone. He pointed the screen of the ringing phone in my direction. "Is Matt calling you from the department phone?" I honestly have no idea why the department phone is calling me other than the fact I'm not at work yet. I'm guessing it's the Chief making an official call wondering where I am. He shall be known as the Chief from now on after what Matt and Jax told me. I briefly thought back to our last moment together in Brian's office. If we were together, this wouldn't have happened to me. He'd have been here to protect me. Fuck.

"I don't know, Danny. I see the same thing on the screen you do. It's just a phone number, I have no idea who is on the other end." Which is true, but I probably shouldn't be so snippy with him since I'm tied up at the moment with what feels like a nasty shiner forming.

"Don't get shitty with me, bitch. Maybe it's that boyfriend of yours, the new Chief. I've seen his truck here a few times. You fucking brothers, you dirty little slut?" He laughed at me and touched my face softly. I jerked away at his touch, it made my skin crawl. When I jerked away, he slapped me again. *What the fuck is with him hitting me? I had no idea how fucking vile he was.*

"He's not my boyfriend, he's my boss," I hesitated. "And my friend." I was running out of ideas to get out of this, and Danny was getting fucking creepier by the minute. He grabbed me by the hair on the back of my head again, pulling me up to him. I let out a little wince, he was hurting me and I was getting even more scared, which I didn't even think was possible. I was starting to feel like I would pass out.

"I see. Just your boss. So who are you fucking, Jo?" He whispered in my ear, still holding me in place by my hair. I could feel his breath on my neck, and it felt like bugs crawling all over me, I was disgusted.

"That's none of your business," I whispered and tried to jerk away.

"How about one more fuck for old time's sake? I did enjoy that tight little pussy of yours," he looked me in the eyes. He was actually serious? I thought I'd throw up, and before I could, he shoved his tongue in my mouth and tried to kiss me. With my hands still tied behind my back, I pulled away and squirmed out of his grip for a moment, ending the disgusting attempt at whatever he had in mind.

"NO! Get away from me!" I screamed. I felt tears start to fall. I didn't want to cry, but I was so scared, and so angry I just couldn't control it.

"Oh, I see how it is," and he hit me again, hard, in the same spot as before. I saw stars this time, and fell backwards onto the couch, reeling from the pain. "I'm not done with you yet," he said, yanking me back to him, and hitting me again on the other side of my face. "Not so pretty and feisty now, are you?"

This time, I stayed down, and he didn't pull me back up. He left me on the couch, where I could see blood dripping from my nose onto the couch cushions. I could also taste the metallic tinge of blood in my mouth. This was bad, and I didn't know what to do at that point to get out of this, but I didn't want him to hit me again. He had me overpowered, and the only chance I had was for someone to show up and help me.

He'd gone back to my dad's desk unsatisfied with what he was finding. "It looks like your dad was lying to me. There's nothing here that implicates me in anything. Such a shame I'm going to have to kill you over nothing. But now you know the truth, and that can't get out and ruin my career."

"You don't have to do this," I said. That's what you say when you know someone is going to kill you right? What the fuck else do you say?

"Yeah, I never considered myself a killer, hun, but I can't let this ruin my career. I've worked way too hard to let a little thing like skimming off the top of the county send me to jail. Besides, I'm way too pretty for jail," he laughed. "I'll be back, you stay right there," he got up and walked to the door. "Don't try anything, Jo. I'm serious."

I just stared at him as he walked out of the house. I looked around for my phone but couldn't see it. He must have had it. Shit. It was time to pray.

BRIAN

"Did you try calling her?" I snapped.

"Of course I did. She isn't answering, and that's not like her. Something's up," Matt said.

"Yeah, she changed her mind, and isn't going to show up. That's what happened," I didn't really believe that she would just ditch work. Even if she didn't want to see me, she wouldn't do that to Matt or the other guys. But what do I know? Here I am, giving her space, all the space she needs but maybe what had happened in my office sent her running.

"That's not it and you know that. Something must be wrong. Maybe it's that shitty Jeep of hers or something," Matt was clearly grasping at straws, although her Jeep could use some work.

"I'll try calling her from here. Maybe she's ignoring you," I tried to make a joke, even though I was having a slight pain in my gut telling me something was wrong. I tried calling her from my desk, and it just rang and rang, then went to voicemail. "Well it's ringing, so maybe she's on her way or something." If this is bullshit, I was going to have to lecture her on her first day about being on time, which I really didn't want to do.

"Let's give her a little bit. I'm sure she'll show up," Matt looked nervous, and I was definitely getting the feeling it was something else. We both got up and went to the kitchen to get some coffee, and avoid the elephant in the room which was the fact that we both know Jo is not only always on time, but to her, on time is early. She was already forty-five minutes late, and that was way out of character.

"Chief, did you find my gear request that I gave to, uh, Jack?" Jax came into the kitchen to get some coffee too.

"I actually did just find it this morning. I signed the approval, but it's got to go to the commissioners, so I sent it over electronically and requested they expedite it. Sorry, it's taken so long, the paperwork is a real bitch," I complained. I didn't think being a Chief was pretty much all paperwork. I didn't want to complain too much about my job to the guys, it was an honor, but I was really second guessing that this was for me so early in my career. Yes, I've been a firefighter since I was eighteen, and that's nineteen years, but I'm nowhere near ready to give up fighting fire and going on scenes to basically doing paperwork full time. I had those goddamn budgets to look forward to later in the week.

"No problem, Chief. I'm sure that coming into all of that suddenly wasn't exactly an easy task," Jax replied. He's a good guy. He always had his shit together, he's safe, and he's smart. He also follows orders, and rarely, if ever, questions anything. He's always keeping himself busy at the station training, watching videos of other stations fires on the internet, and keeping informed on the latest in safety technology. He's a class act too.

We all stood around the kitchen chatting, having our coffee, but all the while I was really getting worried about Jo. Even though I didn't think she'd reply, I pulled my phone out to text her. Something is wrong, I know it is. I can feel it.

Are you okay?

I didn't get a reply, which didn't surprise me really, but it did still concern me. I started to think of all the realistic explanations for why she wouldn't be here by now. I honestly couldn't think of a single one other than that something was wrong, something happened to her. If she was in an accident, we would've gotten a call, so it wasn't that, but something was definitely wrong, and it was nagging at me, bad.

"Hey isn't Jo supposed to be here today?" Jax asked.

Matt replied, "Yeah, I'm not sure why she isn't here yet. If she's not here by ten, we should just take the truck over there and see what's up. It's just too weird, and I've called like ten times. I'm a crazy stalker now," he laughed. His laugh had a hint of nervousness too.

Then the tones dropped. "Engine 23, Rescue 23, Ladder 23, Active fire reported at 243 Old Seminole Road. Victims unknown."

FUCK.

I dropped my coffee cup and made eye contact with Matt. It smashed to the ground spilling coffee and shards of ceramic everywhere.

"GO!" he yelled. "We're right behind you!" I ran to my truck without saying a word. It was Jo's address. Her house was on fire. *FUCK.*

Something *was* terribly wrong, and I needed to get to her immediately. I hit the lights and sirens, which escalated my adrenaline even more. I've always been a stickler about safe driving, but I didn't give a shit about any of that. I've never driven a department vehicle faster in my life, and I thanked God and Jack in that moment for insisting that we get a pickup with a huge engine as I hauled ass to her house. She was about seven minutes away on a good day, and today there was a lot of traffic. Every sound that my truck could make from the sirens was employed, I was beeping like it was a third world traffic jam, and hitting the airhorn as often as humanly possible. Traffic parted around me like the red sea, and while it felt like a hundred years, I'm sure it was just moments before I turned the corner to her street where I could see smoke billowing in the sky.

Oh, God no. This is bad. This is a real fire, please don't be home, baby, please don't be home, I prayed. The moral dilemma of being a firefighter is that we truly do love fire. We love when something is really burning because it gives us a chance to finally put our training to use. The downside is this. There are lives at stake. As I got closer to her house I could see her Jeep in the front where she always parked. *No no no. She's home. She's here somewhere.*

There was fire coming through the front windows, which had blown out already somehow. I could hear the sirens of the other trucks coming in the distance. I grabbed my helmet and my coat, but didn't bother putting my bunker pants on; I wasn't wasting one second getting into the house. I knew she was in there, and I knew she needed me. I grabbed an axe and ran through the smoke to the front door and tried the doorknob. It was locked, but with one blow of the axe to the door it crashed open, and a huge billow of smoke hit me immediately.

I started coughing, and put my face in the collar of my coat as I ran in. "Jo! Jo! Where are you?" I ran into the front room, where the fire had clearly started, it was extremely hot. Jack's desk was completely engulfed in flames, and it had spread to the walls, and curtains, which must have caught fire causing the windows to blow out. I ducked low and continued calling her name, coughing. "Jo! Baby, where are you?"

Then, I heard it. "Brian?" My heart lifted immediately at the sound of her voice and I started scanning the room.

"Baby, where are you? I can't see anything! Help me find you!" The smoke was getting very thick, and I didn't have anything with me but an axe.

I could hear her coughing, and then hoarsely, she called out. "On the floor, by the couch! Help!" I ran to her, she was only fifteen feet from me and she was on the floor, tied up. *What the fuck happened here?*

"Baby, I'm gonna get you out of here, hang tight," I grabbed my knife from my belt and cut off the restraints on her wrists and pulled her to me. She grabbed me and held on.

"Oh, my God, Brian, thank you," she was coughing, and her face was black and blue. Someone had done this to her, and I was going to kill them.

I touched her face gently and looked in her eyes, she looked so scared. I had to get us out of there now. "We gotta get out of here, baby. I want you to hold on to me as tight as you can, and put your face in my coat," the fire was getting hot and the front room was now almost fully consumed with fire. We needed to go out the back.

"We can't go out the back, it's on fire too," she said quietly, while coughing a bit. She started to sit up. "I can walk," she said, but as she started to get up, her knees buckled, and she couldn't stand up. Probably a concussion judging by the marks on her face.

"We're going to run for it, the guys are on their way." I could hear the sirens loudly now, and knew they were only moments away. "Hold on to me." I scooped her up in my arms, and she buried her face into my chest. I was starting to cough more too, so it was time to get the fuck out. I wrapped my arms around her head and face the best I could while carrying her, and I ran for it.

Through the front door, we ran into what was a bit of fire, but God had given us a little pocket where there was a safe enough opening to get out of there. I carried her out to the front yard and dropped to my knees in the grass as the trucks showed up. I laid her down gently, tossed my helmet to the side, took my coat off and balled it up to put under her head.

Her face was covered in bruises, and dried blood was crusted around her nose and the corner of her mouth. I felt a rage inside me like I've never felt in my life, I was going to murder whoever did this to her. The guys ran by me, setting up and getting water on the fire, doing what they do. Matt made eye contact with me as he took over the scene, and I nodded to him, signaling that I was staying with Jo, and the fire could be someone else's responsibility today.

I was inspecting her, checking her for other injuries and being as gentle as I could while I kneeled holding her to me. She looked up at me and I saw her eyes start to well up with tears, "Brian, I'm so sorry," she whispered to me.

I can't imagine what she could be sorry for, "Baby, who did this to you? I'm going to kill them, who did this?" I touched her face gently, looking into her eyes.

"Danny," she whispered. "He didn't think I'd be home. He was looking for something in my dad's stuff but he didn't find it," tears started to fall from her beautiful gray eyes. "I'm so sorry."

"Baby, what are you sorry for?" I leaned down and kissed her gently all over her face right there in the front yard for all to see. I couldn't keep it a secret anymore, "I love you, Jo, I love you so much, and I'm so sorry I didn't get here sooner. I'm sorry I didn't tell you what you mean to me. I can't believe I almost lost you today…" I pulled her to my chest and felt the sting of tears welling up in my own eyes. It was just then that the paramedics came rushing over to check us both out.

"Chief, we can take over now." They tried to push me out of the way.

"I'm not going anywhere, I'm staying with her," I clutched her even more tightly. I was never letting go.

"Chief, we need to check her out, and you for that matter, please let us do our job, you know we need to," that little medic, June, the sister of Detective Cruise pleaded with me, putting her hand on my shoulder.

"Okay, okay, but I'm staying with her," I relaxed my grip on Jo, and set her back down propping her up a bit on my coat.

June kneeled down and assessed Jo's injuries, her face was swollen and she was coughing from the smoke. June put an oxygen mask on her, and her partner came around to me.

"Sir, I'd like to put an oxygen mask on you as well," he said.

"No, I'm good. I wasn't in there very long," I shooed him away and looked at June. "How bad are her injuries?"

"Doesn't look like anything's broken, but we need to take her to the hospital for x-rays just in case," she looked down at Jo. "Jo, we need to take you to the hospital, do you want me to call anyone for you?"

Jo looked over at me and I shook my head side to side. "I'll ride with you to the hospital and I'll make any calls we need to." Jo smiled under the oxygen mask and I squeezed her hand.

While June and her partner loaded Jo up on a stretcher, I stood up and looked around at the scene, the fire was mostly under control now. Matt came running over to me as they were starting to wheel Jo away to the ambulance.

"What the fuck happened here, man?" he burst out.

"Danny Russell did this. He beat the shit out of her too, Matt. I'm going to fucking kill him," I was so filled with rage. "I need you to look for Jack's iPhone inside, and then call the police station and ask for Detective Isabel Cruise, the girl you met the other night, and tell her to meet me at the hospital. Bring the phone, it's important. I'm going with Jo; I'm not leaving her alone." I was praying it didn't get burned up in the fire.

"Holy shit. Yeah, man stay with her. I'll handle it, and I'll meet you there as soon as we're done here."

"Yea, thanks. I gotta go," I grabbed my coat off the ground, and started to hustle my ass to the ambulance they were loading her into.

"Yo, Brian," he called after me.

"Yea?" I turned around quickly.

"The cat's out of the bag now, so just take care of our girl," he flashed a smile at me.

I felt the corners of my mouth curl into a smile as I ran to the ambulance, "Will do. Thanks for handling this," I waved at the scene and took off. He's right, the cat's definitely out of the bag now. I'd told her I loved her, and kissed her in front of everyone. I'd do it again in a heartbeat, and planned on doing it every day from now on.

JO

I felt weak all over, and my face was throbbing. I closed my eyes while June and her partner loaded me into the rig, I was so exhausted and everything felt like a dream, like it was in slow motion. Did Brian save me? Was that real, or another dream? I wanted to sleep now.

"Jo! I need you to stay awake!" Was that June Cruise yelling at me? It felt like a really strange dream. Then I opened my eyes and realized it wasn't a dream at all and I tried to get up. I needed to get the fuck out of here, and I'm strapped down to this stretcher. *What the fuck?*

"Whoa, whoa, baby, where do you think you're going?" I looked over and saw Brian, he was grabbing my hand. He was covered in soot and sweat, and then I remembered everything that happened and I started panicking. My chest tightened, and I started hyperventilating. I had never been a passenger in an ambulance before. I knew this one, I started looking around and I knew I'd ridden in it on a duty crew before.

"Jo, you gotta calm down. Lay back. Take a few deep breaths," June said, as she adjusted the height on the stretcher, raising me up a bit, then looking over at her EKG machine. I knew she was checking my blood pressure, which had to be through the roof right. I did not like being a patient.

I looked up at her and nodded, then looked over at Brian. His eyes met mine, but he looked different, he looked calm but scared. He leaned close to me, still holding my hand on top of me and whispered, "Baby, I'm here. You're going to be okay. I won't leave your side, okay? Just try to stay calm, and look at me."

I tried to talk, but my throat hurt so bad, and the stupid oxygen mask was annoying me. "I..." was all I could get out without coughing uncontrollably.

"Shhhh, don't talk right now. You ate a lot of smoke, babe, your throat is going to be hurting. Just relax and breathe," his voice was so calming that I forgot I was pissed at him. I squeezed his hand and nodded, and took a deep breath trying not to cough uncontrollably again. I just kept looking at him, and trying to take deep breaths which was calming me down, even if I was pissed at him.

I think we got to the hospital pretty fast, it felt pretty fast. The doors opened and the heat hit me right away, making me feel sick and I started to gag. I yanked the oxygen mask off, and kept coughing. God my face hurt, I wondered how bad it looked. The coughing was making everything hurt and I was getting angrier.

"Get this thing off me, it's suffocating me!" I yelled through coughs.

Brian was still right by my side, and chuckled. "You're going to be a pain in the ass about this aren't you, Jo?"

"You shut up!" I said through more coughs.

"Ah, feisty. You're gonna make out just fine, baby," he smiled at me. I was mad now. I was in pain, and what the fuck is he even doing here with me? Why didn't Matty come? He's my best friend. Why is Brian here?

"I'm not your baby," I coughed and shot him a nasty look, scrunching my face in his direction, which hurt quite a bit.

"You are. We can discuss it later," he squeezed my hand and I tried to yank it back but he had a tight hold on it.

"Chief, wait here with her a minute while I give a report to the nurse," June said to Brian, and she and her partner left me with Brian at the ER entrance. This was bullshit, I need to get off this fucking stretcher. I started to undo the straps and sit up, and Brian realized what I was doing before I could get up completely.

"Jo! Enough! You need to sit still; you have to get checked out. That's an order!" He was serious, yelling at me in front of the entire ER.

"Why are you here? Why isn't Matty here with me?" I pouted and of course, coughed some more.

"Matt is running the scene and gathering some evidence. He will be here in a little bit. And I'm here, because you're mine, Jo."

"I'm not yours," I snapped.

"You are. You just don't realize it yet. You will."

"Oh really? Well what about the hot cop you're going to bars with?" He gave me a stunned look, his eyes opening wide. Yeah, I caught you, asshole. Everyone can't be yours. I started coughing uncontrollably, and he helped me sit up more.

"Detective Cruise?" he asked.

"I don't know what her name is. Whatever it is, obviously you're fucking other people, so I'm most certainly not yours." Fuck my throat hurt. I wanted to scream at him, and I could barely get my words out at all, everything was coming out as a raspy whisper.

He leaned in close and whispered in my ear. "Josephine Meadows, you are *mo chroi*. There's no one else but you. There will never be anyone but you." He stood back up looking down at me. I felt paralyzed, not able to move or speak.

"But..." was all I could muster. And a stifled cough.

"Baby, I will explain everything soon. Detective Cruise is going to be by to talk to you about the fire, and about what that motherfucker Russell did to you. I've been helping her gather evidence against him, which your dad had actually started, we just couldn't figure out where it was right away. Now please, lay back, and let the staff here take care of you. I'll be right here, I promise," he said softly.

I was so confused. June and her partner came back over with a nurse who resembled a linebacker, as well as a pretty tiny little nurse trailing behind her. They wheeled me into a giant exam room, and moved me adeptly from the stretcher to the hospital bed.

"Jo, we gotta run, but I'll call you tomorrow to check on you, okay, girl?" June called out as she gathered her stuff to leave. She was on duty, she had to get her rig back in service and I totally understood that. It's always tough when you transport someone you know.

"Thank you, June," I hoarsely called back. I looked around, and the big nurse, the tiny nurse, and Brian were all staring at me.

"What?" I said.

"You need to put the oxygen mask back on, miss," the big nurse said. The little nurse was checking Brian out. *Seriously, bitch?*

"Fine, but let's get this moving, you need this bed for sick people, and I'm fine." I snipped at her and allowed the little slutty nurse to put a new oxygen mask on me while I tried to stifle my cough.

"I need to ask you some questions about what happened, and then we're gonna take you straight to x-ray and get some pictures of your face. Were you traumatized anywhere else?" She asked.

"No." I replied. I watched Brian as I answered the nurse's questions one after another. He stared at me intently the entire time.

"Were you sexually assaulted?" she asked me. I looked over and saw Brian's hands clenched into fists and he took a step closer to me.

"No." I replied.

"Are you sure?" she asked.

"Yes, I'm sure," I snapped at her, then looked back over at Brian. "Brian, he didn't do anything else to me, he just hit me," I didn't want him to have a stroke right there even if I don't understand what's going on with him right now.

"I think we have everything we need. Let's get you down to x-ray now. Sir, you're going to have to stay here," she motioned to a chair for him to sit in.

"That's not happening. I'm staying with her." He didn't move.

"Sir, it's not negotiable, don't make me call security. You're already overstepping here," she meant business.

"Brian, it's okay. I'll be fine, and I'm sure we won't be gone long," I looked at the nurse for confirmation.

"No, you won't be gone long. Audrey here is going to take you," she pointed to the little nurse who couldn't keep her eyes off my man.

"Audrey, I'm Brian Cavanaugh, the Fire Chief," she blushed and smiled as Brian spoke to her. "This woman is a firefighter, and my girlfriend, and I love her more than anything in this world. Please take care of her and bring her right back to me." Audrey the slutty nurse immediately changed her demeanor to professional and nodded at him.

My mouth dropped wide open. I felt it happen and I couldn't stop it. He just said he loved me, in public. Out loud. The slutty nurse heard it too. I could tell it wasn't my imagination by the look on her face.

Well, holy shit. Brian leaned down and pressed his lips to mine softly. "I'll be waiting right here, baby. I love you." The slutty nurse wheeled me away to get x-rays of my face, which was apparently freaking some people out, so it must have been bad.

BRIAN

I waited for Jo to get back from x-ray in the ER room they'd assigned to her and pulled my phone out. I had a text from Matt saying he had found the phone upstairs in Jack's bedroom, which was unaffected by the fire. He was on his way to the hospital, he turned the fire scene over to the neighboring chief so that he could get there. I can't say I blame him. While this is a special situation because it's Jo, if any one of our guys was injured we'd all want to be here.

I couldn't sit, so I was pacing around the empty room looking at the chaos around me. I'm going to fucking strangle Danny Russell with my bare hands for touching my Jo. Who the fuck beats up a girl in the first place, let alone a girl you were intimate with. The thought made me even more angry. And she was tied up, that sick fuck. My blood pressure was through the roof, when Detective Cruise came rushing in.

"Jesus Christ, Cavanaugh, what the fuck happened?" she questioned me.

"It looks like Russell beat the shit out of Jo for starters," I hissed through my clenched jaw.

"Your brother called me and says he has the phone," she said calmly.

"Yeah, he has it. He's on his way here. I'm going to fucking kill Russell." That needed to be really clear, and she wasn't listening.

"Listen, you gotta let me handle this, I'm serious," she reached out and touched my arm just as the little flirty nurse Audrey I think her name was, wheeled Jo back in.

Jo looked immediately to where Cruise had her hand on my arm and then looked up to my face and scrunched her nose up. I quickly moved to her side.

"Jo, baby, this is Detective Isabel Cruise, she's actually June's sister," I explained. She looked at me quizzically, but I figured it would be best if she talked directly to Cruise.

"Hi, Detective," Jo's raspy voice whispered. She gave Cruise the once over and I took her hand, leaning over the railing of her hospital bed. She weaved her fingers through mine, and I expelled a sigh. I think I've been holding my breath since she was away from me getting her x-rays.

"Hi, Josephine. I'm sorry we have to meet under these circumstances. I was working with your father on bringing Danny Russell down for racketeering, and it seems now we can add assault and attempted murder to the list of charges. Can you tell me what happened?" She pulled out a little notebook, just like they do on TV and grabbed a pen from her shirt pocket.

"Sure, I can tell you what I remember." Jo whispered. I let go of her hand and got her some water from the sink nearby, her voice was so hoarse and I know she was trying to stifle her coughing.

She smiled up at me as I handed her the water. "Thank you," she whispered and took my hand again as Matt walked in, still dressed in his bunker pants.

"Hey, Jojo! You look like shit! You gave us a fucking scare. You alright?" he was trying to lighten the mood and ease his own anxieties, I could tell.

"Hey, took you long enough to come," she whispered at him.

"Had to take care of the scene for this asshole," he pointed to me and smirked. She giggled and started coughing a little.

"Alright, now that we're all here, Jo can you tell me what happened?" Detective Cruise brought us all back.

Meanwhile, Matt looked at my hand in Jo's and gave me a wink, which I replied to with a smirk of my own.

Jo took a deep breath, trying to find her voice. "Danny was in my house when I got home. He said he thought I'd be working, but I had found someone to cover my last shift at 19," she whispered, then took a sip of water with her free hand. "He had a gun, and he was going through my dad's desk looking for something," she stopped to cough. I helped her lean forward in an attempt to make it easier, she needed to get that shit out of her lungs.

"Thank you," she whispered to me and then continued. "He couldn't find what he was looking for but told me that he'd been stealing money and that my dad knew about it. He said that my dad was going to out him if he didn't confess himself," then my heart sank. *God, did he have anything to do with Jack's death?* I squeezed her hand so she knew I was here to support her.

She continued, "He hit me a couple times and then said that since I knew what was going on, even though he didn't find any evidence, he was gonna have to burn my house down with me in it," a tear fell from her eyes. I leaned over and rubbed her back softly with my other hand, it killed me that anyone would make her feel this way.

"Keep going, honey," Cruise said softly.

"He went out to his truck and got some gasoline and dumped it on my dad's desk, and then went to the kitchen where the back door is and lit the can on fire. I guess so I couldn't crawl out that way."

"Then what happened?" Cruise asked, taking notes.

"He yelled at me, saying that this was happening because I came home and it was all my fault, and he hit me again, and I guess I passed out. The next thing I remember is hearing Brian's voice calling out my name," she looked up at me, teary eyed and squeezed my hand which was still intertwined with hers. God, I can't believe this happened to her. I should have been there to protect her and I was sick over the thought I could have lost her. Detective Cruise spoke up again, tearing me from my thoughts.

"You did good, Jo. Your dad would have been proud of you."

"Thank you," she sniffled a bit and sat up a bit. "So what's next? I don't have the evidence anyone is looking for, and now my house is halfway burned to the ground, and he beat the shit out of me, so can you go find him and arrest him anyway?"

"Yes, we can, and my guys are out looking for him now. I was hoping that your dad's phone was recovered at the fire actually. Brian believes what we're looking for is on it," she looked over at me.

Matt walked up and handed Cruise the phone. "I believe this is what you're looking for then. It was actually in a different part of the house, not affected by the fire at all."

She took the phone and unlocked it immediately, scrolling through it and then smiling, "This is it, this is what we've been looking for!" She practically cheered, while the rest of us just stared at each other. Cruise pulled up a video, and turned the phone around to us, and then adjusted the sound so we could all hear it.

What we watched, was a video that was actually aimed at the floor, and you could see uniform pants of the person holding the phone, Jack, and the other person was Danny. What was undeniable though was the audio. It was a complete and fully recorded conversation of Jack confronting Russell, and Russell admitting to everything. All of the bribes he was taking, the inspections he was passing that shouldn't have, all of it. Jack told him that he had twenty-four hours to go to the police himself, or he'd be turning him in. It was everything they needed to put Russell away for the racketeering. What he had done to Jo would make it even worse, he'd go away for attempted murder.

"Holy shit, that's fucking amazing. How did you know the code to unlock the phone?" I asked.

Cruise just smiled, "I didn't know it, I just tried 2323 and it worked. I actually thought I'd have to take it back to the tech guys at the station."

Jo started giggling, and then so did Matt and I. That's Jack. He managed to record evidence with his phone, but his password was so easy anyone could've gotten into that phone. Just then, the big nurse walked in with a doctor and Jo's x-rays.

They both appeared startled by the number of people in the room. "Uh, well hello, everyone?" The doctor asked it like a question then looked over at Jo. "I've looked at your x-rays Josephine, and it looks like there's no fractures or breaks, so that's good news. But you definitely have a concussion from the assault, and I'd like to make sure that if I let you go home, that you'll have someone that can watch you for at least twenty-four hours and make sure you're alright."

"That would be me. I'll take care of her," I spoke up immediately. She was coming home with me and that's all there was to it. I wasn't not letting her out of my sight and wasn't asking her permission either.

"Are you sure?" she whispered up at me.

I leaned down closer to her. "Baby, I'm not letting you out of my sight. You're coming home with me, where I can take care of you and that's an order." As I leaned back upright, still not letting go of her hand, she looked up and smiled at me shyly.

The doctor nodded, "Ok, I'll prepare your release papers. You're going to be in some pain, so I've written a prescription for something to help with that, but you'll be right as rain in no time. The smoke should clear out of your lungs in a day or so, but you're going to have a sore throat, and you definitely need to take it easy for a few days."

"Thank you, doctor," Jo whispered. The doctor left the three of us there again and Cruise shifted her weight back and forth. She was an antsy one.

"Okay, guys, I'm going to take this back to the station, and see where we're at in terms of catching this guy. Hopefully he's not on the run and thinks he won," Cruise put the phone in her pocket and continued. "Jo, we'll probably need to be in touch in the next couple days to get your formal statement, but this is just about over, and you're safe with Brian," then she turned to Matt. "And, Matt was it? Thanks for bringing me the phone." She turned around and left the three of us standing there.

"So, is it safe to assume you two now have things out in the open?" Matt was never afraid to point out the obvious, even if it was uncomfortable.

"Uhmmm," was all Jo could mutter, but she did smile at Matt.

"We are working on that, thanks so much for making it awkward though," I replied and gave him a go fuck yourself look with raised eyebrows and an eyeroll.

"Yes, fuck you as well," he replied with a grin. "If you're going to take Jo home, I'm going to have Jax take me back to the station so I can cover for you. I drove your truck here so you'd have it, and took care of the other things you asked me to. He's out in the waiting room, they wouldn't let any more of us back here. The guys want to see Jo, so we'll probably bring the crew by around dinner time to visit you once you're settled, is that cool?"

She looked up at me for a reply, "Yea, that would be great. Is that okay with you, Jo?"

"Yes, that would be great, thank you." She whispered and coughed a little.

Matt tossed me my keys, and headed out, leaving Jo and I alone for the first time since the front yard. I was suddenly very nervous, she hadn't really said much, but she agreed to go with me, so that was something. I sat down next to her, rubbing her hand that I was holding with my thumb, not quite sure what to say next.

JO

After Matt left, it was just Brian and I there alone in my hospital room. His fingers were still intertwined with mine, and he was running his thumb across my hand softly. I rolled over onto my side and examined him. He looked so worried, and tired.

"Are you okay, Brian?" I whispered. *Seriously, I hate whispering. I hope my voice comes back soon.*

He leaned in closer, placing both elbows on my hospital bed and bringing my hand up to his lips, kissing it softly. "I am now," he sighed out. "I thought I'd lost you, Jo. I don't know what I would have done without you. I'm so sorry for everything, baby. I'm going to spend my lifetime showing you how much you mean to me." He kissed my hand again, and rested his head in his hands, still holding mine.

Those eyes of his, I just lost myself in his beautiful green eyes again. I could see a tinge of hazel in them as I inspected his features while he was talking. "Brian, I'm going to be okay," I breathed out. I remembered everything he said to me in the front yard now, and I was afraid he had said it in fear, not really meaning it. He told the nurse he loved me too.

"Brian?" He looked back up at me.

"Yes, baby?"

"Did you mean all those things you said today?" I had to ask. It was just us now.

"What things, baby?" He smiled.

"You know, that uh..." He was going to make me say it? *Come on!*

"Come on and say it, baby. That I love you?" Now he was grinning and he moved himself to be seated on the edge of the bed next to me.

"Uh, yeah. That. Did you mean all of that? I mean I'm going to be okay now, so I mean if..." he cut me off.

"Josephine Meadows, I am truly, madly, deeply in love with you. It just took me longer than it should have to figure it out. I'm going to spend the rest of my life proving to you how much you mean to me. You're my heart, my mo chroi, and I can't live without my heart."

Swoon! He gave me that toothpaste commercial smile I can't resist, and leaned down to kiss me. That fire, that magnetic pull, it was there and it was intensified by a million. He softly opened my mouth with his tongue, sweeping it across my lips, sending shivers through my spine and waking up my sex. The way this man makes me feel is incredible. He growled a little bit and pulled away, making me pout.

"Come back here," I whispered with my new raspy voice, then started coughing.

"As much as I would like to take you right here in this hospital bed, the doctor said he was going to release you soon, so let's get you dressed, and get the fuck out of here. I want to get you home where I can take care of you better," he took my hand and started to pull me up.

"Kiss me again, and I'll get up," I was going to negotiate more kissing at all times.

He laughed and accommodated my request, taking my swollen face gently with both hands and pressing his lips gently to mine. "Oh, Jo, the things you do to me, even here." He pulled away and adjusted himself in his uniform. He was so fucking sexy. He had soot on his face from the fire, his hair was a mess, and he was beautiful.

He helped me get up, and just as I was finished getting dressed, the nurse came in with my discharge papers. "Now you know all the things the doc wants you to do, right? Few days taking it easy, not a lot of talking until your throat feels better," then Brian started laughing.

"Not talking? That's a good one," he laughed at me and I flashed him a look. When the nurse wasn't looking at me I flipped him the bird, and he winked at me in return.

"Thank you, ma'am. I will do my best," I whispered to her.

"Good girl. Now let this handsome man take good care of you," she patted me on the back and sent us on our way.

We walked out to Brian's truck, it was his regular truck, not his Chief's truck, which I thought was curious. He opened the passenger side door for me and helped me get in, noticing my confusion. "I asked Matt to bring my truck. I'm taking a few days off, so I didn't want the Chief's truck." He explained as he closed the door and walked around to his side, getting in.

"Are you going somewhere?" I asked. He never takes time off really.

"You're still not getting it yet, are you, baby?" He put one hand on the steering wheel, the other up on the back of my seat, staring at me, clearly awaiting a response.

"Uhh, no, I guess not?" I said.

"Jo, you're going to stay with me. Your house was on fire today and you were almost killed. We have catching up to do after the last few days. I'm staying with you and I'm going to take care of you. I've mentioned that I love you, and I intend to spend some time proving that to you," he awaited my response.

I felt my mouth curl up into a smile, he loves me. I think he actually meant it. "I'm going to take your smile as understanding, because you're not supposed to be talking anyway," he let out a little chuckle and started up the truck to take us home. My heart was full. I hadn't replied yet, I didn't get a chance, but I wanted to tell him how much I love him so badly.

The hospital was about ten minutes away at a normal speed which we were doing. We had to drive by my house on the way to his house, and when I saw the scene, I pressed my hand against the glass of the window in shock.

Brian reached over and took my other hand in his, weaving his fingers through mine. "Baby, it's not as bad as it looks. The guys got the fire out really quickly. You can't stay there for awhile, but the damage was only to the front room and the kitchen. The bedrooms are totally fine, just smoky, and that can be fixed. Matt already called the company that takes care of all of that, and they're coming over today to board up the windows and clean some of the damage up."

I looked up at him, tears in my eyes, "It's my home," I whispered.

"Baby, it's just a little damage, and we're gonna get it fixed up good as new. It's going to be okay," he brought my hand up to his lips, kissing it softly. "You're going to stay with me for now and then tomorrow if you're feeling better, we'll go get some of your things and look around okay?"

All I could do was nod. I was in shock. I was so tired, so sore, and I couldn't believe my house was on fire today. Brian was taking me to his home, to stay with him. He loved me. I couldn't find the words. For the first time in my entire life, I was speechless.

BRIAN

She looked so tired, and her sweet, beautiful face was swollen and bruised. It pained me so much to see what he did to her. When she saw her house, she became almost silent, and my heart ached for her even more. I should have taken a different route home, I wasn't thinking. I could really be stupid sometimes.

When we pulled in front of my house, her Jeep was in my driveway where I asked Matt to put it, so I parked on the street. She looked over and smiled knowingly at me, she knows my don't park in my driveway rule. *Good, we got a smile out of her.* I needed to shower, she needed to shower, and she needed to get some rest. The guys were probably going to stop by in a couple hours for their dinner break, and to visit with her, so I wanted to get her comfortable as soon as possible.

I parked out front and got out, while she waited patiently in the passenger seat for me to come around and help her out. God, that made me so happy. I helped her hop out, and grabbed the ring box from my glove box, shoving it in my pocket. I put my arm around her as we walked up to the front door. Just inside the door was a duffle bag with a couple things that I asked Matt to grab at her house. Some clean clothes mostly, so she had something to change into. I would never ask anyone but Matt to do something as intimate as that for my girl and I would have preferred to do it myself, but I just couldn't leave her side.

She followed me to the kitchen silently and looked around. We were both filthy, we needed to get cleaned up. "Baby, can I get you something to drink?" I asked her and opened the fridge to get myself a beer.

She mouthed the word water and smiled, then mouthing the words thank you silently as she took the bottle from me. I pulled her into me, and she melted against my chest as we stood there taking in what had happened. She held onto me, resting her head on my chest for a few minutes and then finally she sighed a big, relaxing sigh, as if she'd been holding her breath for awhile.

"Let's go take a shower and get cleaned up, then you can rest okay?" I said still holding her and kissing the top of her head. She silently nodded her agreement. She seemed downright exhausted at this point, and I couldn't say I blamed her. The adrenaline was wearing off both of us. I scooped her up in my arms and carried her to my bedroom, not forgetting the pink duffle bag of her stuff. She rested her head on my shoulder while I carried her. *God, I love this woman.*

I set her down in my bedroom near the bathroom door. "Go on in and get started, baby, I'll meet you in there."

She reached up, grabbing my face gently with both of her little hands, pulling my face to hers. "Thank you," she whispered, and planted a beautiful soft kiss on my lips before turning around to go into the bathroom. She had yet to tell me she loved me back, but I knew she needed me as much as I needed her.

Frozen for a moment, speechless from her sweet gesture, I was awakened from my daze when I heard her turn the water on. I grabbed her duffle and rifled through it to see what Matt grabbed for her to wear, I wanted to set it out for her. I found two pairs of leggings, a pair of jeans, three tank tops, and basically all of her lingerie. What a dickhead. I appreciate it, but what a prick. He was a funny guy going through her intimates drawer. Ah, whatever, he's my brother, fuck it. I laid out some leggings and a tank top for her, and a sexy as fuck pair of teal panties, and a matching bra.

I grabbed the ring out of my pocket, and opened the box, looking at the ring. I pulled it out of the box and put it on my pinky finger, it only went on about halfway, but that's fine, it won't be on long. I stripped off my filthy clothes and made my way into the bathroom to get in the shower with my woman.

I stepped into the shower to see her examining her bruises. Fuck, she had bruises all over her body. My rage took over, and I pulled her to me under the steaming water. "Baby, you're safe here with me, okay?" She looked like she had been crying. "Are you okay, Jo? Say something. I need to know you're alright," I pleaded.

She looked up at me, her gray eyes penetrating me. "I always loved you. I've loved you my whole life, Brian," she whispered, both of her hands resting on my chest.

She does things to me, things that make my heart soar, and my dick hard, all at the same time. Those words melted my heart, and I pulled her in tight, letting the hot water run over both of us and kissed her gently. After a few minutes, I grabbed the soap and started to wash her, and then myself. She stood perfectly still, letting me take care of both of us. When I was almost done, I took her right hand and looked in her eyes.

I took the ring off my pinky, and placed it on her right ring finger, with the crown and heart facing inward, a symbol that your heart belongs to someone. "Jo, my heart belongs to you. I'm sorry it took me so long to figure it out, but I'll spend the rest of my life showing you the rare and beautiful gift that you are to me." She looked down at the ring, and then looked up at me smiling. "My mom gave me that ring, it was given to her by your dad," I waited for her reply. That might have been awkward to say right then, but maybe she'd understand the symbolism to me.

She looked at it again, then looking up to meet my eyes, she smiled a huge beautiful smile. "I love you, Cavanaugh," she said.

I met her grin with my own. "You're mine, Meadows. Forever."

THE END

COMING SOON

COMING WINTER 2016

BOOK 2 IN THE
BROTHERHOOD OF
DISTRICT 23

FULLY INVOLVED

ACKNOWLEDGEMENTS

My tribe is amazing, and I would never have considered writing a book without their support. Since it's my debut novel, I've got a handful of folks that deserve some public recognition.

First and foremost, even though I know he won't read this dirty little book, I have to thank my brother Jesse Briggs. Without his unconditional support of me pursuing my dreams, I'd still be wandering around looking for my passion. Thank you for always saying, "If you look at the worst possible outcome, its usually not that bad. Just do it." You're my guru man, thank you, I love you.

Carina Adams, who made this whole thing real by offering me the opportunity to do my first signing, setting the schedule for reality. Your book Forever Red, was my first romance read, and we became friends the moment we met. If you hadn't given me this gift I may still be mulling over the idea of finishing this book at all.

Janelle Picard, who reminded me that this book has actually been in progress for 20 years, the length of our friendship. I often reminisce of our days at the Jersey diners, writing, talking, and growing up together. Thank you for telling me to go *write*, not to go right to another bar for more drinks after brunch. We've been friends for so long, you're my family, and I love you. Jaisha Burr, thank you for always somehow knowing what my word count meant and encouraging my happy hour writing habits. The bars of Orlando surely want to thank you as well for my patronage. I love you, your family, and the craft beer tastings at TJ's. Donna Caruso, we were destined to be friends, and I'm so grateful for your friendship, and the ability to curse freely with you. Karen Bryda, you're the Meredith Gray to my Christina Yang, and I love our Skype sessions and ridiculous text chats. I'm so lucky we became close before I moved 1000 miles away. My NJ street team, Hillary Perryman, Stephanie Snock and Abbey Flick; drinks on me next time you're in FL. Thank you for your support through the last several years and thank God for FaceTime and autocorrect.

Aaron Heller, thank you for keeping my scene descriptions honest, and for allowing me to use your network for this book. You encouraged me to become a firefighter from the very beginning, and even with the pushback from some, it was one of the greatest personal achievements of my life. I'm grateful for your support and your tutelage during my firefighting days as well as now. Gene Pullen, Walt Lewis, Dave Hernandez all deserve thanks for their assistance in securing photos, equipment, and other fun stuff for me to help promote this book. I was recently reminded that once a firefighter, always a firefighter, and for that I thank all of my brothers and sisters. Delran Fire Department, Delran Emergency Squad, New Egypt Fire Company, New Egypt Rescue Squad, thank you for the privilege of serving with you and creating the inspiration for my stories.

The newest additions of my family, my writing family, deserves special thanks as well. Kristina Rienzi, thank you for your friendship, and thank you for taking me to a book signing with you. You stirred up my passions and you're an inspiration to me. To the authors that inspired and encouraged me to go from reader to author, MJ Fields, Stevie J. Cole, Carina Adams, Leddy Harper and LB Dunbar; thank you for welcoming me into the writing world with you, and for inspiring me with your smoking hot stories.

Judi Perkins, you're my yoda. I'm your kid now, and you're stuck with me, and I'm the luckiest chick around for it. Thank you for the beautiful cover, and for your no nonsense guidance on how to get this book done. Your introductions to my book family have been invaluable. And thank you for my new sisters, Sasha Brummer & Jess Epps; it's as if we've known each other forever.

My beta readers Kelly Williams (who gives fabulous story feedback and brainstorms with me), Mary Baird (who gave me my first author takeover on her blog and has encouraged me without ever meeting me), Chantal Zodarecky (the gif queen who loves my characters), Steph Gostin (we need some champs girl), and Martin Murphy (thank you for adding testosterone to the mix), your feedback was helpful and hilarious. Tiffany Holcomb, thank you for agreeing to being my PA and for sending me the most hilarious "you should be writing" memes. A special thanks to Jillian Crouson-Toth (who shares a brain with me and is truly my spirit animal), you got to know me and my characters and have shown me such love and support from the day we met online, I don't know what I'd do without you, and you're my friend for life. I'd be drowning without all of you! I'd also like to give a shout out to the bloggers I've met and been supported by; you make the romance world go round, and I've become an addict thanks to your reviews, shares and comments. I thank you from the bottom of my heart.

LJ & CB Creative Images and Services (Cassia Brightmore & Lance Jones), thank you for handling basically everything. I ask a million questions a day, and Cassia is always sweet to me even though I'm annoying as hell and a total control freak.

Thank you to my TR family from all over

the world. Seth Miller, Laz Jefferson, Matt Salandra and so many more, your support and encouragement to take massive action and to go for it in every way means more than I could ever express. Ho'oponopono. I love you, thank you.

Lastly, and most importantly, thank you to my readers. I started as a reader, and your support, shares, love and kindness makes all of this worthwhile. I look forward to creating more book boyfriends for all of us!

ABOUT THE AUTHOR

Amy Briggs is an Orlando based writer, consultant, and entrepreneur. Leaving the corporate life behind, Amy runs several small businesses from the comfort of her home while spinning realistic, thrilling and romantic stories. Formerly a firefighter and EMT in New Jersey, living next to a military base, Amy was drawn to creating a stories around emergency services and the military, and draws on her experiences to show the depth and emotional side of that life.

To stay in contact with Amy, follow her on Facebook at https://www.facebook.com/amybriggsauthor, on Twitter @amybriggs23 and on Instagram @amybriggs23. Amy loves to hear from her fans, and you can email her at amybriggs.author@gmail.com.

36104686R00243

Made in the USA
San Bernardino, CA
13 July 2016